Of Gods And Monsters

Ever Chace Chronicles
Book 8

SUSAN HARRIS

OF GODS AND MONSTERS

.

ISBN: **978-1-63422-420-8** (paperback)
ISBN: **978-1-63422-419-2** (e-book)
Cover Design by: Marya Heidel
Typography by: Gem Promotions
Editing by: Chris Kridler

This book is dedicated to the readers:
Whether you've be with me since the beginning,
or have recently joined the EC family ,
thank you for all the support for my paranormal crime series
and the characters that I adore.
This one's for you guys!

PROLOGUE

Centuries ago, a young Valkyrie princess made a deal with her father, Odin, in order to try and put a halt to his quest to remake the world. If he could take her life seven times, then she would hand him the keys to Valhalla and usher in the new dawn of mankind, rebuild the world anew after Ragnarök wiped the slate clean.

Throughout the course of time, she was aided by her trusted sister, the daughter of Tyr, and her one true love, a Viking warrior who held her heart who was forced to die beside her each time her father succeeded in ending her life and the cycle began again.

Now, with only one life left to give, the Valkyrie must call on those who have become family, her werewolf mate, the vampire queen, the psychic vampire, the truth-seeker and the mind reader, along with her Valkyrie sisters.

The final battle is upon them; the fate of the entire world falls upon their shoulders. Only fate knows if they will prevail, and upon the culmination of the endless night ... who shall be left standing?

In the time of Gods and Monsters, the end is only the beginning ...

CHAPTER
ONE

Derek

"*It's the end of the fucking world.*"

Loki's words echoed through Derek's mind and had done so, on a loop, for the last three days. It had been three days since Odin had appeared at the edge of Cork city and sent his berserkers to ravage all that stood in their path. For twenty-four hours, war raged upon the streets of Cork while Derek stood helpless against it, his need to protect his family conflicting with the need to protect the city that was his.

The Valkyries proved why they were some of the most ferocious of warriors, their battle cries heard all over the city. Humans had little time to barricade themselves into their homes, too fragile a species to fight this war, and those who were unable to escape the destructive path that came their way were snuffed out in mere moments.

The dawn never came, darkness a blanket around them as Odin watched on, perched on Sleipnir, his eight-legged horse, which Derek was shocked to learn was another of Loki's children. The horse seemed to hover in the air, steam flaring from its nostrils as it stomped its hooves against the nothing.

A warning had blared throughout the city, a national broadcast advising all those unwilling to fight to remain indoors but calling to arms any able-bodied fighters. The army had been called in to set up a blockade, and Derek had done what he could from the position he was in.

After twenty-four hours of endless night, the fighting suddenly stopped, the berserkers retreating to their master, where they then stayed by his side for almost two days. Derek set up a mobile command center from Ever's hospital bed, rotating between reading reports on damage and death and tending to his newborn daughter.

And still his mate remained asleep.

Derek stood and stared out the window, his eyes focused on the god who was determined to end them all. Derek had always felt protective of the innocent, of his team, and more recently of Ever, but even though he wanted to be on the ground fighting with his team, he couldn't leave his daughter, especially with her mother in a coma.

"Boyband, catch."

Derek snapped out his hand to catch the packaged sandwich Erika tossed in his direction before the Valkyrie strode over and placed a kiss to Ever's temple. Then she glared at him for two minutes straight until he unwrapped the plastic and began to eat. The petite warrior's face was covered in blood and gore, her eyes dark, her clothing torn, but she paced the hospital room for a few minutes before she leaned against the wall and swept her braid off her shoulder.

"It's driving me crazy having the asshole just standing there. Like make a move. I wish you all would just let me take a shot at him. I can kill him."

This was an old argument, the Valkyrie determined to have her slice of revenge. Not only had Odin forced Erika to witness Ever's death over and over, but Odin had also made the woman kill Derek as well. It had initially put a strain on their relationship, but when the end of the world was upon them, petty things such as murder took a back seat among family.

"I mean, it would be a simple sneak and stab. I don't know why everyone is against it," she mumbled, her voice a growl in the quiet of the room as Ash shifted in her sleep.

Derek placed his palm on the baby's chest, and she stilled in the cot. "No one is disputing your skills. Yet none of us want to have to tell Ever when she wakes up that her father has killed you. And that's even before we factor Loki into the equation."

As Erika rolled her eyes, Derek remembered the first time Erika had suggested going after Odin, when the fighting first ceased, and Loki had lost his temper. It was the first time Derek had seen him so unraveled. The power that was contained in that lean frame was too much for a normal man to hold within himself.

But Loki was not a mere man; he was a god.

Erika had pulled him out of the room, returning half an hour later. Loki was calm again, but Derek wasn't even going to think about what Erika had done to calm that storm.

Derek shot off a text for the team to check in and got immediate responses. Ricky and Melanie had gone to check on Zach, who was at Ricky's mom's house. Caitlyn and Donnie had gone to try and corral the vampires, some of whom thought the endless night was the perfect time to skirt the rules and feed without care for humans. Caitlyn was trying to persuade the others to join the fight, using her queen of the vampire's title to do so.

Derek himself had sent a call to arms, reached out to the werewolves, knowing Odin's phobia of wolves might be a sure-fire way to take him, and he was still waiting for the packs to vote on becoming involved in the war. But even the council had said this was a matter that was so far above the scope of their relative species that they dared not intervene unless absolutely necessary.

Fucking idiots that they were.

And while Derek had always been one of those supes who followed the rules, if there was ever a time for action, it was now.

As another being sauntered into the room, Derek turned to

see his time traveling teenage daughter, who was in the same condition as Erika, her clothing torn, her skin spattered with blood and dirt. She had a cut to her lip that made Derek growl in his chest as the young woman sighed.

"I'm okay, Dad. It's nothing. Just some idiot who tried to take a cheap shot. It'll be healed by morning."

Ash grabbed a bottle of water that was over on a side table and drained it, then, just as Erika had done, went to kiss Ever on her forehead. Then she walked over to the window and stared out at her grandfather.

"You guys should just let me and Erika take a shot at him. All I need is one shot with Mjölnir and he'd be dazed enough for Erika to gut him."

Derek glared at Erika, who held up her hands in protest. "I haven't said a thing, Boyband. Your daughter is bred of warriors. Of course her first instinct is to attack. Nothing to do with me and my willingness to sacrifice myself for the greater good."

The conversation was cut off as a nurse came in and checked Ever's vitals, then gave baby Ash a once-over before asking Derek if he needed anything. When he said no, she left and then Caitlyn came in, her face drawn in a frown. She was swearing in her native French before switching to English.

His oldest friend stood in the center of the hospital room, her hands on her hips, her shoulder-length black hair pulled off her face in a braid not too dissimilar to the ones that the Valkyrie were wearing. Her body was sheathed all in black, making her gray eyes seem darker as she frowned, shaking her head.

"Fools. Every single one of them fools."

Derek didn't have to ask, considering she had gone to Chester's to find out if the vampires would fight against Odin or continue to cause extra trouble that the Paranormal Investigations Team had to clean up. Even the vampires were reluctant to get involved in the fight.

Ash began to fuss in her cot, and Derek turned to reach for her, stopping when a uniformed officer came to stand in the door, his eyes wide. Without a word, Caitlyn strode forward and picked up the mewling babe and began to sing to her in French.

Derek had been worried that he would not be able to share his joy at becoming a father with Caitlyn, that his joy would somehow add to the pain she already carried inside her. He could scent her sorrow, knew she thought of her own children and their deaths, but grown-up Ash loved Caitlyn so much that Derek knew his daughter was in safe hands.

Derek strode over to the uniformed guard, who held out an envelope with his name on it. "This is from the commissioner, sir. He told me bring it straight to you. The reinforcements from all around the country are stuck outside the city. It appears that some sort of magic is preventing them from coming in. There's no getting in or out of Cork."

Derek tucked the envelope into the back pocket of his jeans, then he thanked the guard and went to return to his spot by the window when the guard cleared his throat. Derek turned back to him.

"The commissioner would like to see you face-to-face, sir. He is happy to come to you but does not want to force the issue. We don't know how to deal with all the supes. The garda can't cope."

Derek took one look at the worried expression on the face of the young guard and felt annoyed with himself that his own personal dramas had made him dismiss the letter as if it meant nothing. Derek hated to bring any more people to Ever's room when she was so vulnerable, yet he could not turn his back on the police force and the legacy of Sarge, the man who had saved his life. Sarge would have wanted him to do all he could to stop what was coming, the monsters who knew the Paranormal Investigations Team would come for them if they skirted the laws, now that their attention was diverted to stopping the apocalypse.

"Tell the commissioner to come meet me in a few hours. We can talk then, once the team is assembled."

The young guard nodded before leaving, and Derek wondered if this was what he thought he would be doing fresh out of Templemore, the place where those who wished to become a guard went to learn.

Derek leaned in the doorway as Ash checked her phone, let loose a sigh and moved toward him.

"Kenzie texted. She needs backup downtown. I gotta go."

"Be safe."

Ash leaned up and kissed his cheek. "Yes, Dad."

Then his daughter was gone, her long braid a mixture of blond and brown as she left Ever's hospital room and crossed over to another room, slid open the window, glanced over her shoulder with a smirk and held out her hand, that hammer of hers whistling as it sailed through the air. His heart was in his throat as she stepped off the ledge and disappeared into the night.

Erika walked past him to go into the other room to close the window before coming back in. The Valkyrie tilted her head to the side as she stood in the doorway beside him, folding her arms across her chest.

"You need to eat more. No point in her waking up and kicking my ass because I didn't make sure you looked after yourself."

Derek huffed out a breath. "I ate the sandwich, didn't I?"

Caitlyn, who was cradling his newborn daughter, turned in their direction. "Donnie has gone back to the house to get some food and clothing for you, mon loupe. You look like you need a week of sleep and a good meal."

"Mother hens, the lot of you."

That dragged a chortle of laughter from the two women as Erika's phone went off. She barked out a curse. Her whiskey-colored eyes darted to Ever as she muttered, "Wake up, Ever. We need you. You hear me? Stop being so goddamn lazy and get your ass off that bed. We don't need a martyr; we need our queen."

Then Erika bolted down the hall without another word, her boots like thunder on the ground before she flashed and vanished from view, leaving him with Caitlyn. The vampire offered him a small smile as he came to stand beside her, following his gaze to where Odin stood.

"I understand his grief. I really do. We have all lost while we have traveled this world, and yet, we do not seek to rebuild it. I have made friends with my demons, made what little peace I can with the darkness. And though I have lost, I can still see that there are reasons to keep going. You can, even if it is in a week, a month, or a century later, find a new purpose. There is light that can penetrate the shadow of loss if you allow it."

Derek shook his head and reached out to touch his child's feet. "Something twisted in Odin when he lost his love. He focused on that grief and decided that the rest of us were incon-sequential to that loss. When you were lost in your grief, you sought to ensure that others were not forced to endure the pain that you carried with you. That path was harder, and possibly crueler, until you found your way to cope. Odin considered himself all-powerful and refused to allow himself to be affected by pesky human emotions. In the end, it was his damnation."

"No one is immune to suffering, even the gods of old. Perhaps it is another reason for us to feel pity for him, for them, because they spend all of their lives trusting that they are beyond the rules of mortals, yet, when faced with human emotions, they know not how to deal. If Odin was not trying to end the world, I might feel some sort of sadness for him."

Reaching out to cup his friend's cheek, understanding the compassion that shone in her eyes despite her words, Derek said softly, "You would still feel sorry for him, Caitlyn, because that is who you are. You might not agree with his methods, but you know what it is to feel the loss until you cannot breathe. We were lucky to be let in when you had tried to close off your heart, but Odin refused to let that happen."

"A bloke could get jealous and demand you unhand my mate."

The smile that curved Caitlyn's lips reminded Derek of how far she had come because of the vampire who strode into the room, carrying enough food to feed an army and setting it down on the table. Donnie O'Carroll had chipped away at the armor Caitlyn had come to wear, helping her battle her demons and being exactly what she needed to heal.

When Caitlyn had tried to slip off to kill her maker by herself, Donnie had gone after her, unwilling to let the woman he loved succumb to the demons of her past without him. Donnie was the steady calm Caitlyn had needed, the passion she deserved.

"Jaysus, D, first your kid, now you. I mean, the mental flirting is a bit much," Donnie teased with a teasing smile as he pulled out delicious food that made Derek's stomach grumble. With a chuckle, Donnie pushed the table in Derek's direction, lifting a chair. Derek dropped his hand and took the chair offered to him.

Derek ate the food without really tasting it, knowing he needed to build up his strength in case Odin decided he was tired of waiting for Ever to wake and let the berserkers run riot again. While he ate, Derek watched as Donnie walked over, wrapped his arms around Caitlyn's waist, rested his chin on her shoulder and smiled as she cooed at baby Ash.

The pang in his chest would have been enough to buckle his knees if he hadn't been already sitting. The fact that all he wanted was to be with his own mate, his arms around her waist as she cooed over the tiny being they had created, made him feel terribly guilty, because if his little Ash could bring anyone even a sliver of peace and contentment during this nightmare of a time, who was he to begrudge his friend that? He was disappointed at himself for these jealous feelings, but he so desperately wished it could be him and Ever. But she remained lying in that bed, unmoving.

Donnie glanced in his direction, having read the thoughts in Derek's mind, his power both a gift and curse. Donnie's brow raised as he went to untangle himself from Caitlyn but stayed when Derek growled. Derek kept on eating until Caitlyn had Ash sleeping once more and settled his daughter in her little cot again. Then she leaned into her mate's embrace for a second before she slipped from Donnie's arms.

The lights flickered overhead, and they all froze, half expecting the world to erupt into chaos once more, but after a few minutes when nothing attacked them or made a surprise entrance, they relaxed a little.

"Maybe I should let Erika loose and see if she can wound him?" Derek asked. "Am I selfish enough to let her try, even if it might mean her death? Loki might just kill me if I let her, but I think a surprise attack might be our best shot at ending him. Am I a horrible person for even considering it?"

Caitlyn shook her head. "Non, because it is not a bad option. Yet when push comes to shove, we would not sacrifice our family like Odin has. Odin and Cain, they are not dissimilar in the fact that they would happily stand by and let others bleed for their purpose. People were pawns to be used to accomplish a goal, and whilst you may think on it for a time, there is no part of you that would do as they have done."

Derek wanted to believe Caitlyn, wanted to take stock of her words and truly reassure himself that he was not like Odin and would protect all of those he considered part of his family, his pack. And while he would never order Erika to do what she'd been itching to do for days, possibly even centuries, if the Valkyrie made up her own mind to go rogue and make an attempt to stop Odin, would he even try to dissuade her further?

Dear god, he hoped so ...

CHAPTER
TWO

Ever

T he water lapped against her feet as the waves crashed against the sandy beach. Even in the never-ending night, Ever could see it as clear as if the sun shone high in the sky. The scent of salt and water in her nose with every intake of breath felt familiar, like a sliver of paradise. It was like she had never left, the sights, the sounds, the scents all so utterly reminiscent of the place she used to call her home.

But then there was her actual home, and she needed to get back to there. She just wasn't entirely certain how.

Behind her, the trees swayed in the breeze, the rustling of leaves like voices in the forest, of warriors uneasy, restless as the final battle approached and frustrated as the pull of the Allfather did little to drag them free of the confines of Valhalla and onto the battlefield. Ever was surprised to feel the pull herself in the pit of her stomach as she lay between life and death, as if Odin could command her to his side and force her to fight against her family and friends.

That would never be the case.

When she had spoken to Donnie when he had dream-walked her, Ever had been honest in her assessment that she needed time to heal. However, as she stood now staring once more out at the ocean, Ever was unsure if she would wake from this healing slumber.

"Wake up, Ever. We need you. You hear me. Stop being so goddamn lazy and get your ass off that bed. We don't need a martyr; we need our queen."

Ever smiled as she heard her best friend and general chastise her, *as if those words alone could drag her from her sleep to answer Erika. She heard them all: the soft little cries from her newborn daughter, the reassuring strong tone of her mate, and even the hauntingly beautiful French lullaby that Caitlyn sang whenever she fussed over the baby. A gust of wind swept over the island, causing a shiver to tremble through her. Glancing over her shoulder, she could feel the presence of the fallen, the warriors who would be called forward by her father to fight the final battle, yet somehow, even as she felt the pull herself, they did not leave. Rather they waited, ready to once again take form and rage against the night.*

Ever walked along the shore, her toes in the fine grains of sand. Over the last few days, as if by magic, her clothing had changed to an outfit she had worn many centuries ago, when she was nothing more than a Valkyrie princess and warrior. Skirt of tough leather, cut into strips, the same material across her chest, Asgardian metal to her wrists and shoulders. Even the daggers she had worn as a youngling running across these very sands with Erika were sheathed at her waist.

Yet it did not feel like reality, as if this was merely a construct of her mind. A howl in the distance snagged her attention, and she lifted her head to the sky and howled back, well, as much as any human could. She was not sure why those in Valhalla kept their distance from her, why they did not come and spar with her, why she could not see who watched her from the forest.

It struck her all of a sudden, a memory of running through the forest, leaping over branches and brambles, ducking behind trunks as her systirs came in pursuit of her, her heart beating like a drum inside her chest, trying to keep her breathing even so as not to give away her position, even as Erika flashed in front of her and smiled smugly before disappearing once again and foiling any sneak attacks her systirs had in mind.

The joys of youth, of growing up in paradise, had been snuffed out shortly after that memory when Freya began their training vigorously and childish playing was cut short. Hide-and-seek became war games; pretending to be Asgardian warriors with wooden swords became spar-

ring with the real thing. There were no lazy days and long nights, no friendly camaraderie. It was early mornings and competitiveness, the bonds of sisterhood strained.

Ever had always imagined she would grow to be like her hero, the most famous Valkyrie of all time, Brynhild. Ever had seen her once, meeting with Freya, when she was a child and had been awestruck by her obvious strength and poise.

Built like a Viking, she towered over Freya and was all hard angles and muscle. And then she was gone, before Ever could even speak a word to her. Yet over the years, Brynhild had been the subject of many a story as Freya had told them that even the greatest of Valkyrie could be felled by human emotion, for Brynhild had fallen in love, been tricked into forgetting her love, then once the trickery was revealed and having already sent someone to kill the man she truly loved, Brynhild threw herself upon his funeral pyre and went to Hel with her love.

Ever had wanted to be like the Valkyrie who had paved the way for her and her systirs. She wanted her name sung in ballads of glory and spoken of in prose by scholars. She wanted her name to be the first to come to mind when someone mentioned Valkyrie. She was the daughter of gods, of Odin and Freya, the sister of Thor and Loki. Her name would be written beside them in the history books, and for that, she needed to do something worthy of being written about.

Perhaps when she had made the deal with Odin to live and die seven times over, it was with the hubris that this would be her tale of sacrifice and victory. Never in a million years would she have imagined that the stories told about her would be of death, of loss, of the end of the world.

She had been cocky, even as Odin stabbed her the first time, kicking off the curse, believing that she could somehow beat her father, end his silly little quest, and become famous. Instead, she was now down to one life, a life she desperately wanted to cling to.

She thought of all the iterations of who she had been, so many cities she had lived in. Every single one of her six previous lives, other than this time, felt separate from her, like watching someone else's memories. Even the memories she had of growing up on Valhalla felt like she was watching a movie of someone else's life, even if it was her face in all of them. She wondered what might have happened if she had remembered sooner, had found Derek and Erika and been able to best Odin, but would that have cost her and Derek the love and support of their chosen family? Would Melanie have died rather than been raised once more as a vampire? Would Caitlyn have succumbed to the darkness in her soul? Would Erika have found her partner in Loki?

She had so many questions and struggled to find the answers.

"Maybe that is why you still sleep?"

Ever turned with a smile to see her brother standing beside her. Thor was dressed in his Asgardian metal and his long red cloak. His red hair was pulled messily off his face, and his feet were surprisingly bare as he rocked back and forth beside her.

"I wondered when you might appear."

"It is not like you to brood. Especially when you have a family that needs you."

Ever rolled her eyes. "Perhaps I thought I should remain here in order to give you the chance to chastise me some. I miss you, brother."

"And I you, sister. I even miss that troublemaking little guttersnipe."

Ever laughed, and before her eyes, the water seemed to calm, as if the sea was controlled by her emotions. The wind stilled, and peace settled in her bones.

"I regret not being able to hold my niece with my own hands."

"And yet you gave her the gift of the gods. It is a blessing and maybe a curse all in one." Ever sighed, shifting her weight.

"She has the capacity for greatness. Had it not been bestowed on her, Odin could have granted it to someone else, and I could not enjoy the feasting I have earned in Valhalla knowing that the Mjölnir was in the hands of someone less worthy. It was either the child or ..."

Thor trailed off with a faint tug upwards of the corners of his mouth, and Ever knew her brother would not spill any more details, even should she press him. Turning her gaze toward the forest, she felt the dead of Valhalla again with their wish to be free, yet they still did not slip the confines of their immortal resting place.

"I do not understand why they do not answer his call. I feel it, the pull, yet they remain."

"You will." That was all her brother said, no hint on further answers on his face, his features impassive so Ever could not decipher his words. His lack of answer sparked anger in her chest, but was that not what older brothers were for?

Ever huffed out a breath. "It would seem that you have learned Loki's skill of evasiveness. Can you not just tell me what lured you away from the mead and the shieldmaidens to come and mess with my head?"

Thor laughed, the sound like a rumble of thunder in the dark. "This is not my quest, nor is it my place to advise you. Some decisions must be made by yourself. Some paths must be walked alone. My time as Midgard's protector has ended. A successor has been chosen. I have fulfilled my destiny until I do get the chance to fight once more, which should be soon."

Thor rested a hand upon her shoulder. "Your destiny is your own. The future is not written in stone. It is time for you to be just who you were meant to be."

"And if I wish to remain here, forever, with you?"

"Then our father wins and our brothers he has slain in his pursuit of his goals will forever be restless. Your daughter will grow up without a mother, possibly raised by a woman who despite being the goddess of love has forgotten how to love. Your mate will grow cold and distant and trundle down the path away from those who keep him human. You know this. You know you cannot stay here. So say what it is that you wish to say and go home."

Thor had never been one for many words, never one to speak when actions prevailed, the swing of his hammer all he needed to get his point across. If he was taking the time, whether his appearance was *real or a figment of her imagination, to lay all of the cards on the table, Ever had to listen to his words and accept them. She had considered that perhaps those she called family would be better off without her, yet if her death was the catalyst for more pain, she could not remain here, safe from harm or hurt, and live with that choice.*

Thor turned away from her, making huge strides across the sand as he headed toward where the fallen warriors waited. Tears sprang to her eyes as she called his name, her big brother casting his eyes over his shoulder at her.

"Will I ever see you again?" Ever asked, sadness like an anchor in her chest.

"I will see you in the final battle, but I am never far from you or my niece. I shall watch you from Valhalla and await your arrival, when we will toast to our lives with much love and revelry. Though I hope that not be for many eons."

Then her brother was gone, leaving her alone in the sand, tears streaming down her face. By the gods, it hurt to say goodbye. Yet, as Ever placed a hand over her heart, felt the steady beat of it, she knew that she would carry her brother with her until they were reunited in immortality.

"Hail and farewell, dear brother. Hail and farewell. May we meet again."

And Ever finally let Thor go, let go of her grief at his loss and the desperate need to keep him here with her. But she was Asgardian, and death was not to be feared. It was the end of one's destiny, and Thor, he would be rewarded and worshipped in the great hall. He would be feasting with Tyr, with Baldur and Heimdall. It would be a party like no other.

Heat flushed her face, and Ever lifted her face to the sky. Through the dark clouds that had fallen over Valhalla, a little slice of sun had managed to cut through, resting upon her skin and heating her bones. It felt like an embrace.

As Ever wondered how the sun had managed to slip through, the sun reflected off something along the shore, and Ever crossed the sand, but as she did, whatever was glinting in the sand went farther and farther away.

With a snarl, Ever swore, wondering what else she had to do in order to get to her destination. Her thoughts were jumbled, even after she had freed herself from the burden of the loss of Thor. She had such guilt in her, for Tom, for her systirs who had died, even for Derek, who had died six times already for her quest, for her destiny.

When she had first laid eyes on him, a slain warrior in Valhalla, training with the rest of the fallen warriors, she had been captivated by him. She had wanted him even then, wearing clothing befitting a Viking warrior, his skin sun-kissed and his strength obvious. When their eyes had clashed across the sands, a spark had coursed through her, and sure as if she had been struck by a bolt of lightning, she knew that she should be his and he hers.

Why was she standing here, brooding over the past, when her future was waiting for her to snap out of herself? Why was she maudlin over things she could not change? For so long she had been reluctant, indifferent to her very past. She moaned and groaned and felt sorry for herself, for the way her life had transpired.

For too long, she had pushed down parts of herself that made her who she was. She tried to be past iterations of herself, yet they were all part of who she was now. Instead of being this kick-ass warrior she had always wanted to be, she had become a whiny, watered-down version of herself.

She had run from battle instead of facing it head-on. She had allowed weakness to soak into her bones and fear to paralyze her. She had forgotten that she herself was a goddess and not human. She had let herself be controlled by her perception, and it had crippled her.

The clouds above her parted more, the darkness receding, and once more the sun shone on the shores of Valhalla. Her skin tingled, her palms sweated, and when she glanced down at them, little cracklings of lightning crawled over her skin. Her chest felt as if it would explode as she sucked in a breath, as power was unlocked from deep inside her, sending her to her knees on the sand.

A surge of power forced her hands into the sand. Magic like she had not felt before flowed from her hands and out into the sea, which shifted under her grasp, the very earth beneath the sea rumbling.

Ever closed her eyes, and she could feel every soul that inhabited Odin's great halls of the fallen as if they were a part of her, as if every grain of sand on this beach she had constructed in her mind was representative of all those who craved battle. Her spine locked as another wave of power cracked deep inside her, and she cried out, her voice carried by the wind, and the black clouds vanished.

The wave of power ebbed and flowed under her skin as Ever darted to her feet, raced across the distance and yanked the sword from the sand. The moment her palm clasped the hilt, she sucked in a breath. The runes on the sword blazed for a moment before Ever smiled.

Cocking her ears, she listened in to the world where her mate and daughter waited, her mate speaking to Caitlyn as she cradled her daughter. Ever's heart constricted. Her arms ached to hold her child, to hug and kiss her mate.

The time for wallowing was over. She needed to wake up. She needed to wake from her slumber and protect her family.

After all the centuries trapped in confusion about who she really was, Ever was ready to embrace her true self.

"Derek, something's happening with Ever."

Donnie's voice sounded in her ear as Ever took off across the sands, her sword firm in her grasp, knowing that she was the only person with the power to wake herself up. She was finally ready, body and soul, her newfound power simmering under her skin, to face her father and end centuries of death and destruction.

"Ever? Ever?" Derek's voice called to her. "It's time to wake, babe. I'm waiting for you."

And he always had, his soul tied to her on the most primal of levels, their fates intertwined, their love transcendent, one that defied death and curses and megalomaniac fathers. No matter where in the world they were separated, Derek always found her.

Machines beeped, her heart rate racing, as Derek called her name.

But Ever came to a halt, the scent of a berserker hitting her nose as the creatures in the room were distracted by her human body. As her corporeal self tried to rejoin her body, the scent of brimstone and ash hit her, the shores of Valhalla disappearing under her feet as Ever slashed out with her sword and opened her eyes.

CHAPTER
THREE

Ever

E ver's eyes opened to a white ceiling, machines blaring all around her, her heart rate racing as the cries of her daughter turned her head. Caitlyn was clutching the child, Donnie shielding her as Derek pressed the button for the nurse. Her fingers coiled inward, her right hand grasping the sword she had pulled free of the sands of Valhalla as a berserker used the chaos and noise to trudge into the room.

Derek snapped his head around and snarled, charging for the berserker, who tossed him aside like he was a mere human. Twisting her hips, Ever sprang from the bed and crouched on the ground with her sword in hand, a feral snarl on her lips. Her newfound power pulsed in her hand, the runes on her sword flaring as the berserker roared and came for her.

Ever slid across the floor and slashed his legs with her sword. The creature shrieked, its wolflike maw snapping at her as he struggled to stay upright. Getting to her feet in front of the berserker, she watched patiently as the creature buckled, his knees on the ground, bringing its face level with Ever's.

He slashed out with claws as Ever jerked back, the lightning in her veins sending currents along her sword, and the berserker's eyes widened even as she felt the power in her own eyes.

"You have your father's eyes," it said in old Norse.

He surged forward, but Ever was already swinging her sword, the blade cutting through the creature's neck as if it were butter. His head hit the ground with a thud as Ever heard a caw from near the window, where her father's ravens watched her.

Ever gripped the head of the berserker in her free hand and regarded Huginn and Muninn as if they were a direct line to her father. "I'm ready whenever you are, Father. Come face me, one on one, and let us end this. This is a matter for gods, and Midgard does not need to be caught in our war."

You think yourself a god now, daughter?

Muninn ruffled his feathers, his beak moving as he spoke on Odin's behalf.

Ever dropped the head and gripped the blade of her sword within her hand, slicing her palm, her blood dripping to the ground with a hiss, lightning in her eyes as she gave her father a sinister smile. "We shall see. On the battlefield, we shall see."

Then Ever banged on the window with her bloody palm, the birds shrieking as they flew away, a ripple of power shaking the glass as she shielded the room from her father's eyes. Turning back to the people in the room, she offered Derek a smile as he stumbled toward her. Her eyes widened at the scarred flesh on his neck and chin. She made to ask him what had happened when her mate closed the distance between them and kissed her until she was dizzy.

When he broke the kiss, his eyes were wolf amber as she stroked up his neck, her fingers touching the burnt and healed flesh gingerly for fear she would hurt him. "What happened?"

"Phoenix. Long story. He's dead."

"Good. That's one less person I need to kill. I love you."

His eyes blazed as he held her, his strong hands on her hips as he leaned his head down to rest his forehead on hers. "And I love you."

She stayed in his grasp, in his arms for a few heartbeats, until footfalls sounded behind her and a voice said, "I know someone who has been waiting to meet you."

Ever turned to Caitlyn, dropping her sword as the vampire's

gray eyes rested on Ever as she handed Ash to her. The moment she held her daughter in her arms, she sucked in a breath as her daughter opened her eyes, and in them, Ever saw streaks of lighting before they closed and Ash stilled.

"It's okay, sweet girl. Mom's back, and I'll never leave you again."

Ever felt arms around her waist as Derek pressed a kiss to the side of her throat. "She's perfect, isn't she?"

Ever agreed with her mate one hundred percent as Ash fell into a slumber. She cradled her child within her arms and knew that she would destroy the world to keep her child safe. It was that instinctual bond that Ever had not witnessed before with her own parents, yet her human parents had shown it, Tom had shown it and even Ricky and Caitlyn, who had found children, some of blood and some created as their own.

Lifting her gaze, she smiled at Donnie and then cast her eyes in Caitlyn's direction. "I know now why Ash loves you like a second mother. I heard you singing to her. I heard you comforting her while I healed. I felt your heart and the sadness for what you lost. Yet you held her to you despite that. You have my eternal gratitude."

The vampire swallowed hard, even as her own mate took her hand in his. "I was a pale substitute for her mother." Clearing her throat, heavy with emotion, she changed the subject. "Now, before we have Valkyrie and more trudging into the room, perhaps you would like to dress in more suitable clothes?"

Ever glanced down at her hospital robe and laughed. "Ya, I guess I assumed I'd wake up and be dressed. I mean, I did manage to bring the sword through."

But then Ever didn't move, loath to remove her daughter out of her arms now that she was finally holding her. Derek sensed her unease, kissed her throat again as his voice rumbled in her ear. "The sooner you dress, the faster you can hold her again."

Reluctantly, Ever handed Ash over to her father, who rested

the child against the bare skin of his arm. Donnie held out a duffle bag for her as she slipped into the bathroom, removed her hospital gown, and stood looking at herself in the mirror. Her pregnancy belly was gone, replaced with a smooth, flat stomach with just a little cord of muscle. She was surprised to miss the protruding belly, having had little time to enjoy it as most mothers would, even with the short pregnancy.

She told herself that next time she would be free to enjoy it.

Ever dressed quickly, pulling on leggings and a tank top, then throwing a leather jacket over her shoulders. She took the time to brush her hair and then plait three braids into her hair, then pulled the rest of it off her face. When she felt like she was suitably dressed, Ever opened the door and stepped outside.

On the edge of her hospital bed sat a warrior with hair the color of whiskey, eyes of the same shade, her lips curled into a mischievous grin as she ran those eyes over Ever and then quirked her brows.

"What the hell took you so long?"

Ever laughed as she strode forward and embraced her oldest friend. She felt the tiredness in the Valkyrie's bones, smelled the death that she had no doubt dealt on her skin. "I was making sure not to steal your glory. For when they sing sonnets of us, your name should always come first, my sister."

Erika chuckled, taking Ever's face in her hands before she pressed her lips quickly to Ever's, earning a growl from Derek and an amused chuckle from Loki, who appeared in the doorframe and watched her with those eyes of his that saw everything.

"Come now, brother. Come give me a hug."

When Loki refused to come to her, Ever rolled her eyes and strode over, punching him in the shoulder before she embraced him. After a moment of hesitation, he returned her hug.

Lowering her voice, knowing everyone could still hear her, she said, "Thor came to me in my sleep, and he is content with his warrior's death. He misses you, though, and waits for the time when we are all together once more, in the great hall."

Loki plucked at the ends of her braid. "I almost believed you until you made claim that the great oaf missed me."

"If it helps, his exact words were that he even missed that troublemaking little guttersnipe."

Loki's smile was brilliant as he shook his head. "Now that sounds more like our brother."

Stepping away from Loki, she returned to where Derek sat in a chair with Ash on his chest. Perching herself on his lap, she leaned in against the curve of his scarred neck. She wanted to know what had happened whilst she slept, yet if her mate wanted her to know, when he wanted to tell her, she would be there with an ear to listen.

"I can scent your worry. I am at peace with the outcome. Neville Morris is dead. I killed him. My friend who I thought was dead was actually a phoenix, and he did that to me. Then Loki killed him, and I came to you. That is the bones of what happened."

She didn't question him on it, for she heard the resolve in his tone and knew he really was fine with what had transpired. Ever heard a scrape of metal as Erika leaned down and picked up her sword. "I didn't think I'd see this again."

"Neither did I. It was hidden within the sands of Valhalla. Perhaps it returned to its rightful place after those Vikings were done with it."

Erika's lips slowly curved into a smile as she angled the sword out in front of her. "At least those Lodbrok boys took care of the sword. It looks as good as the day it was forged."

Ever patted her daughter's back. "And that is why you never try to outdrink a Viking. You end up drunk and somehow losing your sword in a bet."

Erika chuckled as Donnie's eyes darted from Ever to Erika. "Now that is a story I need to hear."

"Sure, once we survive the end of the world, we'll have a few beers and tell you about how we lost Ever's sword to the world's most famous Viking," Erika teased before she glanced toward the door and muttered, "Incoming, in three, two, one ..."

Teenage Ash came around the corner and spluttered to a halt, her eyes going to the bed before traveling to where Ever sat, her eyes widening. "Mom?"

Water glistened in her eyes as Ever got to her feet, held out her arms, and then she was engulfed in a hug that caused her to take a step back. She felt Ash's tears on her skin as she smothered the girl's hair and tried to reassure her that she was fine.

Ash detangled herself from Ever, then her amber eyes studied her for a second. "Your aura is different."

"Is that a good or bad thing?" Ever asked with a smile.

"Good. This is how I know you."

Ever cupped her cheek for a second before dropping her hand and turning to those in the room. "Odin knows I'm awake. Probably felt the upgrade in my magic. He won't wait much longer, and that dead berserker is not going to be the last to come for me. We need a more secure location."

"We can use the warehouse. Me and Cait had already set up a sort of mobile command there. Ricky has set magical alarms all around the building so we know if anyone crosses the threshold."

Ever nodded at Donnie. "Okay, we need to regroup and see what we've got to fight with. Erika, any Valkyrie wounded?"

"Danae took a knock to the head, but it was already hard to begin with. Kenzie is a little tired, still not used to her wings; however, she refuses to rest. She definitely was destined to be one of us. Other than that, it's all minor cuts and bruises that will heal. I think seeing their queen up and about will give them a refreshed appetite for blood."

Ever glanced at Derek, who slowly got to his feet with baby Ash still in his arms. "Is she okay to be moved?"

"Ya, we just decided that it was better to stay here with her ma until we could leave as a family."

The heat in his gaze nearly melted her bones, and she stepped forward, leaned up and pressed her lips to his. A rumble sounded in his chest as Ever heard Ash groan.

"Please keep the PDA to a minimum, please."

Ever turned away from Derek as Erika tossed her sword in her direction. She caught it easily, like it was an extension of her arm. Donnie slipped from the room and returned seconds later with a car seat, settling it on the bed. Derek strapped the tiny being inside.

"I could just flash her to the warehouse," Erika said, a statement that made Ever think. Closing her eyes, Ever willed herself to stand by the door, and when she pried open her eyes again, she was standing where she wanted to go. She had only been able to flash once, when she had spoken the words out loud that she was a Valkyrie and left Derek and Erika behind in order to save them from Odin.

Now it would seem that she, too, like Erika and Ash, had the power to flash.

"Looks like you finally found the power." Erika mused.

"I did."

Derek slipped his arm through the handle of the car seat before glancing around. "Right, let's get moving."

"Hang on, Boyband. Don't you have to meet the commissioner in the next few hours? You stay here, and we can bring Ever and Ash to the warehouse."

"No." His tone was dangerous, as if he was barely containing himself and his wolf.

"Derek ..." Ever began before he cast his amber-filled eyes in her direction.

"I'm not leaving you or her right now." His voice was a growl that had Ash's eyes flaring and a snarl curling her lips.

Ever walked over and patted his arm. "Okay. Then we stay

until you've spoken to the commissioner. It's fine. Erika, you and Ash go to the warehouse and make sure we have everything we need. Loki, can you go with them and double check that Ricky's wards are strong enough to keep Odin out? I'm gonna stay here with Derek and baby Ash, and maybe Donnie could keep me company."

Derek seemed to relax as Ever squeezed his arm. Erika, Loki and teenage Ash vanished without another word.

Caitlyn pulled out her phone, frowning. "I must go speak with Chester."

"I'll tag along if you need me," Donnie said, resting his bulky frame against the doorframe.

Caitlyn smiled, her face softening as she walked over to Donnie. "I will always need you, yet it will be a quick trip to Chester's. I will be at the warehouse before you arrive."

His eyes held Caitlyn's for a moment before he nodded his head, then dipped his head to allow Caitlyn to kiss his cheek. Then she slipped from the room, her boots making no sound as she left, and Ever knew that Caitlyn was as deadly a hunter as Erika.

Derek pulled an envelope out of his pocket, ripped it open and frowned. "We need to go down to the emergency room. That's where he'll wait for us."

Derek cradled the car seat as Ever picked up her sword and glanced around the hospital room, wondering if she should grab some stuff to take with them. A nurse stumbled into the room, her eyes widening at the sight of Ever, then at the dead berserker, before Donnie took her outside and spoke for a few minutes before coming back in.

"I told her to lock down the room and we would send someone to clean up the mess. And get any clothes and stuff you guys need. Most of her onesie things are in that bag, and I made sure that the warehouse is stocked with nappies and formula and things."

"Thanks, Donnie."

"I just got what Caitlyn told me to get."

They made their way down to the eerily quiet emergency department, where a tall, thin man rose when they came through the doors. His face was grim, and the two guards that were with him had haunted expressions on their faces. Derek set the car seat down and strode over to where the man stood. They shook hands as Ever felt a strange pull from Donnie.

She glanced at him and narrowed her gaze. "What have you that calls upon the power of gods like a beacon?"

Donnie frowned as he fished in his pocket and withdrew a compass. Ever felt the power in the compass even as she reached out and placed her fingers on it.

"I went to Asgard when I was unconscious, and Lady Sif left this for me to take. Tyr was working a spy in Odin's camp in the hopes that he could find a way to end the war. I'm not sure how or why, but he knew I would come and that I was to use it to find what we needed to end it all."

Ever felt grateful that Tyr had not in fact turned against them, felt the sorrow for her beloved general who had found her father, only to lose him before she knew him. Why the hell had Tyr left this for Donnie to find? And what weapon would it lead him to in order for them to get the upper hand in this war?

The ways of gods were confusing, like sun when the heavens opened on the earth and rain fell. Ever knew from the magic in this little compass that Donnie had to figure out how to get the compass to work.

Now that she was awake, the time for war would come sooner rather than later. If Tyr had found a means to kill Odin before the final reset of Ragnarök was set in motion, only to die before he could tell them his findings, then it looked like the god of war had entrusted his secret of the compass to the brave vampire standing beside her.

"I don't feel very brave," he muttered, lowering his eyes to the compass.

But Ever knew that when the time came, he would be brave, and in the end, when all was said and done, that was all they could hope for.

~

ODIN SAT UPON HIS EIGHT-LEGGED HORSE, THE STEAM OF ITS BREATH warming his skin as his ravens flew back and perched upon his shoulders. His daughter was awake, her newfound power a pulse across space and time, sending ripples of discord among his berserkers. He had held them at bay for the last two days and nights by sheer force of will, and yet they grew restless.

He heard the flutter of wings as his young Valkyrie floated in the air beside him, her eyes on the wings of her kin who fought to keep the monsters of this world under control. He felt her longing, her sadness that they considered her a traitor; however, he would kill her or send her to be killed once she had served her purpose.

"What do you need of me, Father?"

Odin ran his fingers through his white beard. Always willing to please, his Marya, still not even two centuries old, and in human years, she was perhaps fifteen. He smiled at her, wondering why his own child could not be as obedient and obliging.

His daughter was far too like her headstrong mother.

"Kill the babe. You need to kill the babe, and then my daughter will crawl on her knees for me to bring about the end of days and, with my beloved Frigg, bring her child back from the dead."

"As you wish."

She flew upward into the blackened sky, her wings a mixture of gray and red, like a streak of blood against the sky, before she shot forward and toward either certain death or victory.

At this stage, Odin wasn't sure he cared which was the outcome.

CHAPTER
FOUR

Derek

Derek was having a little trouble getting Ash settled into the car, having not had time to scrutinize the instructions before the arrival of his newborn daughter, and now the edges of his temper were fraying. The calmness that had shielded him while Ever slept was dissipating, and he wasn't really sure why something as trivial as a car seat was making him want to unleash his claws. He had only been aggravated by the meeting with the commissioner that had just ended.

"There's a trick to it, man. Mind if I give it a go?"

Donnie's voice broke through the quiet as Derek retreated from the battle with the car seat and frowned. Donnie offered him a sheepish kind of smile then held out his hands to take the car seat. An irrational fear coursed through him, and he fought the urge to clutch Ash to him.

A growl rumbled in his chest. His eyes flashed amber.

Donnie held up his hands, still smiling. "You know, when I was a teen, I spent one summer working in a toy store that sold nursery stuff. I must have fitted a dozen car seats just like that. We had to have special training to be able to do it. I'm sure that with all the new health and safety regulations, it would take a rocket scientist to get that thing in place."

Derek arched a brow, and Donnie chuckled. "Or maybe someone who has done this before. I get wanting to do this stuff yourself, D, but everyone needs a little help sometimes."

Derek knew what the vampire was doing, could read it a mile off. Donnie was keeping a check on Derek's emotions, being that rock-steady soundboard that he always was to everyone. Donnie was not someone he should be cautious of handing his daughter's care to. The vampire would walk into the midday sun before he would harm a hair on her head.

Handing the car seat to Donnie, Derek took a step to the side and watched as the vampire bent down, half into the back seat of the car, set the seat into the slot and, after a few clicks, ducked out of the car and straightened.

Donnie reached in and gave the car seat a little jostle, but the seat seemed glued in place.

"See, nothing to it."

"Does that mean we have to pretend that you're a rocket scientist now?" Derek grunted, annoyed he couldn't do what Donnie had but thankful at least one of them had been able to solve the mystery.

"I'm pretty sure Ricky could have done it too but no need to make you feel any worse."

Derek laughed, easing the tension in him as Ever shook her head at them over the roof of the car. She slipped into the back seat with Ash as Derek got into the driver's side and Donnie took the passenger seat. They drove in relative silence, the radio off, heading from the hospital to the edge of the city, where Caitlyn and Donnie had purchased a warehouse. The couple had intended to renovate the building to live in, but after a discussion, they knew they could not leave the home that they had lived in together.

Even if it meant Ricky and Melanie would be building a house right next door.

"Are you going to tell us what the commissioner said?"

Ever's voice broke through the silence as Derek huffed out a breath and dragged his fingers through his hair. "The city is mine to command. He handed over control of the Garda, the defense forces and the navy to me. I told him it wasn't up to me to lead them, and his response was that a human commander could not lead during this war and they needed a supernatural who understands the world."

Derek kept his gaze forward. A muscle ticked in his jaw before he felt compelled to lift his gaze to the mirror, where blue eyes watched him with pride that made him feel like he could take on the world.

"There is no one better to lead them, Derek. It was always going to be you, once he retired, and now, no matter the outcome, perhaps this is the start of expanding P.I.T., just like Tom wanted."

Thomas "Sarge" Delaney had been more of a father to him than his own had, had been the man who had dragged him from his depressed state and given him purpose. He had a knack, did Sarge, for finding those most in need of guidance and setting them on a better path. Derek wished he was here now to offer that guidance once again.

The warehouse came into view, as did the vampire standing outside waiting for them. They parked outside the building, and everyone got out. Caitlyn walked up to Donnie and stepped into his body. Derek watched as he wrapped an arm around her waist. Derek had known Caitlyn a long time, had spent many a night walking under the stars and moonlight as they talked through their fears, their hopes. He was glad that she had found Donnie, that she had not let her self-perceived darkness ruin her chance at a little happiness.

Ever had walked around to the other side of the car and removed Ash's car seat with little difficulty. When she caught him looking at her, Ever smiled. "What, like it's hard?"

Melanie laughed. "Never in a million years would I have thought I'd hear a *Legally Blonde* quote from a Valkyrie queen's lips."

His mate curved her lips. "Elle Woods rocks."

Despite the gravity of the impending war and violence, they all shared a laugh as they made their way inside the warehouse. Just inside on the ground floor, it looked like a shell of a place, but Caitlyn led them up the stairs and pushed open a door, then stepped aside to let them enter.

Derek was blown away by the mobile command center Caitlyn had managed to get in place. The full length of the warehouse was covered in clusters of people, boards, evidence on the walls. You had witches and warlocks tracking violence in the city, shifters led by former teammate Fionn breaking off into teams with the vampires and arming themselves.

"I think, once this is over, that P.I.T. needs its very own building. We were all too cramped in that room." Caitlyn stood beside him, her arms folded over her chest as she took in the hustle and bustle as someone shouted that there was an incident on North Main Street and Chester had called for aid. Fionn and his team headed out with a brief nod to Derek.

"I'll miss that old room though. For many a year, it was the only home both you and I knew," Derek said with a sigh as he shoved his hands into his pockets.

"Home, I have learned, is not a place. It is more the people that are in that place that make it a home."

Derek flashed his oldest friend a toothy grin. "You've become very philosophical in your old age."

Caitlyn simply rolled her eyes as a hush fell over the group gathered, as if they had just realized that they were being observed. The warlocks and witches were not looking at him, however. They were looking at his mate.

Oblivious to the attention, Ever cradled Ash to her and paced, having set her sword down next to the car seat. Derek himself smiled as Ever turned, halted her movements when she realized everyone had eyes in her direction.

"It's like she shines just like the sun."

Derek had not been paying attention or else he would

have scented his best friend and partner stride up beside him. Ricky's black hair was pulled back off his face, his green eyes flaring for a second before he sucked in a breath. Derek knew that his friend was having trouble with his newfound psychic vampire status and controlling his powers. He felt a tinge of sadness for Ricky, for his road had not been easy, yet he was alive and happy to be raising his son with Melanie by his side.

"Looks like your missus has had a power upgrade. She feels more like teen Ash now, like she uncorked her power. Ever could give Loki a run for his money now. Her aura is golden, burning as bright as the sun. I see it. So do the rest of the idiots staring at her."

There was a whoosh of air around the building as Erika dropped to one of the window ledges and raised her brows. "Incoming in three, two, one."

The warehouse all but shook as the beat of wings sounded like thunderclaps outside. One by one, the Valkyries tucked their wings away and entered the warehouse. A sheen of wetness in their eyes once they spotted Ever, they fisted their hands over their chests and bowed their heads.

They were dressed, all but Kenzie, in leather skirts and armor made with Asgardian steel. Their weapons, which ranged from axes to daggers and spears, had been forged by master dwarfs from a place called Nidavellir.

Power crackled in the air as Ever strode over and handed Ash to Derek, the little baby curling into his chest, resting her head where his own heart beat.

Ever walked back over to where the Valkyrie waited, taking her sword in her hands as Kenzie came through the window and almost stumbled, would have done so if Erika had not caught her. The former blood-kissed girl who had been just as much of a victim of Cain as Caitlyn had been was now a Valkyrie, even if her status was relatively knew. She had been struck by a Godbolt, yet Ever had managed to mark her as Valkyrie, making her kin, so to speak.

Derek knew that Valkyrie numbers had dwindled over time. Some had died and others were lost, and now, as Derek watched the five legendary warriors staring at his mate with such reverence, he was proud of her for finally accepting that she was indeed worthy of being a kick-ass Valkyrie queen.

The Valkyrie dropped to one knee as the hulking brute that had taken Kenzie under her wing began to speak. "We held the line until you were ready to return, my queen."

Danae, that was her name, had blood and gore clinging to her skin, much like the other Valkyrie. Kenzie even had a nasty bruise to her eye, which was swollen but didn't seem to bother her.

Ever closed her eyes as her birth mother landed in the window and stepped down to watch what was unfolding. When Ever opened her eyes again, her blue eyes seemed to shimmer. "You held the line well, all of you. And now we shall once and forever more, until our last breath, defend this land as if it were Asgard itself until my daughter is old enough to hold the line herself. Now rise, for we Valkyrie kneel before no master, even a queen."

Yet the Valkyrie did not rise.

They were showing their respect and their loyalty, and Derek felt his wolf howl in agreement with them, even as Ever turned her head, as if lured by the call of the wolf.

Erika got to her feet first, clapping the Valkyrie on the shoulders so that they would rise. Ever sheathed her sword as he watched Erika incline her head to Freya.

"The old bat's been worried about you."

Ever snorted, shaking her head. "She is more concerned what will happen if I should die. Don't be fooled that it is motherly instinct rearing its head, Erika. Freya is who she is. I understand more than ever the urge to protect one's child. There is nothing I wouldn't do for Ash. Perhaps Freya did what she did for her own self-preservation. It matters not when the world is on the cusp of ending."

Caitlyn cleared her throat beside him. "Perhaps we should take this conversation a little more private."

They left the little command center and went up another flight of stairs to what looked like a living area. Donnie sank down onto the couch, as did Ricky, who pulled Melanie into his lap. Caitlyn perched on the arm of the chair beside Donnie, who placed a hand on her thigh. Derek still had Ash in his arms, still fast asleep, when he felt a presence beside him.

"I had forgotten what it was like for a babe to be that small."

Derek glanced down at Freya, Ever's mother, studying Ash with curiosity, just like Ever was watching Freya with equal parts curiosity and maybe a little fear. Ignoring the other conversations that were happening around them as Loki and teen Ash came through the door, Derek pressed his lips together before he asked. "Would you like to hold your granddaughter?"

Freya jerked back, as if the title surprised her, as if his question had surprised her. "You would trust me with her?"

"I don't know you well enough to trust you. But there are enough lethal supernatural creatures and Norse deities in this room to cut you down should you even breathe wrong in her direction."

Derek held out his daughter to the goddess, who gingerly took the baby and cradled Ash in her arms. The baby squirmed, opened her eyes for a split second, then went back to sleep.

Freya began to sing in a language that Derek did not know, her voice sounding as if the heavens had opened up and angels sang a choir of words to his little girl. Derek fought the urge to stay close as he walked to where Ever and teen Ash had eyes wide in disbelief.

"It is told," Ever said with a soft smile, "that Odin was lured to Freya because he heard her sing and he had a need for beautiful things. Her voice was the most stunning in all of Asgard, yet after I was conceived, Freya never sang again."

Derek cupped her cheek as he glanced at Ash. "Maybe this is when she starts to become the grandmother that you know and love."

"You were kind to her when you didn't have to be," Ash said sharply, and Derek could scent her anger in her emotions.

"I think the world could do with a little more kindness in it. We have given her the opening to change. It is up to her to accept it."

Derek nudged his daughter with his shoulder, then strode to where the rest of his family sat. Melanie was dozing, her head buried in the curve of Ricky's neck, his hand tangled in her mass of red hair. Donnie still had one hand on Caitlyn's thigh, but his other one ran over the compass in the palm of his free hand, his thumb tapping on the glass.

"I just wish that I knew what I was meant to do with this bloody thing," Donnie growled, his eyes flashing red before Caitlyn placed a hand on the back of his neck. Her vampire mate calmed instantly. "Ever said that this thing called to the gods like a beacon," Donnie continued as he looked at Derek "but I am no god, Derek. It doesn't call to me in the slightest."

"Perhaps I can be of some assistance, nightwalker." Loki of Asgard, Ever's adopted brother and a god in his own right, held out his hand to Donnie, who placed the compass in the god's hand.

Loki shuddered, a serene look on his features as he closed his eyes. "The power you need to unlock the secrets of the compass is in your blood. The compass knows it belongs to you, and it waits to be awakened. Though the path to answers will not be easy."

Loki handed the compass back to Donnie and opened his eyes. "I believe that you will be following the compass soon.

Might I suggest that you take a traveling companion with you? All of the best quests in history are duos."

Then the god winked, walking back to where Erika, his own mate, stood.

"What do you think he meant?" Melanie murmured, still a little drowsy as she lifted her head.

"Who the hell knows? I kind of get the impression he knows I need to go and not go alone and the secrets of the compass are in my blood." Donnie glanced down at the compass.

"I'll go with ya," Ricky said loud and clear, a look of sheer determination on his face.

"Nah, Ricky, mate, you can't do this with me. You have Mel and Zach to think about."

Ricky rolled his eyes. "And you have Caitlyn to come back to. We will both make sure that we come back to those we love. I'm not about to let you go off after a magical compass with no one watching your six. Fuck that shit."

Donnie shoved to his feet as if he was struck. "I know what I need to do."

Derek stepped back as Donnie kissed Caitlyn hard. "I will come back to you."

"I will hold you to that promise, Donnie O'Carroll," Caitlyn replied with a small smile.

Ricky was kissing Melanie as if they were the only people in the room, and when they broke apart, Ricky winked at her. "Hold that thought."

Stepping away from Melanie, Ricky and Donnie stood in front of Derek, and he embraced them. "Stay safe, you hear me? Don't do anything reckless."

Ricky chuckled. "You realize who you're talking to, right? Reckless is my middle name."

Derek watched as Donnie snarled, letting his fangs elongate. Then he pierced the flesh on his palm and placed the compass in his blood. For a moment, nothing happened, then Donnie reared back his head and screamed as a flash of black light like a shadow leapt from the compass and tore a hole in the fabric of the universe.

Derek glanced into the tear, and he saw nothing, felt nothing but cold and nothingness. Ricky took a step toward the tear, cast a glance over his shoulder at Melanie one last time before he smirked in Donnie's direction.

"Let's go, Frodo. Mordor awaits!"

Then the fool dove through the tear and vanished before their eyes.

"I guess I gotta go now and drag his ass back. Fucking Frodo, my ass."

Then Donnie charged after Ricky, his bulky frame slipping through the tear, and then the blackness shimmered and crackled before it folded in on itself and, like the two supernaturals who had gone through it, vanished from view.

They all stood frozen for a minute, unsure of what to do next until Caitlyn rose from her seat. "I find I am in need of a fucking drink."

Melanie barked out a laugh at the same time as Derek did, then watched as Caitlyn pulled a bottle of whiskey and glasses from a cabinet tucked away in the corner.

"They'll come back, right? Derek, they'll come back, right?" Melanie asked quietly.

Derek found he couldn't answer the truth-seeker's question, for he did not want to lie to her and for her to know that he had lied. Instead, like he would his own kid, he wrapped his arms around the young vampire and simply held her, hoping, for now, that could be enough until her mate came back.

If they came back at all …

CHAPTER
FIVE

Ever

After Ricky and Donnie had vanished through some sort of portal, the mood had turned somber, yet Ever knew that decisions needed to be made. Caitlyn had offered her a drink, but she declined, wanting to keep her mind clear and focused. She was also struggling to shield her own emotions as Freya still held baby Ash and seemed like she had no intention of returning the babe.

Derek came over to her, his keen eyes taking everything in and reading her like only he could. "Go and get her if you like. But we do need to figure out how we go forward. We cannot take her to fight Odin."

Ever had been thinking the same thing, but the thought of being separated from her child was splitting her in half, where one part of her wanted to end her father's reign of terror and part of her wanted to protect her daughter.

"I have a suggestion," Melanie said softly as she came to stand beside them.

She glanced at Derek, who nodded for her to continue. "Zach is with his grandma right now, and Killian has warded the house to keep anyone out that might want to hurt them. I know she would look after the little one until it's safe for you to go get her. And Killian had called in Samhain to fortify the wards as well for extra protection."

Ever shook her head. "Ash's power is like a beacon. I won't endanger Ricky's mom or Zach to Odin."

"Then we cloak her power. Shield her from Odin's eyes."

They were all a little startled to hear Freya speak as she came over and placed the stirring child in Ever's arms. Erika joined them. Freya glanced at Erika, letting out a sigh as she said, "When Erika's mother gave her to me to train, I knew who her father was. Anyone who looked at you as a child and felt that coil of war inside your veins would have known. I used an old spell to dampen your aura. I had intended for Odin to never know whose child you were, but I cloaked you from even Tyr, which was not my intention. We could do the same with Ashlyn."

Erika frowned, rocking back and forth on her feet. "Much as I hate to say it, Freya's idea is good. We flew by the Moore estate, and the only magic we could sense was the warding. Add Freya's spell to that, and Odin will never find baby Ash."

Ever glanced at her mother. "Thank you. I will flash with baby Ash to Ricky's mom's with you and Erika, and we will get her settled and you can perform the spell. Can you remove it or tell me how to remove it?"

"Of course."

"I'm coming too," interjected teen Ash, lightning in her amber gaze. "I want to check in on Zach."

Ever handed Ash to Derek, allowing her mate to say goodbye as she stepped away from the father and daughter, gathering up her sword and sheathing it along her spine before saying to Freya, "Thank you for offering to shield her."

"Perhaps if I had done so with you all those centuries ago, we would not be standing on the cusp of the end."

Ever let loose a sigh. "The past is the past. We are not the fates to change it. We can only ensure that the future is secure. If you keep on looking backwards, you will lose the chance to truly live. We march toward the future; it is the only direction that matters now."

It was as close to absolving Freya of her sins as Ever could muster. Now was not the time for rehashing old arguments or grudges. Maybe, once the war was over, she and Freya could have an honest conversation and settle things.

Derek kissed their baby on her forehead, then placed Ash in her arms. His wolf was very close to the surface, his eyes filled with amber as he growled. "Go. Take her now before my wolf decides that it should not be separated from its pup."

"I'm pretty sure that's the man, not the wolf, thinking that as well. I love you."

"I love you too," Derek said, gravel in his tone as she held her daughter to her chest and flashed from the warehouse to the grounds of Ricky's mom's house. Melanie had been right. The wards around the house were rock-solid, Killian obviously as powerful as his older brother. Ever took a step toward the house, felt the ward push her back, and that reassured her that little Ash would be safe here.

The door flew open as Erika, Ash and Freya all appeared beside her and a small woman with graying hair waved her hand over the door and the ward around the door shimmered.

"Melanie rang ahead to let us know you were coming."

Ever passed over the threshold, and once they were all inside, she closed the front door and the ward fell back into place. Ricky's mom gave Ever a warm smile, and Ever knew she would look after Ash as if she were her own.

"Thank you for agreeing to look after her for us."

The older woman dismissed her thanks with a wave of her hand. "Nonsense. That mate of yours is like a brother to my son. I always wanted to fill the house with grandkids, so your little one will always be welcome here."

"I have my own room," Ash said softly, then clamped her mouth shut as the older woman glanced at Ash, her eyes wide.

"My Ricky told me that you came from the future. I'm not much for all that science fiction thing, but it is obvious who you are. It warms my heart to know that you are so special to us that you have your own room. Now, come, let's get the little you settled."

They were led to a large kitchen that seemed to be the hub of activity. A young man in his early twenties was crouched down by Ricky's son, detailing how Zach could use his magic and push it into the wards. The little boy turned, and on seeing Ash, he darted away and right up into her arms.

Ash balanced him on her hip, then came to stand beside Ever, who was still cradling baby Ash.

"Hey Zach, remember when I said that when you are grown, me and you are bestest friends? Well, this is me right now, and when I go home, I'm gonna need you to look out for me."

The little boy nodded his head of black hair so hard that the strands went into his eyes. "I promise. Dad said I could use my cat claws if someone tried to hurt baby you."

Ash laughed and pulled his nose. "Good idea, Z, good idea."

Killian had gotten to his feet, his dark hair and eyes not as dark as his brother's, nor were they as filled with mischief like Ricky's were, but Ever felt as though the young man was wise beyond his years.

"I need to hold her to work the spell." Freya broke through Ever's thoughts as Ever handed the child to her mother. Then the goddess looked at Ricky's mom. "I need some sage and some jasmine oil."

"I'll get it," Killian answered as he opened cupboard doors and got the ingredients that Freya had asked for.

"Why is a goddess asking for items to work a spell?" The clipped tone of her adoptive mother Samhain didn't so much as surprise Ever but reminded her of a childhood that seemed like a distant memory. Ever angled her body in the direction of the voice, her pulse quickening at the sight of the woman who had raised her during this life cycle.

"To keep the child safe. One would think you would want our granddaughter safe, yet your tone says otherwise."

Freya's own tone was blunt, and Ever had not been aware that Freya knew who Samhain was. But it looked like Samhain had added everything up and taken one look at Freya and seen the resemblance.

"You mean like you should have from the moment Ever was born? Don't take that tone with me when I raised her."

The atmosphere was quickly becoming more hostile than Ever had anticipated. Her lips parted to ask them to stop the pettiness, but Ricky's mom got there before her.

"There is enough fighting out in the world right now. If you two cannot be civil, then you should both leave. I will not have a besting match in my house."

Killian stepped in front of Freya, a slow smile on his lips. "You need me to get you anything else?"

Freya blinked, frowning, then shook her head. When she reached for the sage stick, Killian took it first, clicked his fingers igniting a spark to light the sage. Then he handed it to Freya, who was looking at Killian like she had taken a punch.

Dear gods, was Ricky's brother flirting with her mother?

Freya snapped out of herself and waved the sage over the baby, then dabbed the jasmine oil over her tummy.

"Is that it?" Ever asked, her nose crinkling at the scent of sage.

"That is just to mask the scent. The other part is next. General." Freya held out her palm. "You've been wanting to make me bleed for centuries. Now is your chance."

Now Ever truly believed the world was ending because Freya was making jokes.

Then again, knowing Freya, she probably was being serious.

Erika pulled a dagger from her waist and, instead of cutting her palm, slashed a small cut across Freya's finger. Blood and magic flowed from the wound, and then Freya placed her bloody finger on baby Ash's forehead. Freya's lips moved, yet she did not speak as Ever felt the shift in the air. Then the baby's aura disappeared.

Freya removed her finger, held her granddaughter out to Ever. The moment Ever took Ash from Freya, her mother's knees buckled, and she would have face-planted if not for Killian catching her.

Freya's own magic aura, seemed to dim as Killian helped her to a seat, then started to immediately brighten once she had a moment to rest.

"She is now masked. You asked me how to break the spell. It will break the moment she leaves my side, as it once did when Erika first left Valhalla without me. The first moment we are separated by distance, the spell will fade."

Ever stared open-mouthed at her mother. "But that means you will not fight on the battlefield with us."

Freya smiled, and Ever understood for the first time why there were poems and sonnets about her mother's beauty. "My fight is not with Odin. I will do as I once should have and protect the next generation. Should the battle spill from the city, I will defend the children with my life. I will hold the line."

Then Freya pushed from the chair and strode from the kitchen, leaving Ever with tears in her eyes. "She deserves the chance to fight. She should not be sidelined here."

Erika placed a hand on Ever's shoulder. "She doesn't see it as being sidelined. She is the next line of defense. I pity the fool who dares come knocking on this door with all the power barricaded inside."

Ever watched as Killian grabbed a bottle of water from the fridge and headed out after Freya. Well, this was not expected.

"It's okay, Mom. Grandpa Killian knows how to handle Grandma ..." Ash's voice trailed off as her eyes widened and she realized that she had divulged another fact about the future that she really shouldn't have.

Erika chuckled. "Good. It's about time she got some."

Ever shook her head. "Even I don't know what to say to that."

Zach yawned, sagging a little in Ash's arms as Ricky's mom took the little shifter. "Think it's time the kids went to bed. Come on, Ever, I got down my boys' old Moses basket for Ash. She can rest in my room so I can keep an eye on her."

Ever followed the older woman out and up the stairs and waited in the hallway as she settled Zach in bed. Then Ever was led to Ricky's mom's room. The room was small, modest, filled with pictures of her sons and some new ones with Zach. There was even one of Ricky and Derek, her mate smiling and laughing beside Ricky with an even bigger smile on his face.

"I'll leave you to settle her. Take as much time as you need. The peace and quiet is probably welcome."

Ever turned to thank the woman, but she had already slipped out and closed the door behind her. Ever glanced down at her child, the one who held her heart even though she knew she once had thought it best she not be born. Ever couldn't imagine a life without her now as she paced the floor and looked out the window.

Killian sat on the fountain in the courtyard, an easy smile on his lips as Freya glared at him. She said something, and Killian threw back his head and laughed, causing Freya to get that "I've been punched" expression again.

"Odin took away her chance at happiness. In her own way, Freya sacrificed her future for ours. I understand it now. I do."

Ever kissed her daughter's forehead, then laid her down in the basket. She was caught between snatching her up again or running away as fast as she could. Ever found it harder to walk away, even if she knew it was for the best.

Before she could change her mind, she ducked out the door

and closed it softly behind her. Her heart was pounding in her chest, and she felt like she was about to vomit.

"Leaving your child for the first time is scary."

Ever lifted her gaze to see Samhain waiting on the landing. Her face was stern, as it always was, yet her eyes were softer.

"I wanted to apologize for my behavior when you came to tell us that you were pregnant."

"Is that you, or did Dad tell you to apologize in case we all die?" Ever said sharply, folding her arms across her chest.

"It's me. I have tried to protect you since Tom first brought you to us, and when you charged off and took a wolf as yours, I felt like I had failed you. I pushed you away, telling myself that it was easier to lose you now than to watch you die. I should have known that you were more than a mere human, destined for greater things."

Ever sighed and shook her head. "There is nothing wrong with being human, Mother. Right now, humans are fighting a war that I started and dying to protect the city. And you didn't fail me ... I failed myself. But I will stop him because I need to see her grow up to be the smart, beautiful woman she is today. Hopefully, you get to see that too."

Ever descended the stairs as Freya came back inside, her cheeks a little flushed, glowering at the warlock who came in after her. Freya glanced at Ever, inclined her head, then stepped into a lounge area. Ever blew out a breath, made to follow Freya, then paused to look at Killian.

"You as smooth as your brother?" she asked an amused Killian.

"I learned from the best."

"Good," Ever said before she offered him a smirk. "You hurt her and I'll break both your kneecaps."

Killian just grinned and walked down the hall. Ever shook her head as she joined Freya. The goddess had her back to Ever, her shoulders tense as she continued to look out the window.

"Do not underestimate Odin's power. He is born of the first gods, and he will not be so easily felled. And if he is, we do not know what will happen to the world of men, of gods and monsters if he is slain. It might just unravel the fabric of the universe itself. You are brave of heart, my daughter. Do not become a monster to kill one."

There was a hitch in her tone that made Ever itch to hug her, but she refrained from doing so.

"Freya?"

Her mother didn't answer her, so Ever tried another tactic.

"Mom?"

That had Freya turning round to face her, and Ever took her shot. "Thank you for staying to protect her. It means a lot. It matters. But remember that Odin doesn't get to keep you as his victim. And if that means getting naked with a certain warlock, then I say go for it. Life is too long to walk the road in loneliness."

Ever left her mother standing there with a shocked expression as she went to the kitchen and thanked Mrs. Moore once again. She waited as Killian opened up the back door, watching until they stepped outside before he pulled across the patio door and sealed the wards.

Freya inclined her head to Ever as she entered the kitchen, then Ever felt the urge to spread her wings. Erika, her general, grinned, then unfurled her night-black wings and flapped herself up into the air. Ash held out her hand, calling forth Mjölnir, the hammer flying through the air and into her outstretched palm. Then Ash whirled it around for a couple of spins and launched herself into the air.

Ever felt her own wings itch along her spine, and she shed the magic that allowed her to hide them inside her body, much like she had felt when she felt her toes in the sand at Valhalla. Unfurling her own wings was like a homecoming of sorts. They sprang from her back, feathers of gold and glitter, brighter now than she had ever remembered them to be. Stronger too.

She flexed the wings and then, after Erika called her name, she flew upward toward the sky and was joined in their flight by her Valkyrie sisters, their wings beating in sync with hers as they traveled the night sky.

CHAPTER
SIX

Ash

Ash dreamt of blood and death, the screams all around her as she tried to fight against the never-ending force that she fought alone. Her arms and legs ached, tiredness made her dizzy, and hunger gnawed at her bones. The chains on her ankles chafed her skin as she punched and shoved at the invisible attackers, trying to stop them before they tore innocent humans to shreds.

It was futile, her attempts. However, it was not in her vocabulary to give up even when all seemed hopeless.

"Do you see what your slip-ups could cause, Ashlyn?"

Ash whirled round, grunting as the chains hampered her movement, her eyes going to where three females stood among the bodies of the slain and simply ignored them like it was nothing that they had not seen before.

And considering these were the fates themselves, she supposed they had seen it all before.

Urðr was the youngest of the trio, appearing as a child, though one look into the fate's eyes would tell you that her eyes were old, even if her body appeared not. Her hair was dark blond in color, her clothing simple and plain.

Verðandi stood beside her, a woman in her mid-thirties, the same hair and eyes. It was only when Skuld stood among her sisters, slightly hunched with her hair as white as snow, when the three pillars of the fates were aligned—the past, present and future—did you notice the resemblance.

"*You have evaded us once again, Ashlyn Eversdótti. The magic your cat displays is impressive, yet you flout the conditions in which it was possible for you to return, as does your mate. Even now, you meddle in the course of destiny for Freya. What say you?*"

Skuld's voice grated on her like nails on a chalkboard.

"*It was a slip of the tongue. I meant no harm when I misspoke. I shall endeavor to keep my mouth shut until the battle is over.*"

"*This is not your battle to fight in. That time has not yet come to pass,*" Verðandi advised Ash, the fate's eyes swirling as if she was checking to see if Ash had caused any more disruption in the timelines.

Zach was the one who understood the concept of traversing the timelines. He watched enough superhero movies even before he started working on repairing the Bifrost bridge. He had warned Ash not to interfere in things that did not concern her, to not alter the future in any way other than to ensure her safety. As the shard of the Bifrost in her pocket made her want to take it out and go home, she felt that she still could help in the fight without changing too much.

Urðr tilted her head to the side, as if she was reading Ash's mind and pondering her thoughts. She smiled for a split second, then her expression darkened.

"*You know the outcome should you think yourself greater than fate itself. We stand outside the rule of Odin himself, not beholden to any god. We are instruments of the past, present and future and are duty-bound to ensure it comes to pass. Do not dare think you are better than we.*"

Ash felt the chains around her ankles tighten before there was a sharp tug forward, yanking her to her knees. The fates were suddenly standing around her. They reached out, gripping her hair, yanking her head back, and then, with claws not too unlike a wolf's, they slit her throat.

Ash jerked awake, clutching her neck and gasping for air as the darkness continued to loom outside. After enjoying flying with her mom over Cork city, Ash and the rest of the Valkyrie had returned to rest before Odin's forces struck out again. She had loved every minute of it. Despite not having her own wings, she had flown in her own way and never once had the Valkyrie look at her like she was any different from them.

Sitting up, Ash withdrew the shard of the Bifrost from her pocket, hoping that her slips would not impact the cat at the other end of the shard, waiting for her to return.

Maybe she should go back now and be done with it. Ash knew she was hiding from Grey, hoping distance would dilute the mate bond, but the idiot had followed her back in time, which, to be fair, was a major spoiler no matter how you looked at it.

She was a little worried that if she returned to her present, something would have altered in such a way that she would want to go back and try and fix it again. Zach told her plenty of times she had a hero complex, that being named as Thor's heir had put it into her head that she was solely responsible for fixing everyone's problems.

Ash rested her elbows on her knees and stared at the shard for some time, caught between wanting to stay and wanting to go home. Right now, her da would be going absolutely mental at her disappearance, her mom the same. She had hoped to be back before they even realized she was gone, but weeks had passed now and she was still here. Zach could only fend them off for so long.

"You are brooding now like your father used to do."

Ash lifted her gaze to where Caitlyn stood, her body tilted so that she looked out into the night and at Ash at the same time. Caitlyn gave her the space to figure out what she wanted to say before she said it.

"I'm trying to decide if I should go back now and face the music. I'll be punished for my actions, but part of me doesn't want to go back. Does that make sense?"

Caitlyn offered her a smile. "It does. But why will you be punished? Can you simply not return to when you left?"

Ash snorted. "Time travel is weird. Especially when you factor in the Bifrost. Zach could explain it way better than me. He's super smart when it comes to stuff like this, but I think the Bifrost makes it so that time still goes on."

Ash heard the sadness in her tone even as Caitlyn asked, "But do you not miss your Zach? Your parents? You had a whole life before you decided to come back. Do you not wish to return?"

Ash considered Caitlyn's words, knowing she did miss the life she had. "It's nice getting to know my parents as they are now. There were stories told that I didn't believe, things Zach told me because he got to witness things that I didn't and I always wanted to know. Dad's always been strict but reasonable. I would ask to do something, and he would have me explain why it was important that I did it before he said yes or no. Mom was a straight, flat-out no."

With a smile tugging up her lips, Ash palmed the shard. "Erika still calls Dad 'Boyband.' Now, I know why. Mostly, though, you know I said before that I tried not to get jealous that Z saw parts of all of you that I never did. I mean, I never knew what happened to you until I was a teenager."

"The past is not a happy place for me, little one. Perhaps I was grateful to have one person who looked at me and did not see the broken shards inside me. I am much like that piece of glass you have been clinging to."

Ash snorted. "I never saw you as broken. Even when I did find out, it made me hero-worship you even more. I understood all the lessons you tried to teach me even more after I knew. I can't tell you what happened for me to find out, but I can tell you that after it did, you had this look of fear in your eyes, and I knew you were terrified that I would be afraid of you. In all of my sixteen years, I have never, ever been afraid of you."

Caitlyn looked away for an age, and Ash wondered if she had said too much. Her fears were assuaged when Caitlyn began to speak. "Zach and I have that special bond because he was the first child I held after my daughter. I could not resist those eyes of his, so like his father's. I considered I would feel resentment towards Ricky for the gift he had been given when I had lost mine. Yet I did not. I was equally afraid when I held you, a beautiful baby girl, that the memories of my past would push me back to a place I had clawed myself out of."

Craning her neck as if she were trying to get out a kink, Caitlyn looked at her with those gunmetal-gray eyes of hers. "Getting to know you and Zach has unlocked a piece of my heart that I feared would never be free. I found myself wondering the other day what a child of mine and Donnie's would look like. It sounds quite silly, now that I say it, yet that is the truth."

"It's not silly, Auntie Caity. You love Donnie. But as you once told me, there is no point in dwelling on what-ifs and maybes. You cannot change what is inevitable, so why waste time thinking on it if it hurts you?"

"Perhaps you should consider your own advice. Thinking of the inevitable will not change what is meant to pass. And although none of us want to see you leave, your place is not here in your past, Ashlyn Kyria Doyle. While we lose you in one way, those of us who make it to the future are missing you now."

Ash glanced down at the shard, then sank back on the chair as Caitlyn left her to her melancholy. Her eyes remained on the shard until she felt a presence behind her, and she darted to her feet and glared at the deity giving her a smile that was very wolfish.

"You said that you were leaving."

"I did leave. Your wolf called to me. She likes me more than you seem to."

Ash closed her eyes, hoping her mind was playing tricks with her, but as she cracked them open slowly, Grey was still standing mere feet from her, his scent washing over her. She licked her lips, and his eyes traced the movement, heating the blood in her veins. Grey took a step toward her.

"My dad's in the other room."

"I am not afraid of your father."

Ash rolled her eyes, slipped the shard back into her pocket, then took a step back as Grey watched her with that intense stare of his. She hated the fact her body was all for closing the distance and giving in to the mate bond.

"Have you decided to come home yet?"

His tone was even, but his voice always held the hint of violence in it, no matter what. She was never afraid that he would hurt her—the mate bond prevented that from happening —but Grey was volatile.

"I'm considering it. I'm struggling to say goodbye."

Grey narrowed his gaze, his expression falling to the one he got when he couldn't understand her emotions, because his own were pretty much nonexistent. One day, she hoped to figure out how or why he was the way he was, but that day would not be today.

"It's not like you belong here, Ashlyn. You have to come home eventually."

Ash inhaled, then exhaled slowly. "Do I? I could stay here. I could protect Zach and little me and have a whole life before …"

Her voice trailed off as Grey blinked slowly. "You want time away from me."

"I don't know," came her honest reply as Grey began to walk around the couch to come into her field of vision. Ash made herself stay where she was as he came to stand before her. Ash drank in his handsome face, from his strong jaw and chiseled cheekbones to sinfully curved lips and even to his tousled hair that looked like he had just gotten out of bed.

"You do know, when you look at me like you want to lick me, it doesn't persuade me that I should give you space."

There was a smugness in his tone that prickled on her temper. His proximity always set her off-kilter.

"I'm a teenager. I have hormones. And I never said that you weren't pretty. I have eyes."

A slow smile crept over those lips. "You think I'm pretty."

"I also have said that you're psycho, but focus on the pretty if you want."

Grey continued to smirk, flashing his teeth. "I will use any tools at my disposal to make you accept the mating. Have I forced you into anything you have not wanted? All I have done is lay claim to my mate and allow her the freedom to grow. Apart from when I found you after you left me in the present, I have not so much as kissed you without your initiation of it. You were the one who felt the tug and came to find me. You were the one who brought us together. I might not understand many social norms, but I cannot be the only one to blame for the bond snapping into place. Tell me, Ashlyn, what do you want?"

Right now, Ash didn't want to think about going home, didn't want to think about mating bonds or fate. She just wanted to set her soul on fire. Grey closed the distance between them and cupped her cheek almost tenderly, tilting her face up to his. "Tell me."

She didn't so much as tell him but show him. She dragged him down until his lips collided with hers, and she groaned, her bones melting as Grey took control, nipping at her bottom lip so he could sweep his tongue against hers. Her body trembled against his, begging for him to touch her, yet maddeningly, Grey held back.

She slipped her hands down his torso, her wolf needing skin to skin as she pulled his tee from the waistband of his cargos and placed her palms on his abdomen, the muscles tensing at her touch.

Breaking the kiss when her lungs needed air, she kept her

hands on his taut stomach, her amber eyes clashing with his, now tinged with red. His own chest was heaving, much like her own, a slow, sexy smile on his lips.

"That does not convince me to leave you alone, my she-wolf."

Ash opened her mouth to retort with something snappy, but a throat cleared from off to the side. Her dad lingered in the doorway. His eyes held a hint of amber as he watched her and Grey. Ash made to step away from Grey when her dad stepped toward them, but Grey reached for her hand and held it.

"Did either myself or your mother tell you about how we mated?"

Her dad's voice was soft, whimsical even, as he continued. "I was dying after chasing an unsub, and your mom, she used her powers, even though she didn't know they were hers, to keep me alive. It made her weak and drained her, and I almost lost her. I'd been denying the bond until I had no choice but to surrender to it."

Ash knew that her parents' mating bond had snapped into place before they even got to know one another, much like her and Grey, but her parents had this bigger destiny at play.

"I was the one who forced it in place, and I was worried that I had trapped her in the bond. I was lucky enough that she was stupid enough to love me. The mating bond is magic unto itself. I can feel the tie that binds you, and it is true."

Derek stepped up to Grey. "You might be tied to her, but that also ties you to us. You hurt her, and she has me, her mother and a whole pack of aunts and uncles who will gut you if you harm a hair on her head."

Grey flashed her father a feral smile. "Ashlyn is my mate. I would never harm her. She may think me a little psychotic, as she puts it, and perhaps I am. But I would rather be restrained again against my will than harm her. Though I would love to go toe to toe with any of her so-called aunts and uncles. See how long they last."

Derek barked out a laugh. "Ash is right. You are psychotic."

Ash pulled her hand away from Grey. This was not what Ash had wanted, for her dad and Grey to bond. She growled and stalked away, heading for the door, stomping down the stairs and then out into the never-ending night.

Taking in a few gulps of air, Ash sat down on the curb, dropped her head to her knees and groaned. Her mind was already in a mess over everything, but the fact that her dad all but gave Grey a green light to pursue her would now make him impossible. She was madder at herself for kissing him when she knew each kiss was addicting her to him.

Her dad came and sat down beside her, stretching his legs out onto the road. "I've done something to upset you. I thought my understanding of the bond might help you with Fenrir."

Ash lifted her head, then leaned it against his shoulder. "It's not you. It's me. I'm confused and have been confused. We mated, and then I started to fade and I came here, and now, I want to go home, but I also want to stay. I want to go back to being that carefree teenager who thought herself invincible. I'm scared to stay, but I'm even more scared to go home."

Her dad wrapped his arm around her shoulders and pulled her even closer. "I wish you could stay. Selfish of me, but I love having you here. But now, I have the knowledge that I get to spend time with you like this in the future. We raised a smart, beautiful, fearless daughter who has more courage in her fingertips than most people have in a lifetime. I hate to send you back, but I know that me in the future is probably going out of his mind missing you. Mom too."

Ash said nothing else, just continued to lay her head on her dad's strong shoulder, wondering how the hell she was gonna say goodbye.

∾

ZACH BANGED THE DOOR OF HIS APARTMENT CLOSED, PULLED HIS *pocketknife out and slashed across his palm, then slammed his hand against the wall where he had drawn some wards, not strictly warlock-learned but ones that would keep even a rabid wolf monster out.*

Breathing hard, he shoved his glasses up his nose as he darted down the hall and into his little cave of nerdiness, as Ash called it, flung open the door and lunged into his chair. He had ten monitors all linked on a server to monitor the nine realms and anything else that he might have to find. His vamp mom had seriously hooked him up and taught him everything he knew, even if some of it was strictly not legal.

Pulling the shard of Bifrost from the inside of his jacket, Zach slipped it into the device he had designed and created to control the magic inside it and send Ash to the past.

"Come on, A.K., come on." He urged the shard to spark to life, hoping his friend would feel just how much he needed her here to help him.

"She does not want to come home just yet."

Zach jerked around at the sound of that smug voice, and Zach stopped wondering how the hell Fenrir had gotten past his wards.

Outside, he felt someone try to force their way through the wards, and Zach growled. "You could at least try and be helpful, Fen."

"I promised not to harm you. I did not offer to aid you, cat."

Then the fabled wolf vanished into thin air as someone else tried again to break past his wards.

"A.K., I need you. Please come home."

Silence was his only reply.

CHAPTER
SEVEN

Donnie

T here was nothing but darkness, a vast yawning stretch of black that seemed to go on for the span of eternity. For a moment, Donnie thought that he had merely clamped his eyes shut to soften the uneasiness in the pit of his stomach, yet his eyes were open, and he saw nothing but obsidian. His body felt like it was falling, though he heard no whisper of sound, no whistle of air … it was as if the compass had taken him from a living, breathing world and cast him into another.

He was surprised at how calm he was. A sane man would be panicking right now. A sane man would be trying to fight his way out of whatever hellhole the compass had sucked him into. Instead, Donnie just rode the sensations as if he were lying on a field in Musgrave Park after a serious knock to the head and the doctors were checking for concussion.

His face hit solid ground a second later, leaving him to shake out his head to clear his vision and hearing. He blinked, and the black began to fade to an even more ominous ashen color. Donnie heard Ricky swear near to him and knew his friend was grand.

Getting to his feet slowly, Donnie roamed his eyes over the place where they had landed. Everything was devoid of color, like he was staring into an old noir movie. The trees were gray and the leaves withered. The grass that should have been a rich green in color looked like razor blades, with everything devoid of its usual vibrance and washed in various shades of gray. Even the mist that lurked around them, sneaking in and out of the trees, held the promise of threat and menace.

"Why couldn't that bloody thing have taken us to Disneyland instead of this shithole?" Ricky grimaced as he came to stand beside Donnie, his hand twitching to reach for his gun, which was still at his hip.

Donnie glanced down at the compass, still in his bloody palm, the needle pointing north. To be fair, Donnie was unsure if he wanted to venture deeper into the overcast forest. But he knew of no other way to get home, to his love and to his family, so he jerked his head up and watched as the mist seemed to travel the path in which they needed to go.

"I see that look in your eyes, Donnie. You need us to go deeper into the creepy-ass forest, right?"

"It's okay, Gretel. I'll protect you from the wicked witch."

Ricky laughed, shaking his head as he raised his right hand. "No need. I can just burn the bitch."

Donnie waited as Ricky tried to summon the flames to him, but as his friend growled in frustration, Donnie realized that Ricky might not be the only one affected by whatever magic held the forest together.

Donnie couldn't hear a single thought in Ricky's head.

It felt like a blessing and a curse at the same time.

When Ricky gave up trying to get his magic to work, Donnie told him that he wasn't the only one who couldn't use their powers, which seemed to comfort the warlock a little. Donnie glanced down at the compass, the heat searing into his skin until he took a step toward the opening, where two tall, thick trees formed a sort of archway into the forest.

"Come on. We better get going," Donnie said as he crossed through the archway and into the fog and mist. His footsteps were almost as silent as the forest itself; his boots were heavy and should have made some sort of sound as he stalked down the path in the direction the compass led him.

Donnie was starting to feel like one of those idiots in a horror movie who ran up the stairs instead of escaping out the front door. He kept on walking and walking, Ricky stalwart by his side, allowing him to lead and to have his back.

Donnie made sure that he cast his eyes over the far reaches of the wood, waiting for some kind of nasty to leap out and attack them. The mist seemed to swirl around him, as if it was sentient, and perhaps it was, for the mist kept grazing his face, his arms. The shock of ice cold on his skin felt like a burn.

They walked deeper still into the forest until Donnie heard a rush of water, the only sound he had heard apart from the ones they made themselves. He jerked his head toward it, motioning for Ricky to follow him as Donnie veered off to the right, toward the sound of water, doing so when the compass flickered in the direction of where the water sounded.

The compass in his hand began to heat, searing his skin, but he could not let the thing go. Instead, Donnie gritted his teeth and broke into a jog, trying to reach the water quicker.

The dark of the forest suddenly had a sliver of light toward the end, and Donnie broke through the ashen mist and fog and ground to a halt before a quantity of bubbling water.

Ricky stumbled over his stop and would have gone into the spring had Donnie not grabbed the collar of his jacket, snatching him back from the water's edge. A bubble drifted toward Donnie, popping in his face, and the water stung the skin on his cheek.

"Well, that seems out of place," Ricky said as he leaned forward and tried to get a closer look. The water itself was as gray and white as the fog and mist, and while the water appeared to be hot enough to burn, there was no hint of that, no steam, no obvious heat identifiers.

"This whole forest seems out of place."

The compass flared in Donnie's palm as he spoke, pushing him in the direction of the opposite side of the bubbling water. Donnie nudged Ricky forward, his friend humming the melody to R.E.M.'s "It's the End of the World as We Know It." Donnie shook his head with a smile tugging at his lips.

That smile began to fall as his eyes fell on a point of reentry into the forest and what sat in front of it, with eyes the color of the darkest black.

"Is that what I think it is, or am I fucking hallucinating?" Ricky asked softly, a slight waver in his tone.

"Naw, mate. It's exactly what you think it is."

A fucking dragon … a massive, black, scaled dragon blocked their path, its eyes trained on them, and as Donnie swore, he could have sworn that the dragon smiled.

Well, its lips curved to reveal teeth as sharp as blades, as white as the finest ivory.

The dragon lifted up off the ground, rising to almost fifteen feet high, its scales rippling as it shook itself out, and the ground shifted underneath Donnie's feet. Donnie's first thought was that the dragon was beautiful in a lethal sort of way. Its body was sleek, probably armored scales and flesh. Its feet were the size of a truck, and those claws looked like they could gut Donnie without much effort.

"I don't have enough bullets for this," Ricky muttered beside him.

Donnie clasped him on the shoulder as he replied, "I don't think our puny guns would do anything but piss it off, Ricky."

They glanced toward the dragon, who snorted, a stream of steam coming out of its nostrils.

"The nightwalker is correct. The bullets will only piss me off, and it has been many millennia since I have dined on beings such as yours. Come, join me a moment, and I will aid you on your quest." The dragon's voice boomed across the lake, sending a shiver down Donnie's spine.

When neither Donnie nor Ricky made an attempt to move, the dragon shook itself out and its scales rippled, the scent of magic in the air. Its massive body began to shrink before their eyes until a woman with hair of obsidian stood naked on the other side of the lake. She pulled a bearskin cloak over her shoulders, covering her skin and the scales of black that still lingered on flesh that appeared human and was not.

Ricky sucked in a breath, then began to walk around the bubbling water and toward the dragon. She sucked in breath herself and unleashed a blast of flames from her lips, lighting a fire and holding her hands over the flame.

The warlock was the first to reach the dragon and the fire, and he did as the dragon did, putting his hands close to the fire. His face instantly relaxed as the heat hit his skin, and he let loose a sigh, then glanced at the dragon.

"It is okay, Firestarter. It is disconcerting to be free of your magic when it is a considerable part of who you are."

Ricky flashed the dragon an apologetic smile. "I used to want it gone, the magic, but ya, I understand what you mean."

Donnie saw the dragon smile as if the two were sharing a secret, but then the dragon turned her focus on Donnie. "Come closer, night stalker."

Knowing better than to disobey what was obviously an order, Donnie stepped closer to the dragon, who lifted Donnie's palm and flicked her tongue over the blood staining his hand.

"Yes, yes, Tyr chose right. This quest is true. Once your resolve is tested, then the weapon you desire is yours."

Donnie slowly took his hand back. "Can you tell us about why Tyr would have sent us here?"

The dragon smiled, a feral gesture that reminded Donnie of death. "This world was one of the first two realms ever created, not by Odin and his brothers, but from Ginnungagap, the great and yawning emptiness that existed before the time of the gods and monsters. In the beginning, there was nothing but darkness, and thus, Niflheim came to be."

Listening to the tale from the dragon made Donnie feel like he should have done more research on the mythology surrounding Ever and her father, yet there was something utterly magical about hearing the story told, by a fucking dragon nonetheless, that had Donnie keeping his lips clamped shut as the fire crackled.

"I am Níðhöggr or in your Midgardian tongue, Nidhug, the guardian of the spring Hvergelmir, which is the source of all the eleven rivers. Hvergelmir is the origin of all that is living and the place where every living being will go back. It is also said that from the rivers, Yggdrasil took root and Hvergelmir is one of its sources."

Ricky rubbed his hands together, then frowned. "Isn't Niflheim the closest to Hel?"

The dragon smiled, and it was all teeth. "It is. Hel was created in the shadow of the darkest realm. One does not venture here unless they must."

Nidhug gestured toward the forest. "You must decide if you wish to take this quest upon you, and I am responsible for conveying the consequences of failure. To be deemed worthy to pass through to the other side of the realm, to find what it is that you seek, each of you will step into the forest alone, each on their own path."

The dragon ran her dark gaze over Ricky. "However, I promise to return you to your own world if you forgo this quest and lay with me. It has been an age since I was in flesh, and you are not hideous."

Donnie nearly laughed and would have done so had it not been for the serious expression on the dragon's face. Ricky grinned at her with that charming smile of his, then let his face appear sad.

"In another space and time, I would have taken you up on

that offer. But I have a mate at home that I adore, and I would never cheat. I'm flattered you think I'm not hideous, but I have to decline."

The dragon nodded as if that was all she needed. "Each of you must pass the test to come out the other side of the forest, and when you do, the weapon you need will be within reach. But the path must be walked alone."

The dragon waved her hand, and the foliage shifted, revealing a second pathway. Donnie and Ricky glanced at one another, then Ricky rolled back his shoulders. "So we walk in and just walk out again? What's the catch?"

Nidhug mouth widened displaying teeth.. "This realm is the realm of darkness, of mist and fog, of ice. But mostly darkness. Every being carries darkness within them, the capacity to allow the darkness to take over and let it control them." The dragon glanced at Ricky. "You once succumbed to the darkness, and it was the light of love and family that roused you from it."

"That darkness will always be a part of me. I can't change what happened to me. But it does not define me."

Donnie glanced at his friend, knowing exactly how dark Ricky's mind had gotten and how they almost lost him. Donnie was proud of the fact that Ricky had gotten the help he needed, and now, he was a much better father and mate for it.

Ignoring Ricky's fighting words, the dragon edged closer to the forest, which seemed to grow darker the closer she got. "Each of you must choose to follow the path yourself. Alone. If you do not pass the test of the realm, then, like all living things that are created here, you will be trapped here for all eternity, never to leave."

Donnie suppressed a shiver, trying to push down the nerves in his stomach as he considered her words. Sure, he could turn back now and the world could end anyways. He thought of his Cait, his reason for being. They had traveled a rocky path to get to where they were now, and he would be damned if a god would stop him from his forever. One such person, a vampire who thought himself a god, had tried to take away their forever once before, and Donnie was a stubborn SOB.

"Let's do this."

The compass fizzled and turned to ash in his palm.

"The compass has led you here, completed its purpose. It is no longer needed."

Donnie eyed the dragon as Ricky strode up to the forest entrance and took a quick look inside. Taking a step back with his lips curved up, he held out his fist for Donnie to tap.

"Why the hell are you grinning?"

"This shit will make us legends. Whatever happens when we step inside, you and me will fight to the death to get to the other side of it. Failure is not an option. You don't come out, and I don't go back. We ride together. We die together."

"Bad boys for life." The last part they said together, an easy smile on each of their faces after years of shared memories, of triumph and loses. There was a truth in the way people said that blood doesn't always mean family, and Ricky and him were brothers in all the ways that mattered.

"Don't be getting sentimental on me now, Donnie. I'll see you on the other side."

Before Donnie could say anything more, Ricky rolled his shoulders and marched into the forest. He had barely gone a few feet when the mist and fog engulfed him and Donnie could no longer see his friend.

Donnie peered over his shoulder at the dragon, her scales shimmering as she shifted her naked flesh under the heavy bearskin. Donnie wished for a minute that his heart still beat, for he didn't trust the eerie calm that settled in his bones, the resolve that steadied his nerves and straightened his spine. He stepped closer to the mouth of the forest, thought he could hear whispers on the wind.

A sane man would feel fear. A sane man would not feel the

simmering excitement that felt like a rush of blood to his head. He had spent his human life running headfirst into situations that heightened his emotions, whether that was on the field, in a bar, or life in general. He had sought death or oblivion before with the same calm as he felt now, and Donnie wondered why he wasn't more terrified of not succeeding.

"Failure is not an option. You know you must succeed. In your human life, it was the calm rage in you that meant winning or losing. The field is different, but the outcome is the same. If you waver, then Odin may well win. If you succeed, then crowds will rejoice and the sun will rise once more on your Midgard."

Donnie swallowed hard, not wanting to return to the shell of a man he had been before Caitlyn had saved him, but the dragon spoke the truth. Failure was unthinkable. He would succeed. He would play his part and help save the world.

"You step on that field, O'Carroll, and erase all the thoughts from your mind that tell you that you can't win. You pray to whatever god you want, and once you put your boots on that grass, you play as if the blood of gods runs through your veins, because on the field, you are a machine and a god all rolled into one. Fear cannot win."

The words of his former coach played in his head as Donnie nodded at the dragon, whose eyes gleamed as Donnie muttered, "Fear cannot win."

He repeated the mantra over and over like he once did, when his heart beat and blood quickened his pulse. He strode into the mist and fog with his head held high, let the sharp coldness wash over him as it seemed to seep into his veins, his bones and then his heart, piercing him like a shard of a blade as he gritted his teeth together and let himself be dragged farther into darkness.

CHAPTER
EIGHT

Ricky

R icky felt the frigid cold of the mist in his veins, felt it as completely unnatural to him, considering the fire that usually simmered under his skin. Then it had an iron grip on his heart that had him squeezing his eyes shut and sucking in a sharp breath against the pain of it.

"Are you still a wimp, boy?"

Ricky's eyes sprang open at the sound of a voice that had haunted him for years, and he took an involuntary step back. Xavier Moore stood in front of him, the same black hair, the same scowl on his face as he had worn throughout Ricky's life. His eyes were the same green as Ricky's.

"You look frightened, boy. Are you not happy to see me?"

"Looks like not even death meant I was free of you," Ricky snarled as he took in his surrounds.

They stood on the landing in his childhood home, where many an argument had taken place. He'd been standing there the first time Xavier had lashed out at him, when he had tried to deflect his father's anger from Killian. The first time Xavier had lamped him square in the jaw, Ricky had lost some teeth. He'd been eight years old at the time.

Ricky shook his head and made to descend the stairs when his father called after him. "Still running away from things, I see. Always such a disappointment, boy. And now even more so."

Ricky ignored Xavier and went downstairs until his feet took him to the fridge, and he took a beer from the fridge. He was already drinking it when Xavier walked inside with him.

"Don't you dare run away from me, boy. We have things to discuss so I can be free of you."

Ricky lifted his beer in a mock salute. "Xavier, I don't have time to listen to your BS. You're dead. I've made peace with how I feel about you, and because of you, I know what kind of a father not to be."

"I warned you about the cat a long time ago. Now you have an offspring who is neither warlock nor shifter. He defies the nature of who we are."

Ricky's anger coursed through his veins as he set his beer down on the counter. "Now I know you didn't insinuate that my kid was an abomination, right? Wanna know what it feels like to get sucker-punched?"

Xavier laughed as he smirked at Ricky. "You have me here now, boy. Now is the time to say everything that you want to say to me. You sullied yourself with drugs and alcohol so that you would not be like me. Now, you are a leech that preys on others' magic to survive. You have become the son I always wanted. Does that twist you up inside? Tell me, boy, now that you are even more powerful than I could have dreamed of, what say you?"

"I think you talk too much, Da. I'm nothing like you."

Xavier smiled back at him. "If you truly thought that, then I would not be the one here testing you."

Quicker than possible for his father, Xavier launched himself at Ricky and clasped his head at the base of his neck, slamming his head down on the counter and into one of Ricky's painful memories.

Ricky sat at the kitchen table; his fingers clenched together on the wood as his mother fixed a pot of tea while they awaited his da. Unlike any other family he knew, Ricky had to schedule this meeting with his parents over a week ago, his da's work commitments and social obligations meaning any important conversations had to be held at a time that suited his da's hectic day.

Now he could have had this conversation with just his mam, have her give his da the news, but if his da was going to have a meltdown over his decision, then he might as well have his mam for back up. Watching his mam bustle about, fixing tea for the ten minutes Xavier Moore had allocated his eldest son, Ricky felt sad that his mam seemed perfectly happy to be an armpiece when needed.

Xavier Moore came into the house a few seconds later, and Ricky listened as his da completed his home time ritual. Keys pinged as they were set down into the glass bowl on the side. Shoes set down on the hardwood floor before his da slid his briefcase into the closet under the stairs. Ricky could hear Xavier tapping away at his tablet as he strode into the kitchen, pausing to kiss his wife's cheek before he sat down across the table from Ricky.

Only when his da had taken a drink of his tea and set down his tablet organizer on the table did he lift his eyes to look at Ricky. Settling back into the chair, Xavier checked his watch before he spoke.

"I have ten minutes until I have to answer a conference call from an American warlock. Get started, boy."

Boy ... it was always boy ...

"I've made a decision about college, sir."

Xavier's brow quirked at the "sir," knowing full well that his son would rather choke then call his da sir. His mam squeezed his shoulder as she sat down alongside Ricky, and Ricky hesitated with his next words, waiting for his da to question him. A smack to the mouth the last time Ricky had spoken out of turn had given him a split lip.

"I'm glad you have finally been man enough to make an informed decision. I assume business and magical politics will be your main areas of study?"

Ricky swallowed hard. "No, sir."

Xavier's eyes narrowed, his lips pressing together in a firm line. "Well, boy ... what will you be studying?"

Ricky's mam fidgeted with the lace tablecloth, nervous as to how this was all going to turn out. Ricky squared his shoulders and looked his da dead in the eyes. If he was man enough to make an educated decision about his future, then he would sure as hell tell his da the truth.

"I've decided not to go to college at all, sir. I've signed up to join the Gardaí. I'm off to Templemore in two weeks."

His mam covered her shock with a hand over her mouth while his da simply glared at him, expression void of any indication that Ricky's words had affected him. Not a word was spoken for several heartbeats, and Ricky counted them, because he certainly could hear each one like a drum in his ear.

The silence was shattered when his da slammed his fist down on the table. The overly expensive china teacups leapt out of their saucers, splashing liquid onto the wood. Ricky's mam jumped in her seat, but Ricky remained planted to the spot.

"Is your sole purpose on this earth to aggravate me, boy? No son of mine is going to waste his magical talents and join the Garda. You will go to college, and you will gain all the necessary qualities to take over my seat on the council. Are we clear?"

"With all due respect, sir," Ricky said with a calmness in his voice that surprised even him, "I am not the son to follow in your footsteps. I have only ever wanted to be either of two things, a musician or a cop. I have the chance to make a difference within the supernatural community. I'm not a legacy child, Da. I want to follow my own path."

Flipping over the table using the air in the room, Xavier

rushed Ricky, who did not move and took the blows like he did every time, silent and empty. When his da had vented out his rage, he grabbed Ricky by the throat and shoved him, bloody and bruised, against the kitchen wall.

"Xavier, please!"

He appreciated his mam speaking out for him, but a glare from his da halted her protests. "You have made me the laughingstock of the covens, boy. A laughingstock. The son with so much power who wants nothing to do with it. If you continue to live under my roof, you will abide by my rules, or you will never set foot in this house again. You will not see your mother or brother ever again."

His mam was sobbing in earnest now, knowing that Xavier Moore's pledge would hold, for once he promised something, Xavier Moore never went back on his word.

Ricky had to do something that would make his da realize that Ricky would not be a victim of an expectation Ricky would never live up to. Pushing forward, Ricky used the suppressed rage and determination against his da and switched their positions. Xavier grunted in surprise as Ricky got in his face.

"You know what, Da. I've put up with a lot of shit over the years, and that stops now. If you say I can't be a cop and live under your roof, then that's okay with me. I'll pack up my stuff and go. But mam makes up her own mind."

Shoving off his da, Ricky fled the room and took the stairs two at a time, grabbing his already packed bag, his guitar, and about five hundred euros he'd managed to save up. Ricky was just about to stride right out the door when his mam stopped him.

"Don't go, Richard. Please. I'll try to talk your father around."

Giving his mam a long hug, Ricky kissed her cheek and simply said, "I'm sorry, Mam. But this was bound to happen. We are just far too different."

Ricky opened the front door and took a step outside into the night air.

"Remember my words, boy. You will amount to nothing and come crawling back here for the legacy you so easily shy away from. It is my name that has kept you from harm, and now I will make sure that everyone out there knows Richard Moore is not my son."

"And that's the best goddamn present you will ever give me."

Slamming the door shut, he tried to ignore his brother's pleading face pressed against the window while Ricky marched into the night, relief breathing new life into his lungs.

Ricky broke free of the memory and shoved his father away. "You don't get to throw that in my face, asshole. I walked out that door. I made that choice. I could have been bitter and twisted, but I am loved and love in return. When my son wakes during the day and tells me there is a monster under his bed, I am the one who makes him know that he is safe and will always be so."

He grabbed his father by the collar of his shirt. "You beat and mentally tortured us for years because you felt inadequate. You see me walking away as a failure, but it was the best decision I ever made. I went to Templemore and then worked my way to being one of the best. I grew to be that man because of Tom Delaney and Derek Doyle, both men more a father to me than you ever were. When you died, I did not mourn your loss. When Sarge died, I felt like a piece of me had died."

Ricky let go of Xavier before he continued. "I am man enough to admit that I was terrified when Zach showed up at my door because there was this little part of me that still believed I was your son. But I am nothing like you. You prey on people who you think are weaker than you, and I was never weaker than you, Xavier. If anyone was weak, it was you."

Xavier growled, summoning his power of air and dragging the air from Ricky's lungs. His knees buckled from out from under him, and the moment Ricky's knees hit the ground, he shot out his hand and clasped it around Xavier's ankle, using his own instincts to siphon the magic from Xavier.

The air rushed back into Ricky's gasping lungs as he let go of his father and got to his feet, the other warlock staggering back as he tried to will his magic to him. Ricky licked his lips.

"That's not even enough power to call it an appetizer, Da. Did you seriously have so little?"

Xavier frowned as he regarded Ricky, then a slow, deliberate smile crept over his face, darkening his features. "You are a leech. My legacy lives inside you, and you will always be known first as the son of Xavier Moore. You are nothing without that which I passed down to you."

Ricky laughed, a bitter and resolute sound, as he shook his head. "Naw, Da. You've got it all twisted. I may carry your last name, but I am not that angry boy anymore who was a victim of your cruelty. I am a mate, a father, a brother. I am my mother's son. I am what the people who chose me as their family made me. What I made myself. You are an insignificant part of my past that does not taint my future."

"You mean that ..."

Ricky took a slug from his beer. "I do. Therapy is a wonderful thing. You get to tell a stranger all the deepest, darkest parts of your mind, and they don't judge you. I have made peace with what you put us through, and I work to make sure my son never once feels like I don't love him. So if this is the test, you can go fuck yourself, Da, 'cause you are done fucking with my head!"

Turning away from his father, Ricky felt a wave of relief and peace slide over him as he gave his father his back.

"Don't you dare turn your back on me, you insolent git. I am still your father."

Ignoring his father, much like he had done all those years ago, Ricky left his childhood home, closing the door behind him and locking the ghost of Xavier Moore inside. Seeing his father again, or the forest's definition of his father, had been the closure Ricky needed to shut the door with a firm click of finality.

He had never considered himself a victim of his father's or that his father's mental abuse had led him to make a lot of bad decisions in his life, but his therapist had. Ricky would never be the father or husband his da had been.

Ricky felt the gravel crunch under his feet as he kept walking and walking, heading down the hill toward Caitlyn and Donnie's home. The road was long and winding, but he was alone in his travels, though he kept himself on alert in case something decided to jump out and scare the bejesus out of him.

At least no one would hear him screaming like a girl in this fucked-up world he was walking in. The little bit of magic he siphoned warmed him a little, but the flames still would not ignite in his palms as he came to a stop in the drive of Caitlyn's home.

Instead of walking into the house, he walked around the side and on the plot of land where he was building his home with his Lanie and Zach. They had barely had a chance to lay the foundations of the idea when the world went tits up, and he wished he could be curled up on the couch, his vampire girl in his arms and arguing over her need for a tech room and his desire for a soundproof music room ... as well as their bedroom, though Melanie worried that they'd not hear Zach if the bedroom was soundproofed.

He sat down on the grass and rested his chin on his knees and waited. If he was still stuck here, it meant that he had not passed his test, so he might was well just sit here and wait.

After an eternity, Ricky huffed out an impatient breath. Was this it? Had he passed the test, and if so, why was he not leaving this imaginary world?

A chuckle sounded behind him, and Ricky darted to his feet, his gun in his hands in the blink of an eye. That made the laughter in the shadows start again, and Ricky fired off a warning shot.

"I don't have time for shits and giggles, mate. Either nut up and face me like a man or fuck right off and be done with it."

"Do you really think that a bullet could stop me? I forgot what an arrogant asshole you could be."

The voice that taunted him from the shadows seemed garbled but familiar. Ricky took the voice on face value and put his gun away. He held up his hands, and his eyes darted around the driveaway until he saw a silhouette of a person in the shadows.

"I've put away the gun. Come on. I'm as eager to get this over with as you lot seem to be to get rid of me, so let's cut the bull and play nice now. It's not like the world is about to end or anything."

The voice chuckled again, and Ricky felt the hairs on the back of his neck rise to attention. The shadow took a step toward him, then another, as Ricky felt his stomach drop to the floor as he ground his jaw together. He felt his heart beat like a drum in his chest as the man came forward, giving him a clear view of who had been taunting him from the shadows.

Ricky Moore had been terrified of his father when he was a child. Yet as an adult, he had only been really afraid of one person. Facing his father had been a piece of cake compared with the insufferable bastard that stood smirking at him.

The snigger that curved the other man's lips as Ricky stood in shock, knowing that this was his true test, made his blood run cold.

"You understand now, don't you, why Xavier was only the start of your test, right? You know why the darkness chose me as your test, right?"

Ricky didn't have to say the words out loud to know the

answer to that question, because he should have seen this coming. Ricky lifted his gaze to the green eyes staring back at him, swallowing hard as he took a hesitant step toward the one thing in the world that he was absolutely terrified of.

Himself.

CHAPTER
NINE

Ever

Ever tried to steady her pulse and calm her heartbeat as she remained crouched in her hiding place. Her legs began to burn from the constant position in which she stayed, yet Freya had taught her that pain was only an illusion of a weak mind, and she was far from weak of mind.

Inhaling a breath quietly, Ever heard the shuffle of feet along the tiled corridor and gripped her dagger tighter to her chest. She knew the person who came closer still by his gait, the way his right foot stepped heavier than his left because he carried the fiercest weapon in all of Asgard in his right hand.

Anticipation crept into her veins, and adrenaline sent her pulse racing. Ever glanced up to where Erika, petite and agile, crouched in the rafters, her eyes filled with determination as she held up her hand and then counted down from five.

Five, four, three, two, one ... go.

Ever rolled out into the path of their intended victim and swept her feet out so that the male was taken unawares. With a grunt, he stumbled, as Erika dropped down from her perch and landed on the male's shoulders, her arms locked around his neck. She managed some sort of maneuver with her arms as Ever landed a kick to the male's stomach, and he was felled like a tree, hitting the ground with such force, it echoed throughout the halls of her father's home.

Erika rolled to her feet as she joined Ever, standing over the male, their daggers pointed, one at his heart, one at the softest part of his *neck. They grinned at each other as the male on the ground snarled and the two young Valkyrie giggled.*

Thor let loose a rumble of laughter that sounded like thunder as he surged forward, sending Ever and Erika into a defensive position, their backs to one another, daggers raised and the stupidest of smug looks on their faces.

"You have become sneakier while I was gone, sister. Have you been spending too much time with our other sibling?"

Ever laughed, sheathing her dagger and running to embrace her big brother, his thick muscular arms coming around to hold her close as she retorted, "You have not been gone long enough to allow that to happen, dear brother. Besides, I have Erika to mute Loki's influence over me."

Stepping free of Thor's embrace, Ever glanced over her shoulder at her chosen sister, the girl who would one day be the general of her Valkyrie warriors. Petite and curvy, Erika watched the exchange with a sadness in her whiskey-colored eyes, her hands on her hips, lips pressed together in a firm line.

Ever had always been envious of how beautiful Erika was, and at fifteen, both of them were old enough to receive admiring glances from many an Aesir and Vanir. Normally Ever blushed, but Erika snarled until she scared a suitor half to death. Dressed today in sleek black pants and top, both gifts from her own brother from Midgard, Erika already looked like she was ready to lead an army across the sand.

"Come, Thor, and tell of stories of your trip to the mortals." Ever said eagerly.

"Yes, Thor, come bore us with tales of mortal men and women," a voice drawled behind her brother, and then Loki stepped out of the shadows with a smirk on his lips. Ever ignored Thor's rumbled snarl, hugged Loki to her and stepped back to allow Loki to join the conversation.

Loki's eyes of stars and galaxies glanced toward where Erika stood, a slight tinge on her cheeks as Loki ran his eyes over her best friend.

Erika shifted her weight, the only sign she was uncomfortable at all, because her expression did not change.

"General, a pleasure to see you again."

Ever shook her head, about to tell Loki to leave Erika be, when footsteps thundered down the hall. Baldur came around the corner, his face filled with an anger that should not be possible for the god who never was without a smile, beloved by all the other gods. His hair was the same color as Ever's, his eyes the same blue, like their father.

Baldur had always been kind to her, yet she was not as close to him as she was to Thor or even Loki. As he spotted them standing in the halls, he ground to a halt and tried to rein in his temper, greeting them with a smile.

Thor hoisted Mjölnir over his shoulder. "You've been with father."

It was a statement rather than a question as Baldur ran his hand through his hair. "It is the extent of his anger that even Mother cannot reason with him. But what has transpired can wait for another day, brother. I feel the need to spar. Care to join me?"

Thor chuckled, then his eyes lifted, joy and love in his gaze, and Ever turned to see who had stopped Thor in his tracks.

Her gown was a simple white, off-the-shoulder dress that looked elegant and serene at the same time. Rings of Asgardian gold traced up her bare arm. Her skin seemed to shimmer. Her long braid was draped over her shoulder and down the front of her dress.

Lips curved into a welcoming smile. Her eyes held little speckles of gold in them, her aura like the midday sun as it warmed Ever's own skin.

Ever had always considered her mother to be beautiful, that Erika was drop-dead gorgeous, yet they all paled in comparison to Frigg, who strode in bare feet toward them. Ever watched with a lump in her stomach as Frigg kissed Baldur on the cheek, then waited for Thor to bend so she could do the same. Even Loki wore a different kind of smile on his face as he waited for his adoptive mother to kiss his cheek as she had her other children.

Ever's heart skipped a beat as Frigg turned her attention to her.

Frigg had never treated Ever differently, considering Odin, Frigg's husband, had slept with Freya while they were married in order to further the Valkyrie race, yet Ever felt awkward about running into Frigg, considering that her presence was a constant reminder.

Frigg kissed each of her cheeks with a tenderness that Freya never had. Then she turned to Erika, tilted her head and laughed, the sound like songbirds in the morning.

"Greetings, Erika of Valhalla. I believe you are keeping all of my children safe."

"Yes, ma'am."

Frigg inclined her head, and Ever felt her heart soar at being referred to in the same affection as her brothers. Stepping between Baldur and Loki, Frigg reached out and twirled a strand of Loki's raven-colored hair. "My son, you need some cutting shears."

"I find that the ladies like my luscious long locks, mother. I would hate to disappointed them."

Frigg laughed again, setting a flutter in Ever's stomach.

"Your mother would like you to settle down with a nice girl and allow her to be present at your marital blessing."

Loki rolled his eyes; then Ever was certain she saw his eyes flicker toward Erika before he schooled himself. "Once I have found the right person, you will be the first to know. Besides, Thor has been seen courting Lady Sif. Perhaps you should inquire about his intentions."

Thor growled and grabbed for Loki, but the God of Mischief disappeared out of view, appearing behind Erika and leaning into her ear. "Protect me from the great oaf, General."

Erika responded with an elbow to the stomach that had Loki laughing as chaos descended upon them. Frigg chuckled, stepping out of the fun as Thor dove for Loki, was tripped by Ever and then held down with a foot to his back by Baldur, allowing Loki to stride down the hall as if he was not in danger in the slightest.

Ever felt a hand on her ankle, then she was on her back with an oomph, grinning as Thor got to his feet and swung his hammer in Loki's direction.

Erika called out a warning, the hammer sailing through the air as Loki ducked, avoiding the blow, but the hammer kept going and was about to crash into one of the statues positioned along the corridor.

The trajectory of the hammer was halted by an outstretched hand. Odin stood outside the archway to his great hall, Mjölnir fisted in his palm, the handle facing outward. Ever's mouth fell open, for she had never seen anyone but Thor wield the hammer, but considering it was Odin who had gifted him with the weapon, it made sense that her father would also be worthy to do so.

Her father's face was enraged as he spotted them, his anger radiating so much that thunder clapped outside the palace and lightning streaked the side.

"Odin, my love, the children were just letting off some steam," Frigg said gently as she stepped in between her husband and us children.

"Three of them are gods and not children. The others are supposed to be warriors. Mayhap I should have a conversation with Freya in regards to their training."

His words boomed like the thunder outside as Ever saw Erika reach for a blade that rested at her hip. She glanced at Ever, who shook her head, and while Erika didn't withdraw her blade, she still remained coiled with tension.

"Odin." Frigg sighed softly before she shook her head and strode toward him. He dropped the hammer to the ground with a thud that sent a crack running down the hallway, along the tiles at their feet.

Frigg placed a hand on his arm, and the thunder stopped, then Odin glared at them. For a moment, Ever thought she saw a glint of madness in his gaze. Then he pivoted on his feet, retreating into the great hall and sucking all the tension from the corridor.

Thor held out his hand to call his hammer, grunted his farewell and then strode away from them all, as perplexed about Odin's temper as the rest of them. Loki had also vanished into thin air, leaving Ever standing alone with Baldur.

"What has gotten him in such a twist, Bal?"

Baldur folded his arms across his chest. "A prophecy has been uncovered that suggests Ragnarök may happen sooner than we expected. I asked Father for the chance to speak to the prophet, for he has indicated that my death will be the spark that ignites the flames. He denied me and said that what comes to pass, comes to pass. Our destiny is already written."

Baldur set his hands on her shoulders. "I have not spent as much time with you as Thor or the trickster, but you are still my sister, Ever. Go back to Valhalla and train. Stay there and do not come back to this place if you can. His sons are tainted by him in ways you cannot even fathom. Do not let his only daughter become like us."

Ever didn't know what to say in response as Baldur kissed her forehead and then walked away from her. She kept her eyes on him as he moved, strong, unkillable.

But in the morning, Baldur was dead, killed by a poisoned arrow shot by Höðr, the blind god. Rumors ran rampant that it was Loki's doing, and Baldur's death ravaged Frigg.

Ever had stood beside Thor as Baldur was laid to rest upon his great ship Hringhorni, and she cried for the loss of him, as did all on Asgard. She felt Loki's presence even if he did not appear in person, but as Ever lifted her gaze, her eyes clashed with Odin's across the burning ship, and Odin was the only one not to weep for the loss of his son.

It made her blood run cold.

"What's got you wearing a frown the size of Texas?"

Erika's voice broke through her memories as Ever shook herself free of the trappings of them. She wasn't sure she was remembering events correctly, though she knew deep down she was, for she never forgot anything.

"I was thinking about Baldur and the night before he died. It struck me that perhaps Odin's descent into madness began before Frigg died."

Erika glanced down the hill at the stone bandstand where they had arranged to meet a handful of gods, away from Odin's great hall and any watchful eyes that Odin may have left to spy on them.

"She cornered me once, you know. Not long before she died."

Ever glanced toward Erika with a frown. "You never told me. What did she say?"

Kicking at a loose stone by her feet, Erika shrugged. "Does it matter now?"

"Of course it matters. You wouldn't have brought it up if it didn't."

Erika barked out a laugh. "Seems silly now, but it was strange. Thinking back now, I wonder if she knew she was going to die. I was sitting on the wall in the training arena, and she came to sit beside me. She told me she was envious of my skills, that she could barely lift a sword. I was over a hundred years old at this stage, but the pride in my chest was immense. Unexpected."

Ever knew what she meant to be in receipt of Frigg's warmth, because Freya, her own mother and the Valkyrie responsible for training them all was not very forthcoming with praise. It was always, "Do better next time."

"She held my hand," Erika continued, chewing on her bottom lip, "and told me that she was happy her son had chosen well and that I shouldn't let the easy smile fool me. Her boy was kind of heart and loved harder than anyone even knew. She asked me to take care of him."

Erika laughed. "You know how I was then. I laughed and told her she was mistaken, for my life was sworn to another and my sword was the only companion I needed. Frigg smiled and said, 'Wait and see.' Then I thought I heard her mutter 'Just like her father' before she walked away."

Ever glanced at Erika. "She knew you were Tyr's daughter, and she never told Odin."

"She protected us all from him."

Erika straightened suddenly and inclined her head. "They've arrived."

They headed down the hill, pursuit in their stride as they reached the bandstand and jogged up the steps to the great Lady Sif. She was as Ever had always remembered her, a warrior who had once knocked her brother to the ground while sparring and Thor had been in love with ever since. She inclined her head to Ever as she folded her arms across her chest.

"Would no one else come?" Ever asked at the sheer lack of gods following after Sif.

Lady Sif shook her head. "They have sent me to hear you out, but after Odin killed Thor and Tyr, even the gods are afraid to stand against him."

Erika spat on the ground. "Fools. They dishonor the memory of those who gave their lives to stop Odin."

Lady Sif sighed. "Those who are predicted to survive do not wish to tempt fate."

"Yet the humans fight harder against Odin than those who have power. It is not right, Sif, and Thor would not have stood for it."

Rage flared in Lady Sif's eyes. "No, he would not. My spear is yours once the battle begins. My sons too. I did what I could by giving the nightwalker the compass. It is up to Tyr's chosen to find his path now."

"Why Donnie, though?" Erika asked, a slight edge to her tone. "Why send a stranger in search of a weapon to stop Odin and not his daughter? Why did he overlook me?"

Ever made to speak, but Lady Sif cut across her. "Tyr did not overlook you, child. He said you were exactly where you should be, standing beside your queen and leading an army. I know not why the nightwalker was chosen, but Tyr had his reasons, and I have faith in them."

"And there is no chance of the rest of Asgard fighting beside us?"

Lady Sif sighed again, and her shoulders sagged. "I will try and convince them in the little time we have left. I will do all I can."

Then her sister-in-law took off with a jog and left them standing on the bandstand. Ever shook her head as Erika hissed out, "Cowards."

"Fear is a powerful emotion, Erika. Freya taught us not to be afraid of war or death and, in a way, of Odin. We stand against him because we do not fear death, and that will keep us in the path of victory."

"You sound confident. Arrogant even. I must be rubbing off on you."

Ever laughed at Erika's words. "That is very true. But with you at my side, just like it was always destined to be, I can feel it in my blood that we will be victorious."

Erika clasped her on the shoulder. "Hell ya. Now, let's go home so your mate can stop worrying about you."

As Erika finished her sentence, Ever flashed back to the warehouse. The team turned in her direction as she came into view, and then Erika appeared beside her, the general's eyes seeking out Loki.

Loki strode over to them, disbelief in his eyes. "They would not fight."

Ever shook her head. "Fear is a powerful thing."

"Cowards," Loki growled, and Ever laughed.

"That's exactly what Erika said."

Loki beamed at Erika, who rolled her eyes as Derek came to wrap his arms around Ever's waist.

"I'm sorry they would not stand with you against them."

Ever leaned into him, allowing her muscles to relax. "Thor would have made them. Tyr or Baldur would have convinced them. But I was never fully one of them, so it's hard for them to buck against everything they believe in. To them, Odin is the center of the world, and they revolve around him."

Before Derek could answer, there was a commotion at the door that had them all rushing to the window. Ever could not believe her eyes as vampires stretched out for miles, some armed, some not, but the hum of magic was in the air.

Caitlyn leaned over the ledge, her eyes wide as a vampire dropped the hood of the cloak he was wearing and looked up.

"I did not expect him to come. After Kenzie, I had not expected them to come," she whispered as the vampire with dark skin smiled, his fangs unleashed.

"I will always come when you call, Lady Caitlyn, my queen. No matter what."

Caitlyn vaulted over the window ledge and landed on the ground with a feline grace that should not be possible for a vampire.

"Bonjour, Marcel."

"Hello, Caitlyn."

∼

Lurking in the shadows, Marya raised the bone knife in her hand, ignoring the slight tremble that betrayed her calmness and showed her true feelings about her mission. She was utterly conflicted, killing her kin, but she wanted what Odin promised her. She wanted to be powerful and worshipped, not dismissed and forgotten by those who were supposed to be her family.

They were distracted now, all eyes on the army of vampires who had somehow managed to slip into the city and were now bowing to a vampire queen. Erika was in the embrace of the god of mischief, and Ever had just stepped away from her mate as he took a phone call.

It would be easy now to slip out from the cloak of invisibility she wore and slide the blade into Ever's spine. The bone knife was coated in Odin's blood and would kill Ever before anyone realized she was struck. She would be rewarded even more so by ending the life of the daughter who caused him so much strife.

Marya took a step closer to Ever, her heart beating wildly inside her chest. She dropped her arm, tightening her grip on the knife, and moved forward, her hand angling the blade to strike the moment she was within reach.

Odin had promised to make her queen, adopting her much like he had Loki, and she would become famous in the new world, when Odin remade it anew.

Marya exhaled as she paused inches from Ever and readied herself to strike.

CHAPTER
TEN

Ricky

"**I**f you don't mind me saying, but we are a handsome bastard, aren't we?"

Ricky looked at himself across Caitlyn's driveway in utter disbelief. This version of himself seemed amused by Ricky's reaction, his green eyes blazing with power. The alt Ricky wore the same leather jacket, a distressed black tee with Black Sabbath on it, and black jeans and boots. His black hair was cut tighter than Ricky had it now, clipped at the back, but still had height at the front.

"Why the hell are you here?" Ricky growled, feeling like a fool for arguing with this version of himself.

"I'm who you are afraid of most in this world. I'm what you can become if you lose control. Or if you submit to the growling power in you. It keeps you awake during the day, this newfound power, as you hold Lanie in your arms, knowing you could suck her dry in seconds. For someone who never wanted magic, you now crave it more than you ever wanted those little pills."

Ricky growled, letting his hands clench into fists as his alt self had a destructive glint in his eyes.

"You spent all those hours talking about your feelings," Alt Ricky taunted him, "and yet you kept this little golden nugget to yourself. You don't end up like your father. You become so much worse than he ever was."

Ricky shook his head. "That's not true."

"Then why don't you seem convinced?"

Ricky clamped his mouth shut, shaking his head as if that would push down the fear inside him that his alt self was right —he was never meant to carry such power inside him, and what if it did twist him into a monster that he no longer recognized?

Alt Ricky snickered. "There it is … the doubt … the PTSD from when you burned down that hotel. When you first popped a pill. Every time you look at our kid and see the magic in him, different, and you fear he will end up just like you."

Flames erupted in his palm as Ricky took another step toward his alt self, who grinned like a maniac, unleashing his own more controlled ball of blue flames.

"There he is. The reckless warlock who acts before he thinks. Who thinks he can stand beside gods and queens and fight alongside them. Will Lanie have to save your ass because you leapt before you could walk? A liability who refuses to accept that he could be a power, a god himself, if only he let the power he so desperately needs into him. I was never weak like you."

Doubt crept into his mind, sending a barrage of thoughts to torment himself with. Despite the fact that Ricky knew this version of himself was here to do just that, torment him, he couldn't help but wonder if he was right, if the magic in him was too much for him to handle and he would hurt those he loved. He felt tense when he held his Lanie in his arms, felt the rush of his new vampiric magic hunger for her energy.

Even when he allowed himself a little taste of her delicious energy, he always wanted more, craved it like a vampire craved blood. He could not keep feeding from gods because the high wore off too quickly and it left him hungry still.

"I can see your mind twisting and turning there, Ricky. Do you remember dying? Do you remember what haunted you while you died?"

Ricky spun on his heels and collided with another woman,

heard the sound of her hiss of pain as she fell to her knees. He dropped to his own knees, reached out and helped the woman up, scolding his carelessness as she struggled to stay upright.

"Gods, I'm sorry. I should have been watching where I was going."

"It's okay. I'd joke and say I was visually impaired, but it wouldn't necessarily be a joke."

Ricky chuckled, his breath hitching as eyes of green held his own. He knew this woman. He knew her. He remembered the teasing conversations, the feeling in him when he was with her. He knew the press of her lips against his. He knew the feel of her body against his.

"Have we met before? I feel like we've met before."

Her red hair glinted in the dying sunlight, a smile curving her lips, and Ricky, damn him, felt the urge to press his lips to hers. He stumbled back, earning a frown from the beautiful woman.

"Nope. Don't think so. I sat in on your magical physics class last semester for fun. But us mere mortals have no place attending magic classes. I'm just here for the techy stuff."

The young woman smiled as she nudged her laptop bag. Ricky returned her smile, and the urge to kiss her and hold her in his arms grew stronger as his headache punched louder in his head.

Brushing the dirt off her knees, she gave him another breathtaking smile. "Well, I gotta go or I'll be late for class."

"Again, I'm so sorry for running into you … Ms. …?"

She held out her hand, and Ricky took it, his brain telling him that her hands were normally not as warm as they were now. "Melanie. Just call me Melanie."

Lanie … she's definitely a Lanie.

Ricky held on to her hand for a moment more, then released it reluctantly. "Well, it was nice running into you, Lanie."

The girl blinked at the nickname, then her lips twitched into a smile as Ricky felt a small pang of guilt for being flirty when he had a wife and kid at home. He stood as night fell upon them, watching the girl walk away from him and wondering why every instinct in him begged and pleaded with him to go after her.

Mate.

Mate.

Mate.

Ricky scolded himself, thinking of his wife back home, turning to walk in the opposite direction of the girl when a bloodcurdling scream from the direction Melanie had gone rendered the air.

Ricky bolted toward the scream that had now gone silent, crossing through the quad, his mind screaming that he was in danger, to call for help, but he could not stop from rushing forward. He rounded a corner, standing in the archway that led to the main building, a cry of anguish in his throat as he spied a mass of flame-red hair sprawled against the reddish-brown brickwork on the ground.

It took Ricky a moment to see the pool of blood staining the ground. He screamed for help as he lunged forward, dropping to his knees and taking the bleeding girl in his arms.

A memory washed over him, a nightmare quite like the real-life one that he was living now, of him holding Melanie in a similar way, close to death but not entirely so. He smoothed her hair like he did in the memory, promising to look after her, but his promises were empty, as empty as the green eyes that looked blankly at him.

He felt the crowd gather around him, but he would not relinquish his hold on the dead girl until a hand fell upon his shoulder, and Ricky dragged his eyes from Melanie and landed on a stern face with eyes of hazel. A sense of unbreakable trust filled him.

"You need to let her go, buddy. We have to pronounce her and try and see if we can catch the monster that did this."

One of the most beautiful women Ricky had ever laid eyes on crouched down in front of him, her face a mask of cold that had him shivering. She didn't so much as look at him when she uttered something beneath her breath in French as Ricky laid Melanie down on the ground. His head ached, and he stumbled.

A strong hand steadied him. Ricky glanced up to thank whoever it was that had held him up.

"Donnie?" Ricky mumbled, his legs trembling as he tried to concentrate and figure out what was going on.

"Do I know you?" Donnie said, the vampire studying him as Ricky stumbled away from them.

"This isn't real. This isn't how it's supposed to be!" He shouted the last part, the pain in his head now almost debilitating. He held his head in his hands and retreated until his back hit the wall, and then he slid down until his ass hit the cold ground. He cradled his head in his hands.

"This didn't happen. We saved her. She didn't die."

Ricky knew he was rambling like an idiot, like someone who was embarking on a psychotic break, but he couldn't stop the words from tumbling from his lips.

"We saved her. Caitlyn makes her a vampire. Ever kills Donnelly. Sadie and Cain are dead. Caitlyn and Donnie finally get together. Derek and Ever know that she's a Valkyrie and Odin's trying to kill her! Melanie's a vampire and we ... we ..."

He could feel everyone's eyes on him and felt warm hands on his shoulders as he peered up to see Sadie standing there with her rounded belly, and Ricky knew he was dreaming.

"Ricky, you are not well. We will take you to the hospital, and we will make it all go away."

Ricky shook his head vigorously, tears now streaming down his face. "There was a crash. I went into the Lee. I don't think I got out. Am I dead?"

Ricky felt arms lift him up, saw the wolf who he knew was his brother and the vampire who was his best friend standing beside him, holding him up as they all but carried him toward the ambulance. He glanced back, and Melanie's body was gone. It wasn't real. He had to wake up … he had to get back to his mate.

Ricky felt his magic surge deep in his body, and he roared as he shoved the supernaturals away from him, the blue flames engulfing his skin as he tossed the flames to the side and ran. He heard nothing but the sound of his feet against the concrete, the rush of blood in his ears, and he ran and ran until he ground to a halt at the intersection by North Gate Bridge.

There were no screech marks on the road, no crumbled wall where his car had plunged into the bitter water. There was no indication that he and Lanie had been here at all. He felt a gust of wind against the nape of his neck and whirled round; the vampires were standing in front of him, the obvious tension there for even Ricky's muddled mind to see.

"Guys, this isn't real. Cain is dead. Kenzie killed him. Your niece, Caitlyn. You and Donnie are mated, and you guys are happy. Caitlyn, you smile when you think no one is watching."

"He really is delusional," muttered Caitlyn, a deadpan expression on her face.

Donnie's gaze narrowed as he observed Ricky, and Ricky wasn't sure any of them would believe him; he wasn't sure he believed it himself.

"Donnie, mate, don't you remember the pub crawls we used to go on? The gigs we played? We went to festivals and couldn't remember what we did for those three days. You've seen inside my head and still kept my secrets. Look into my head now and see I'm telling the truth."

Caitlyn and Donnie vanished, and Sadie stood in front of him, Zach by her side, her hand resting on her stomach. The world around them darkened, the city disappearing as she stepped forward.

"Stay here with us, Ricky. Don't leave us here. Aren't you happy with us?"

Ricky coughed, and water filled his lungs as he stumbled back. His family gone in the blink of an eye. Darkness settled in, the road a vastness of nothing, and his headache burned inside his skull. Ricky screamed, but no sound came out.

The alt him's expression was almost gleeful as Ricky flinched, the memories like a punch to the gut. Ricky hadn't told anyone what had happened while he was dead or remade. He had dreamt of an alternative world where his teammates didn't know him and he was still with Sadie. Melanie had died, and he had broken past the dream. It had hurt like hell to have the team not know him, but reliving it was worse than the first time because Melanie was dead again and he had seen that enough times to last a lifetime.

"Or maybe you're still haunted by how Melanie dragged you up, back from death. Does she know that she yanked you from heaven or Valhalla or wherever it was that we went that made you feel so much sickly happiness?"

Ricky hadn't told anyone what had happened while he was dead or remade.

"Or maybe I should show you what happens in the end."

The voice was at his ear as Alt Ricky appeared by his side and clamped a hand on his forehead.

Flames crackled all around him as he swept his hand to the side and flung the bullet aiming for his chest away and into a patrol officer who happened to have gotten too close. Ricky pulled the magic from the warlocks on the front line, draining them down to husks of skin and bones.

He sent a ball of blue flame out toward the group of agents who were coming up behind him, then used his magic to melt the tarmac underneath their feet, their screams feeding the magic swelling inside him until he felt he would burst.

Another bullet shot forward, dinging him in the shoulder, yet he barely felt it. Using his siphon powers, he drained a shifter of magic, and then the bullet popped right out.

"Ricky, stop!"

Ricky glared at Derek as his former friend came forward. "I can't. I won't. You hunt me like I'm not the same person who was your partner for years."

"The Ricky who was my partner would never have been so casual with life. He protected the innocent. He didn't kill them."

The magic pulsed in his veins as Ricky snarled. "You hunted me down, D. You came after me. I ran. I left. I needed more, and now I have it. Now leave before I leave your children orphans."

"Dad!"

Ricky froze as a familiar voice broke through the noise and the din in his mind and he saw his son break free of Caitlyn's grasp and make a beeline for him. Derek tried to halt him, but Ricky sent a blast of heat toward his former best friend.

"Dad, please don't do this."

Zach stood in front of him, thick-rimmed glasses slipping down his nose as his son let tears flow down his face. He was an adult now, but he was still his baby boy. Ricky reached out and hugged his son to him, for it felt like an eternity since he'd laid eyes on him.

"Dad, please. Don't do this. Let us help you. Mom's waiting for us."

Oh, his Lanie.

It had been so long since he had held her in his arms, too long since his magic controlled him and he went from hunting unsubs to being one. He had to protect them, his family, from all the other evils in the world. This was the only way. He needed to be the most powerful, the most feared.

If he had, then Donnie might not have died and Caitlyn might not have gone insane.

And his Lanie might not have gotten hurt.

He felt his power, his magic lunge at the same time he felt the blade pierce his chest. Eyes wide in surprise, he let a small smile creep over his face as he looked into his son's green eyes, filled with tears and sorrow.

"That's my boy."

Ricky came back to himself as if he had broken free of the icy waters of the River Lee once again and smashed an elbow into the nose of his alternative self. He whipped around and withdrew his gun, but instead of pointing it at alt him, he pressed the muzzle to his own temple.

Alt Ricky tilted his head in a confused state, so Ricky decided that he would explain it for him.

"You see, I might be afraid of the power in me, but that's a good thing. I keep myself in check, and if I don't, I have a family who will kick my ass before letting me become like you. That's the difference between me and you."

"Tell me what makes us so different?"

"I'd rather blow my own brains out than make my son fucking kill me."

Ricky said a silent prayer, closing his eyes before he pulled the trigger, feeling some semblance of peace as he heard the gun click but nothing else.

His eyes sprang open, and his gun was still in his hand, but he was no longer standing in Caitlyn's drive. He dropped the gun like it burned him, eyes darting around while he took in his surroundings.

He stood at the end of the forest, a mountain at his back as mist and fog surrounded him, the yawning silence stretching out to give him little comfort. Picking up his gun again, he wiped the dirt from it, strode to a nearby boulder and sat down on it, his eyes trained on the way Donnie should come through any minute now.

Ricky had passed his test and had survived the sum of all his fears.

He allowed himself a second to pat himself on his back before he sobered and wondered where the hell was Donnie? His friend had nothing to fear, was never afraid of anything in his life, so why had the forest spat him out while Donnie was still inside?

But there was little time to celebrate as Ricky glared at the exit to the forest, willing Donnie to appear. He would hug the son of a bitch, even if he had kept him waiting.

"Come on, Donnie ... come on, buddy."

Ricky waited and waited, and still Donnie did not appear.

CHAPTER
ELEVEN

Melanie

Melanie was trying not to worry about Ricky and Donnie, but something in her gut didn't sit well with her. She had chewed her bottom lip so much it had started to bleed, and even though she was supposed to be getting some sleep, she had spent a solid two hours staring up at the ceiling.

She heard a commotion outside and kicked off the blanket, slipping her feet into her Timberland boots before she glanced out the window to see a contingent of vampires lining the streets. Caitlyn was smiling at a vampire that Melanie remembered from the night of Caitlyn and Donnie's mating ceremony. He was the one she had taken into her human home, long before she was a mother and wife, and cared for him like he was her own.

He was also the vampire who lost his entire family, his husband, because Kenzie killed them. It was Cain's order, but Kenzie was the one who delivered the blow. Marcel had vowed not to lay eyes on Caitlyn ever again because he was denied the blood rite, where he would have killed Kenzie.

Looks like the end of the world changed things a little.

Caitlyn embraced the vampire after a few quiet words, and then Marcel barked out words in a few different languages before the vampires faded into the night and Marcel came into the warehouse with Caitlyn and one other vampire.

The other vampire was quite handsome, with skin almost as

sun-kissed as Erika's, and deep brown eyes and lashes that any girl would be envious of. His hair was the same brown as his eyes, curled behind his ears, that windswept bedroom hair her Ricky had.

From her fourth-floor view, Melanie was able to see the vampires melt back into the shadows. Then she headed down the stairs and into the main area, where they were all waiting. Her friends had their eyes on the retreating vampires, and they did not see the threat that lurked behind them.

A young girl who seemed to be in her teens gripped a wicked-looking blade in her hand as she silently slipped into view, and not a single person sensed her.

Melanie rushed down the steps as the girl snapped her head in Melanie's direction, eyes wide, and then she lunged.

"Ever, look out!"

Ever turned just in time to dodge the strike, a fierce growl rumbling from her throat as she withdrew a dagger of her own and blocked the next strike. Erika circled around the girl, forcing her to divide her attention between the two of them. Erika and Ever shared a look, nodded, and then they *moved*.

It was like watching the physical version of a poem, as smooth and fluid of movement as if the two had been doing this forever and it was as easy as breathing. And she supposed it was, as the girl twisted and twirled, trying to keep her eyes on both of the warriors in front of her, yet that was damn near impossible.

Erika kept her dagger in her hand but reached out to barely touch the attacker's shoulder, and the girl nearly leapt out of her skin. Ever did the same, and the girl looked close to tears. Then Ever inclined her head, and Erika stopped her assault to stand back.

Ever tossed her dagger aside. "I do not need weapons to defeat you, for you are already defeated. You do not believe the fight can be won, so your death is inevitable. Stand down, Marya, and I will have no need to send you to Hel this day."

The girl lunged at Ever, and Melanie sucked in a breath as Ever simply sidestepped, gripped the girl's arm, and yanked it back. The sound of bones snapping was only drowned out by a scream as Marcel and Caitlyn came in. The other vampire standing in the doorway with Caitlyn had to hold Marcel back.

"We must not interfere. This is the way of Valkyrie."

Marcel nodded as Marya continued to grip the blade, then Ever turned into the blade, earning a shout from Derek. Ever didn't even glance at him as Ever yanked the girl's arm, then wrenched her wrist hard, forcing her to drop the knife.

Erika strode around the back of the girl, and with a swift kick to the back, the young girl was on her knees, tears streaming down her face. Erika yanked her head back, and Melanie saw the power that was contained in the Valkyrie for the first time.

"You sided against your own family. Plotted to kill your queen. Odin was not the one to comfort you when your parents left you to our care. Odin was not the one to bandage your cuts and grazes when you were injured in training. Odin did not offer praise. Odin did not put those clothes on your back. You forget those who raised you as if we meant nothing. You are not worthy to be known as Valkyrie. Centuries of training wasted on a traitor like you."

The last few words came out in a harsh snarl as Erika's eyes blazed. Ever reached down to force the girl's chin up so she would look directly into Ever's eyes. Quick as lightning, Ever had the knife at her throat, and Melanie sucked in a breath.

"You will tell me when Odin plans to attack and what he has in store."

The girl jerked her chin out of Ever's grasp. "I go to death with no fear in my heart, for I will be rewarded by him in Valhalla when he is victorious in battle."

"Stupid girl ... the only place you'll go is to Hel, where all the unworthy go."

Melanie was moving forward before her feet could stop her, would have kept going if Caitlyn had not grabbed her hand. "This is the way of Valkyrie."

It was nearly the same thing she had said to Marcel, but Melanie didn't want to watch them kill the girl. The knife held to the Valkyrie's throat reminded her of when she was human, when Stephen Donnelly had relished the way he slid the knife into her flesh over and over until her voice was hoarse from screaming and she passed out.

Melanie sucked in a harsh breath as the warehouse in front of her vanished and she was back in the abandoned call center, strung up like a pig to be gutted. Panic welled in her chest as Caitlyn stepped in front of her, placed hands on either side of her face before she said, "This is not the same. You are safe here. He cannot hurt you anymore."

Melanie shook her head, the past vanishing. She offered Caitlyn a small smile. "I'm okay."

Caitlyn kissed her forehead before she stepped back to give Melanie space. However, now the two Valkyries were looking at Marya with smiles that didn't quite put her at ease. Again, as if they were speaking a language that no one but the two of them knew, Erika nodded with an expression that promised pain.

"I think before we kill you that we are going to get some information from you, even if it kills you."

The girl spat on the ground. "I will not break. You will not get a single word of truth from my lips."

Erika's grin deepened, and Melanie wanted to step back from it, as if the monster in her recognized the bigger monster. Erika's whiskey-colored eyes glanced in her direction.

"Oh, neither myself or Ever is gonna try and get the truth from you, Marya. But she is."

It took Melanie a second to understand that Erika was referring to her.

Ever must have sensed her reluctance, because she strode over to Melanie and stood facing her. "What if I said to you the information we get from her, could stop the war? The bloodshed. That using the powers given to you by the fates could garner just a sliver of info to help me kill my father."

"I can only tell you whether it's a truth or not. If she lies her ass off, then that will do us no good."

Ever regarded her for a moment, but it was Erika who spoke next. "Then you yank the truth from her."

Melanie shook her head. "I can't do that."

"Yet," answered Erika, as she kept an iron grip on Marya. "Just like Donnie can suddenly dream walk and your husband is a weird concoction of warlock and vampire. I heard what Ash said to you. The power is in you. You just have to decide if you control it or it controls you."

Melanie's mind raced, knowing that if she didn't at least try, then the girl was dead. "Promise you won't kill her. Promise me you will let her live, and I'll try."

Ever glanced over at Erika and nodded. Relief sagged Melanie's shoulders. The pair shared a look, but Melanie was too worried about her part in all of this. If she couldn't make Marya tell the truth, then Erika could kill the girl.

For some reason, Melanie didn't want her to die for a foolish cause.

Erika pulled the girl up by her hair, causing her to yelp as Ever dragged a chair across the room and set it down. Loki had come to sit on the couch, stretching out his arms as if he was casually watching a movie rather than an interrogation.

Melanie glanced around the room. Derek gave her an encouraging nod, as did Caitlyn. She wanted Ricky. She needed Ricky. She wanted one of his pep talks where he told her she was a badass and she could do it. He had done that for her since before she had become a vampire.

Erika had the girl sit in the chair, placing a hand on her shoulder as Melanie planted her boots firmly on the ground. She lifted her gaze to Erika. "I need you to ask her a few questions to get the magic flowing. She has to answer, or it's useless."

"With pleasure."

There was something in Erika's tone that made it sound like this was going to be anything but pleasurable for anyone involved.

Lifting up her free hand, Erika beckoned for Ever to toss her the knife. The Valkyrie caught it with ease, then kept it within Marya's eyeline.

"You have already promised not to kill me because the vampire asked it."

Erika chuckled. "I promised not to kill you. I never said I wouldn't hurt you." To prove her point, Erika let go of the girl's hair for a split second, and a different dagger that appeared from nowhere lodged in the girl's thigh.

The traitor screamed, reaching to pull out the dagger, but Erika yanked it out for her. The girl bucked and tried to stem the bleeding as Erika began to circle around her.

"When will Odin strike?"

The girl clamped her mouth shut, then screamed again as Erika slashed at her shoulder.

"I will ask one more time, then I start peeling skin off with my fingers. When will Odin strike?"

"He has no timeframe."

A bitter lemon taste coated Melanie's tongue, the first swirl of magic pumping in her veins. "Lie."

Erika slashed out again, this time on the girl's cheek, and the scent of blood made Melanie growl and snap at Erika.

"I can't fucking concentrate if you keep carving her up and presenting her like a Happy Meal on legs."

"Then I just need to start breaking fingers. No big deal."

Truth.

Melanie knew that Erika was vicious, but seeing it was another thing altogether.

"Does Odin have any other surprises planned?" Erika asked quietly, deadly.

"No."

Again, bitterness on her tongue. "Lie."

Erika had the girl's hand in hers a second later, and she crushed the bone like it was nothing more than a chicken bone. The girl writhed, tears in her eyes, but she did not scream this time.

Melanie needed to hurry this up, stop this interrogation before the girl had any more bones broken or blood spilled. Closing her eyes, Melanie drowned out the voices of the others. In her mind, she pictured her magic like a slice of code for hacking, all lines of data that a normal person would not be able to decipher, then when she tweaked at the magic of it, she felt her skin flush, the magic surging inside her, wanting to get out.

Was this what it felt like for Ricky? In a constant struggle for control with a vital part of himself. She understood him now in a way she hadn't before, because right now she felt drunk on power.

Opening her eyes, she looked at Marya and tested her magic. "Tell me why Odin waits."

The girl shifted in her seat, trying to clamp her mouth shut, so Melanie asked again, with a little more magic in her voice. "Tell me why Odin waits."

"His army is not complete."

Melanie shuddered under the push back from the truth. She kept going. "What does he need for his army to be complete?"

"I don't know."

The girl again spoke the truth, sweat breaking out on her

forehead as Melanie dug a little deeper, blood starting to trickle from the girl's nose.

"Is there a way to defeat him? Odin?" Melanie asked, her feet moving closer to Marya.

"Yes ... but I don't know how. He kept that from me."

Truth in every word. With every word spoken, the magic wanted more.

"Who knows?"

The girl gritted her teeth, the sound of her molars grinding as she tried to keep her mouth shut.

"Tell me," Melanie snarled, not recognizing her own voice.

"No one. Anyone who knew is dead."

"Who knew?"

The girl didn't answer, so Melanie grabbed her magic in her mind and forced it into the girl. She jerked back and forth, fighting the compulsion until she suddenly halted and uttered a single name.

"Tyr."

Then she sagged as if she was out cold, and Melanie stumbled back, a little horrified by what she had done. Her hands trembled, even as relief washed over her. Tyr had known how to stop it, and he had sent Donnie on his quest. The way to winning was within their grasp, and Melanie knew that they would come back.

They had to.

Melanie was happy that it was over. They could lock the Valkyrie up until it was all over and try and rehabilitate her maybe. Odin had brainwashed her, and Melanie knew what that was like. When she was a young woman, Greg DeShane had brainwashed her, disguising it as love, and she had ended up breaking the law for him.

This girl was no different.

"Take her outside, General, and call her sisters."

Wait, what?

Erika had the semi-conscious girl over her shoulder a second later, Ever trailing after her. Loki got to his feet with a little touch of sadness in his eyes as Derek reached out and placed a hand on Ever's cheek.

"Do you really have to do this?"

The expression on Ever's face flashed from stoic to sad while she took her sword in her hands. "It is the way of Valkyrie. She must be punished for her betrayal."

Melanie made to follow when Caitlyn stopped her. "You do not have to bear witness to this. Even if you cannot stop it, you do not have to see it."

Shaking her head, Melanie replied, "I know this is war. I know that terrible things will happen and people will die. I have to see it to believe it. I have to play my part, even if I lose a little part of me in it. I can't run from all the horrible things that are going to happen, even if I think the terrible things are going to be done by family."

They all converged on the street, and Melanie glanced up at the beat of wings as the Valkyrie descended on the street. Melanie saw Marcel flinch as he laid eyes on Kenzie, her black wings nothing more than a streak in the never-ending night.

The hulking Valkyrie Danae dropped first, her cream-colored wings folding into her as she stepped onto the ground. She was followed by Almira, the quiet warrior who Melanie had learned from Kenzie liked books better than blood. Then Rebekah before Kenzie herself dropped.

She stumbled on the landing, a sheepish look on her face as she glanced toward Melanie, then her face froze as she took in Marcel standing beside her, then the younger vampire standing beside him.

Kenzie blinked as the younger vampire ran his gaze over Kenzie before saying. "You have changed since we last laid eyes on one another." His accent was thick, like he had learned English as a second language.

Kenzie rolled her eyes. "You look the same. Suppose that's to be expected with you being a vampire and all."

The vampire chuckled, a throaty sound that sent a blush to Kenzie's cheeks. Then Danae called her name, and she turned her attention back to the scene playing out before them.

Erika had Marya on her knees in the middle of the road, as if she were praying for mercy to her sisters. The remaining Valkyries formed a wall behind Ever, facing Marya as the rest of them stood on the pavement and waited for everything to unfold.

"Marya has betrayed our laws, where loyalty to our sister-hood is absolute. She conspired with the Allfather to kill me, to take the throne for herself." A growl started up between the Valkyries, and they were silenced by Ever's raised hand.

"She refused to speak the truth until it was pulled from her. I promised not to kill her, on behest of the vampire Melanie Newton-Moore. However, her betrayal cannot go unpunished. So Marya will receive the most severe of our punishment."

Marya sucked in a breath, her small frame trembling.

"For her grievous acts of treason, Marya is to be stripped of her wings, her powers and any magic that would mark her as Valkyrie. She will wear the scars on her skin as a reminder that she forsook sisterhood for power. And it was her undoing."

Erika muttered a few words, and wings of white and auburn sprang from Marya's back. Ever lifted her sword, the blade glinting in the moonlight. A caw rang out above them, two birds circling, watching as Ever stood behind Marya, the sword twirling in her hand.

"You will live the rest of your days as a human, alone. And when your time comes, we will see if you have repented enough to gain access to Fólkvangr, for you will never be worthy to enter Valhalla again. Have you anything to say?"

"I go to death with no fear in my heart, for I will be rewarded by him in Valhalla when he is victorious in battle."

CHAPTER TWELVE

Donnie

The midday sun blinded Donnie as he jumped backwards at the sound of a horn blaring. The driver of the bicycle swore at him in a language he sort of recognized, but his immediate panic at the fact he was standing in daylight and not frying his ass off meant his brain was in too much of fight or flight mode to translate it.

He glanced around, trying to get a handle on where he was, why he was able to stand under the full force of the sun and not burn to ash. His eyes darted around as cyclists ambled down the streets until he saw a flash of black curls striding across a bridge straight in front of him.

Caitlyn?

He tore off after her, calling her name as he slipped in and out of the crowd, losing sight of her, but the way men and women turned in the path he was traveling, he knew they were looking at his mate.

For a terrifying moment, Donnie thought he had lost her, yet there she was, standing before an impressive-looking cathedral like the goddess she was, a smile on her lips and a goddamn heart that he could hear beating.

"Perhaps if you lighten the shade of gray in the sky, then the gargoyles would appear fiercer."

The words were spoken in French, yet Donnie understood completely what she had said. Caitlyn was looking at an artist who didn't even glance in her direction when she spoke to him. The idiot snorted at Caitlyn, shaking his head before he retorted, "Mademoiselle, I draw what I see, what I feel ... perhaps, if my art is not to your liking, you should move on elsewhere and leave me to my own devices."

His mate laughed at his words, that throaty laugh that Donnie loved to drag from her. The sound of her laughter dragged his gaze away from his artwork, and he looked at her in surprise. Caitlyn gave the artist a smile, apologized, which his woman never did, and asked if he would have coffee with her to make amends for her ill words.

Extending her hand, Caitlyn introduced herself, and the man took hold of her outstretched hand. She asked him his name, to which he replied, "Sebastian Hardi, Lady Caitlyn. It is my honor to meet your acquaintance."

Donnie sucked in a breath, and the man glanced in his direction. Donnie took in his appearance. It was hard not to compare himself to Sebastian, for it was something he did almost unconsciously at this point, a thing he kept mostly to himself, for he knew how much it would hurt Caitlyn.

Where Donnie was all broad shoulders and thick thigh, this man was a thin wisp of a man, slightly smaller than Caitlyn when she wore heels. His spectacles had slipped down the bridge of his nose, and his eyes held an intelligence that Donnie would never have.

The image of Caitlyn slipped away. The sights and sounds of what Donnie now knew as a Parisian street vanished too, leaving Donnie standing in the midday sun, facing the ghost of the man he feared the most.

"I would have missed her, had she not spoken to me that day."

The other man's voice was gentle, as if he wondered how to talk to him, the other man in Caitlyn's life. Did the fact that

Sebastian claimed her first mean that Donnie was the other man, always in his shadow?

Sebastian chuckled. "Does she know that you see yourself as the other man? I am flattered that I can be nothing but dirt and bones and I still hold sway over people I have not met."

Donnie blinked as Sebastian read his mind and was pissed that he had.

"Now you know what others feel when you take a thought they meant only for themselves, oui?"

Donnie didn't answer Sebastian, yet he walked closer to him as the man leaned against the bridge, his elbows resting on the rail. He glanced to his side, and Donnie followed the path his eyes went to see Caitlyn retreating, but when she peered over her shoulder, a bright smile on her lips, Donnie knew the smile was not for him and it fucking burned.

"I wonder why is it that your mind did not conjure Cain for this little quest. He is responsible for the woman you know now, not I."

Donnie knew the answer before he replied to Sebastian. "Cain never had her heart. You did."

"Yes, I did."

Donnie said nothing as Sebastian pushed off the rail and began to walk, giving Donnie no choice but to trail after him. The man whistled as he walked, hands shoved into his pockets as he ambled along the roads until they came to stand in front of a house.

"This is the home we shared together. Where we first lay as man and wife, where we rocked Jessamine to sleep. She kept it; did you know that? She still keeps a staff on-site. It was the first place she returned to when she came back to Paris."

Donnie hadn't known that, but it didn't surprise him in the least. Caitlyn had known happiness and sadness inside that house, and she would not have been able to sever the ties that bind her for nobody.

"I never had a proper home until Caitlyn found me. I don't understand the need to hold on to a building for sentimental reasons. But Cait is different from me. Sometimes I think she was blessed and cursed to have known love like the one you two shared."

Sebastian chuckled as he pushed his glasses up his nose. "Ah, mi amour always had a soft heart for waifs and strays. She was always trying to feed the world and spending time taking the children off the streets to rehome them. My love was too kind of heart."

Was that what he was, a stray for Caitlyn to adopt? Was that all he was? Why did this still haunt him?

"It is because you are a bastard that no one wanted. Even now, having met your own bloodline, they keep you at arm's length. Tell me, Donnie, when you allowed yourself to be beaten in the streets, did you want to die that night?"

Donnie growled in his throat at the harsh words spoken in Sebastian's gentle tone. "I was good at only one thing my entire life, and that was rugby. When they told me I couldn't play anymore, I knew that I'd probably be dead in a year, and I had no one who would care if I went then or in that moment."

"You didn't fight back."

"No, I didn't."

A silhouette appeared in the window of the first floor, and Donnie knew it was Caitlyn. He knew the outline of her curves, had kissed and touched and coveted each part of her until he knew her skin as well as his own. A peal of a child's laughter rang out, and Donnie froze, watching as the shadow scooped up a smaller frame and they spun, the laughter cutting through him.

"This is the night it started. When Cain first invaded her dreams. Do you think it ironic that the vampire she allowed herself to feel something for has the very same power as the man who stole away her happiness?"

Jesus, that hadn't even dawned on Donnie, that he had somehow gotten the same gift as Cain. It made him sick to his stomach, wondering if Caitlyn would think less of him now. If she would fear him like she had once feared Cain. Would Donnie himself be the cause of her night terrors?

"What if I told you that if you let me walk into the house now, that Cain would never find her. We would welcome our son and perhaps more children. That Caitlyn would never step foot in Ireland. That she would stay human and mine and happy. Would you let me walk inside that door, even if it meant you died alone in an alleyway?"

Donnie was floored by Sebastian's questions, and at first his mind screamed no, no, he wouldn't be all right with never knowing Caitlyn, of never having her say "I love you" or never hearing the way she almost whispered his name when they were in bed.

He thought back to when he had chased after her, when she returned to Paris to hunt down Cain and they had talked, really talked for the first time in twenty years. They talked about his life before, when he was human, how much of a dickhead he had been, and his woman had turned to him and said, "And then I made you a monster."

Donnie had taken her in his arms, positioning her so she looked him right in the eyes as he told her, "I started living the moment you made me a vampire. It was like I was asleep and you woke me up. I became the man I am today because you saved me. Every good thing that happened to me happened after my heart stopped beating. And I will always be grateful that I found you."

And he meant it. His life had truly begun when he died and was reborn. Part of him selfishly didn't want to say yes, to tell Sebastian to walk into the house so that instead of Caitlyn losing her entire family, he would simply lose her. Would she say yes, if given the choice?

"She will never know. It will be as if she simply took another path. The lives she had in Ireland would not exist. Those she impacted would not know of her. Kenzie Blake would have lived a full life with her family."

"But both Melanie and me would be dead."

Sebastian shrugged. "Probably. Maybe. I know only what I know now. If I stay out this night, I meet the vampire Cain and I invite him into our home. He tries to seduce my wife and then, inside that very room where the love of our life dances with her child, her belly rounding with another, she will watch us be butchered. If you had the chance to make her happy, would you?"

A tumble of thoughts and memories spilled into his mind, of breakfasts and dinners, of movie nights, of heated glances and I love you's. He didn't know how he could give them up, because Caitlyn was ingrained in his heart and soul.

"She won't even know she ever loved you."

His mind played out an argument they had, when he had made the foolish mistake of suggesting that they could adopt a child, when Caitlyn had lost her temper and he his, when he had felt so lost and couldn't figure out how to help her, the distance between them more so after they had mated.

"Seeing you with Zach and how happy you were, and I wanted to make you that happy again, because you certainly aren't happy with me."

But Caitlyn had told him she had loved him … was he still that little boy who stood at the children's home and watched other kids get adopted and longed for someone to love him enough to call him theirs? Was he clinging to the only love he had known because it seared him right in the heart to think that he would never hear the words *je t'aime* tumble from her lips?

Glancing up at the window, he studied the silhouette and let his shoulders sag. He would do anything to make her, his Cait, happy, and if that meant he had to die alone in an alleyway, never knowing true love, then so be it.

Donnie looked down the street, a memory playing out in front of his eyes, of them walking hand in hand, anticipation in the air, tension in their limbs, knowing that they could not go back after this night, no matter how hard they tried.

"But that's not when I fell in love with you." Donnie shared with her. *" I fell in love with you one day after you had a nightmare. It was the first time my mind-reading powers manifested, about a year after I became a vampire, and I was powerless to stop what happened to you in the nightmare. You woke screaming so hard that I thought you would rip your vocal cords. And as soon as you remembered that you had an unwanted houseguest living right below, you covered your mouth and screamed on the inside."*

"I never wanted you to see that side of me."

"But I did, and it didn't scare me away. Getting inside your head made me understand you a little bit more. I couldn't understand, with my tiny male brain, why you obviously wanted me but never acted on it. That day, I knocked on your bedroom door, yet you never answered. Defeated, I went back to bed but could not sleep. After a few minutes, my bedroom door creaked open, and your scent filled my nostrils. Cait, you slipped into my bed and curled up on your side, your back to me, and I could have sworn my heart skipped a beat."

"Which is impossible, since it did not beat."

Donnie nudged her with his shoulder. *"Shh, I'm trying to be romantic and shit."*

Caitlyn snorted. *"Forgive me. Carry on."*

"As I was saying." Donnie went on with his tale. *"I lay there staring at the goddamn ceiling, not knowing what to do, your scent waking me up. But you turned to face me then, fast asleep, a peaceful yet troubled expression on your face. I watched you for few minutes. A nightmare began to creep its way into your mind again. So I just acted, slipped my arms around you, pulled you up into my chest, and as soon as you lay your head against my chest, you stilled, the nightmare ceasing. I*

felt like a fucking superhero that day. I had the most beautiful woman in the world asleep next to me, despite the obvious trauma she'd been through, and she trusted me to keep her safe, especially when she could kick some serious ass."

"And I ran out before you woke and neglected to mention or even thank you for keeping the nightmares at bay."

"But you did thank me. The next time that you had a nightmare, after ignoring me for a week, you came back to me, to my bed and let me hold you. That meant everything to me."

They'd been walking for a while now, and Donnie paused to look at her. "I appreciated what I had within my grasp. That you had given me a home, something I never had before. You, Caitlyn, showed me what a family really could be like and gave me a purpose when you asked Sarge to let me join P.I.T., and you gave me you, as much of you as you could. And that made me fall for you."

And he was still ridiculously in love with her and always would be. The woman who gave him a home, love, a family, and he knew in that moment exactly why he had to let Sebastian walk into that house.

Because he had to have a little bit of faith that he and Caitlyn were meant to be. That he could make peace with the ghost of the man who held Caitlyn's human heart as much as he hoped that he, Donnie, had the vampire one just as she had told him after he asked her if she wanted to be married like humans do.

He heard her voice in his ear, as if she were solid and standing beside him. "Sebastian held my human heart, but you, Donnie, only you hold the vampire one. I married only once in my human life, and I will only marry once in the vampire way."

Donnie cast one last glance toward the window and the woman he loved, then he inclined his head to Sebastian and walked away. He didn't dare look back to see if Sebastian had walked into the house or not, because while he could be the person to grant Cait her happiness, he wasn't built of stone, and seeing it would break him.

Rounding the corner, Donnie saw he was no longer in Paris. The cobbled stones of Temple Bar were beneath his feet. His head was dizzy from drink, his heart beating in his chest. He still had his memories, his sorrow of what would never be in his veins.

His feet tangled, and he landed on the ground with a thud. He felt something twist in his hand, however he was too drunk to feel any pain. Lying on his back as rain hit him hard in the face, he laughed, though he was unsure as to why.

"Look at the almighty Donald O'Carroll lying in the gutter, just like his mam left him on the day he was born!"

Rage flooded his veins at the stark reminder of both his birth and the death of his teenage mother, too ashamed to seek help after giving birth to her baby down a Cork City alley. Her family hadn't wanted a bastard child to bring shame to their good name. Growing up in foster care had only added to his anger and self-loathing.

Donnie knew he had been sent down the path that had changed his life for the better, but now, there would be no guardian angel to save him, and he was powerless to stop his actions.

He growled and lifted off the ground, his fists clenching. As he made to punch the sneering Dub, the native sidestepped, sending Donnie crashing to the ground. A boot connected with his stomach, and he groaned in pain before vomiting all over someone's shoes.

"Now that's just fucking rude, Donnie lad. We should make ya lick it clean."

"Go fuck yourself," he replied as he rose to his knees.

His attacker smacked him, open-palmed, across the face, hard enough to draw blood from Donnie's lip. Donnie spat the blood on the ground and, like a madman, grinned up at his assailant, bloody mouth and all.

"Resorting to a bitch slap; that's low, man. C'mon, at least grow some balls and hit me like a man. I've been spanked harder than that."

His comments were answered with a boot to the face, followed by swift kicks from the other men with the Dubliner. Dizziness made him nauseated, and he closed his eyes to calm the feeling. When he felt himself being pulled along, Donnie opened his eyes long enough to realize he was being dragged down an alley.

He knew, in that exact moment, that he was going to die.

The kicks came more frequently now—to his stomach, chest, and his head. He lost count of how many times he blacked out. It hurt to breathe, and he could taste blood in his mouth. After what seemed like an age, two of the men backed away, and he heard one say, "Come on, Damo. You're gonna kill him."

He received one final boot, this time to his face, and felt bone crunch—he had broken his nose so many times, he knew the feeling instantly—but his entire body hurt so much that a broken nose was the least of his worries. He would die in a darkened alley, leaving the world as he'd been brought in— alone and bloody.

Donnie opened his eyes to gaze once more on the sky before he died, but instead of seeing the gunmetal eyes of Caitlyn Hardi, he saw only rain as his eyes fluttered, and just before he died, Donnie uttered, *je t'aime, Caitlyn, je t'aime.*

~

SITTING ON TOP OF HER SKULL THRONE, HEL, KNOWN ON EARTH AS Helen, huffed out a breath with boredom as she contemplated a trip to Midgard to see how the war against Odin was proceeding. She missed her friend Melanie, who, by the way, had not even bothered to send her flowers or a gift for saving her lover.

Then the Thor girl had tried to rough her up, and Hel had not liked that, but the girl smelled of her brother, and she would rather be upset than have Fenrir hunt her down because she had made the puny goddess bleed.

She glanced at Baldur, who stared out into the underworld beside her, his expression blank and joyless as it had been when she dragged him down here. Hel—the place, not the person—had sucked the joy and light from the god.

Awareness washed over her as she darted upright, righting her rainbow-colored tutu and striding to the mouth of her cold palace and glancing down at the army of the dead, who jostled each other as they moved.

Hel blinked as one of her dead vanished, then another, then a handful all vanished before her eyes. "What the ..."

Her words were cut off as her hound, Garmr, howled, a low, mournful sound that sent a shiver along her spine.

"Bad dog, shush!" she chided him, but Garmr continued to howl at the entrance to the underworld as the souls she had kept for eternity began to vanish at an alarming rate.

Glancing over her shoulder just in time to see Baldur disappear, Hel glanced back at her hound and sighed. "Well, that's not good."

CHAPTER
THIRTEEN

Caitlyn

"I go to death with no fear in my heart, for I will be rewarded by him in Valhalla, when he is victorious in battle."

"Mon dieu, foolish girl," Caitlyn muttered at the rhetoric coming from the little warrior's mouth. She knew of those who followed blindly, those who demanded such reverence, and many a young woman who was ruined by it, and it was such a shame that this poor girl now had to face the consequences of when a man had been the master wielding the puppet.

"She may be centuries old, but she has yet to see that not all gods are good and that even the evilest of men and women can have sheep who will follow them blindly."

Caitlyn knew Marcel was speaking of Cain, though his eyes had shifted to where Kenzie stood, her niece stealing looks at the vampire who was stoic by Marcel's side.

"Kenzie saved him. Mateo. From the other vampire who appeared when they killed my Jean. She told him to run and if she ever saw him again, she would decapitate him."

Caitlyn chuckled as this Mateo said softly, "I think she was flirting with me."

"I look at her and I still see the person who murdered my love. I sent Mateo to keep a check on her, waiting for her to make a mistake so I would have the right to have my vengeance. Yet Mateo tells me she has done quite a lot to make amends, even facing down one of her new sisters in a fighting ring," Marcel said softly, so that only Caitlyn heard him speak.

"That bravado almost got her killed."

"Nada." Mateo offered with a mischievous smile. "She moved like a harpy out for blood. It was something to watch."

"What are they going to do to her?" Melanie whispered beside her as Caitlyn slipped her hand into that of her sired child and gave a little squeeze.

Caitlyn did not have to answer, for Danae stepped forward, as did Erika, each of the Valkyrie women holding a wing in their grasp as Ever lifted her hand and sliced downward. Caitlyn saw the way the blade cut through the muscles and tendons on the girl's back.

The scream that ripped from the girl was horrific. Melanie squeezed Caitlyn's hand so hard, she felt her own bones tense. The girl's wing hung loose as Ever sucked in a breath, then slashed down on the other one to the same effect.

Blood gushed from the wounds as Erika and Danae each let go of the wings that they were holding. Then Erika took the sword from Ever and finished what Ever had started. The scent of blood in the air was overwhelming, but it did not stir hunger in any of the vampires.

When Erika had severed the last of the Valkyrie's wings, she handed the sword back to Ever, then with her bare hands, she pulled the wings away from the girl's flesh and Marya lurched forward, vomiting on the ground.

"Nope, that's it … can't." Melanie spun on her feet and was inside the warehouse before Caitlyn could stop her.

Caitlyn lifted her gaze to where Derek was standing, his eyes filled with amber as he watched Ever. This woman was not the same teacher who Derek had claimed as his mate. She was the sum of all the lives and deaths she had endured.

Ever called the other Valkyrie forward as she dipped her hand to the bleeding skin on Marya's back, her fingers dipping into the wound, then she turned, smearing the blood down her face from eye to jaw. Caitlyn watched as one by one, Erika, then Danae, followed Ever's lead, right down to Kenzie, who swallowed hard as she did the same, until the remaining Valkyrie all wore Marya's blood on their skin.

"You are no longer Valkyrie. You are no longer kin. Should we meet you on the battlefield, you will not see the sun rise. We wear your blood as a reminder of the sister we lost and to remember that loyalty to family is above all."

Ever spread her own wings, white and gold as flew up to the sky, the Valkyries all spreading their wings and joining her. They circled Marya overhead, and then they flew away as the girl cried out in agony, her fingers touching her wings.

"We call ourselves monsters. We claim that our ways are archaic. But I will never forget what I have witnessed this day. We may be monsters, dear Caitlyn, yet we will never be as vicious as the way of gods." Marcel offered Caitlyn his opinion.

Marcel might have lost his family to Cain, much like she had, yet this was a kindness compared with what she had witnessed under the catacombs. She didn't correct Marcel as the girl grabbed a handful of feathers and stumbled away and out of sight.

Mateo stepped forward, grabbing a bloody feather and tucking it into his pocket, then he braced himself with a pair of karambits as Ash dropped to the ground, hammer in hand, breathing hard.

"The dead … are … coming!"

Caitlyn could not have heard that right, for if she had, then exactly what did Ash mean?

There was a low sort of moaning, the sound of feet shuffling down the road as Derek went to stand beside his daughter and even Mateo braced himself. The first dead came around the corner, its eyes turning to see them. Then another and another filled their field of vision.

They would be slaughtered.

"Madre de Dios," Mateo swore as he twirled his blades in his hand, a skill that not many could master.

"Everyone into the warehouse. We don't have the numbers to fight them. Marcel, call back your vampires." Caitlyn barked out the orders as Marcel confirmed that he had already done so.

Ash, Derek and Mateo stayed rooted to the spot as the first of the dead lunged, snapping its teeth at Ash, who swung with her hammer and knocked a few back. Derek growled and kicked and punched as Mateo cut through the dead like they were a mild inconvenience.

Derek grunted as one of the dead snapped her teeth right in his face, and Ash kicked the dead with so much force, its knees broke and it dropped to the ground. That did not stop it from dragging its body forward along the ground.

"Where is Rick Grimes when we need him?" Marcel muttered quietly; amusement hidden in his tone as Caitlyn glared at him. She was about to chastise him for being so glib when suddenly an aura of power filled the street and the dead halted their attack.

Melanie rushed out of the warehouse with two guns pointed toward the dead and groaned. "This can't be good."

Ash helped Derek to his feet as they retreated from the dead, who seemed immobile, unaware of anything outside of the frame who marched in front of them dressed in a multicolored tutu, tights with koalas on them and a T-shirt that read, *Baddest bitch in the underworld.*

Her hair was pulled back into two pigtails, and Caitlyn saw they had colored chalk at the ends. Pink flashing sneakers finished off the car crash of an outfit as this petite creature paced in front of the dead.

"That is not the Rick Grimes I was expecting." Marcel chuckled. "I should come to Cork more often. Nothing is ever straightforward."

The being stalked along the line of the dead, holding up her hands as they tried to surge forward, as if she was struggling to hold them back. She seemed to pause, lifting her palms, and popped some gum before bringing her hands together in a large clap.

"Lucy, you've got some 'splaining to do!" Then she stomped her foot on the ground, and the dead moaned.

"That's right, momma is so pissed right now. You all go home now, you hear!"

Caitlyn felt the power in her voice, but the dead did not move. The being looked over her shoulder, her fathomless eyes landing on Melanie, and she waved enthusiastically.

Melanie lifted her hand in response as Ash growled. The being shouted, "Hi, Daddy!" at Loki before she stuck out her tongue at Ash.

The girl turned back to the army of the dead, who began to shuffle again, and then unleashed the first true glimpse of power. "I am Hel, the goddess of death, and you will obey me!"

A few of the dead disappeared, slowly at first, then more, but some still lingered, a fierce growl emulating from the gathered dead.

Hel, goddess of death, sighed, then strode over to her father and motioned with her hand. "Gimmie."

Loki shook his head. "The last time you borrowed it, you caused an earthquake."

"It was only a small one."

"Tell that to the people of Valdivia, Chile."

Loki's daughter rolled her eyes. "OMG, you said you would let that go."

"And what of Pompeii?" Loki said with a quirked brow.

"That was all you, Dad!" Hel stomped a foot, and the lights on her trainers came to life. It was ridiculous to imagine the goddess of death standing in a tutu and flashing runners arguing with her father, the god of mischief, about who had caused which natural disaster.

"So it was … my mistake." Loki looked sheepish at the realization that they were both equally responsible for historic events.

Caitlyn watched the interaction between father and daughter, smiling a little despite the gravity of their situation. Loki sighed again, then held out his hand. A scepter that looked like it was solid gold, with a silver-tipped curve at the end, appeared in his hands.

Hel strode back over to where the dead waited, then she slammed the heel of the scepter into the ground. It trembled at the impact, and Hel repeated the action. This time, the ground did not so much as tremble but quake.

The road cracked, then it was as if the layers were peeled back, revealing a chasm to the underworld. Coldness crept along the street, and Caitlyn shuddered. Derek, Ash and Mateo fell back in line with them. The dead groaned and moaned as if they did not want to return from whence they came.

"Off you pop, now, back where you belong," Hel said with the cheeriest of smiles on her face, and this time, when she glanced over her shoulder, her features flashed, revealing the grotesque skull under her guise. Mateo blessed himself.

The dead ambled forward, dropping into the split in the ground as a hound leapt from the gap and stood beside Hel. This was no ordinary hound, for it was made of fire and brimstone, and when it howled as the dead fell into the abyss, the sound was shrill enough to shatter glass.

Hel reached down and rubbed the hound's head. "Who's a good boy? You're a good boy. Mommy's bestest boy."

"I would not have believed this had I not seen it with my own eyes. That goddess is not quite right." Marcel muttered.

Caitlyn had little comfort to offer Marcel as some of the dead broke off, trying to flee, but the vampires had arrived, and they pushed the dead back and back. The Valkyries returned, and they swooped low and scooped up the dead and dropped them into the ground. Vampires screamed as the dead tore into them, and Mateo retreated as Kenzie swooped overhead.

"La Chica Bella, a lift?" he called out to Kenzie, who shook her head at the vampire before he vaulted over Derek's car and into the air, where Kenzie caught his arms and flung him into the path of the dead. Caitlyn knew the vampire was trouble when she heard him whoop with happiness as he drove the dead into the hole.

Hel beat the scepter into the ground, each touch like a gunshot. Caitlyn helped where she could, fighting against the dead and forcing them back the way they came if one managed to slip away from Marcel's vampires.

Melanie fired off a few shots of her guns, the dead seeming to be impervious to the bullets. It seemed to take hours to clear the street of the dead, and when the last fell into the pit they'd crawled out of, Caitlyn was covered in sweat and gore. They all were.

As the last of the dead was cleared away, Hel stomped the scepter down three times, the ground quaking once again before it closed up, but not before the hound of Hel leapt into the rift.

Hel turned to face them, tossing the scepter into the air. Loki caught it with ease before it vanished from view. Hel fluffed her tutu and then strode over to where Melanie stood, throwing her arms around Melanie, who had yet to lower her hands holding the guns.

"This was awesome! I can't believe Odin called them all from my domain! That's just rude."

Caitlyn wasn't sure if she would describe the fact that the thousands of dead that Hel held dominion over had walked down the streets of Cork city as awesome, but the goddess bounced around like a child hyped up on fizzy drinks and chocolate.

Marcel shook his head and walked over to where Mateo was wiping blood from his face.

Dusting off her tee, the goddess let loose a sigh. "I was trying to hear what was going on, here on Midgard, and I left the door open for him. He shouldn't have been able to sneak my little pets out the door without me knowing. Whoops!"

Hel turned to Caitlyn, looking at her for a hard moment before she frowned.

"I almost had your mate to take Baldur's seat beside me for a hot minute. But I totally was denied. Too bad. I think he would have been waaay more fun than Baldur ever was."

Caitlyn's heart sank to the very soles of her feet as she regarded Hel. "What do you mean?"

"Well," the goddess drawled, "there was this moment where his name appeared on the list in my head. But when I went to get him, I couldn't. I assume that means he's still alive ... or not."

Caitlyn reacted before anyone had the good sense to stop her and pulled Hel toward her with a growl. "What do you know of Donnie?"

Hel's features flashed, as if that would scare someone like Caitlyn, who had faced her fair share of monsters in her time and was not afraid of a little death. The goddess of death inhaled through her nose, and she let loose a moan Caitlyn had no answer for.

"Oh, you could kill me. I can feel it down to my marrow. Death is in your blood, vampire queen. I like the taste of you."

Caitlyn let her go with a snarl as Hel fixed her tutu and then vanished before Caitlyn could reach for her again. She pivoted toward Loki. The lord of mischief had the good graces to look sheepish as he held up his hands in surrender.

"Would you believe it if I said she takes after her mother?"

"Do you know what it is she spoke of?"

Loki shook his head. "I'm sorry, Lady Caitlyn. If I knew, I would certainly tell you."

Everyone had returned to the warehouse to clean up after the fight with the dead, yet Caitlyn remained outside, as if standing outside would bring Donnie running around the corner and into her arms.

Their story had yet to turn full circle, and Caitlyn could not believe that she had endured all she had to lose him now that she had found him. Caitlyn had told Donnie that she loved him many times, though not as much as she should have. When he returned to her, she would not see the sun rise without reminding him that she loved him.

Caitlyn felt something land on her shoulders and glanced up to see Derek drape a jacket around her.

"A watched kettle never boils, Cait. Come inside."

"I should have said more before he left. I should have given him more of me when he was here. I didn't think on it, as I am not as free with public displays of affection as everyone else. Yet I feel the need for him to know that he has all of my heart."

It was safe to say all of these things to Derek, for they had shared many a secret during midnight walks. Derek knew her as much as she knew him, for theirs was a friendship built on trust and loyalty.

"You get to tell him, Caitlyn. Of course you do. Ash proves that he comes back because he's alive for her to tease the hell out of him. You can tell him all that you said to me, all that's running through your head, when he comes back."

Caitlyn pulled the jacket around her, not because she was cold but because she wanted comfort. Derek rested his shoulder against hers, and Caitlyn, who quite often shied away from such a touch, leaned into the offer of comfort.

"We have both been given a second chance, mon loupe," she said. "And I worry that I have squandered it. Your Ever knows that you would leap in front of a bullet for her. Does Donnie know that I would do the same for him?"

"He does, Cait. He does. And if the idiot doesn't, then you get to smack him upside the head so that he doesn't doubt it the next time."

Caitlyn wanted to believe him, to trust Derek, who had not steered her wrong in the decades they had known one another. Still, she lingered outside on the road, as if thinking of her Donnie would conjure him to her side, where she would hold him to convince herself that he was safe with her.

Mon dieu, she prayed that she would.

CHAPTER
FOURTEEN

Donnie

Donnie pried his eyes open, the pounding in his head so strong, for a minute he thought he was lying on some field, having taken a knock to the head. His heart was not beating as he stared up into the darkness, surrounded by mist and fog, a very grumpy warlock staring down at him.

"What took you so long?" Ricky demanded, hands on his hips, his features dark as he glared.

Donnie chuckled, then grabbed his head as he rolled to the side, first getting to his knees, then rather shakily to his feet. "I'm sorry. I was getting my head kicked in and dying. Again."

"Ya, well my kid stabbed me and then I blew my brains out. Don't see me standing here bitching and moaning, do ya?"

Running a hand over his hair, Donnie felt a moment of panic as he tried to feel the pull of the mate bond, but though it was still there, it was diluted somewhat. Relief washed over him, and he staggered, probably would have fallen if Ricky had not reached out to steady him.

"Okay, sit your ass down before you fall over."

Ricky led him to a boulder, and he leaned against it, Ricky looking at him with concern. "You look like death. Paler than normal, as if that's possible. What the hell happened to you in there?"

Donnie took a minute to take everything in before he replied to Ricky's question. "I was in Paris, with Sebastian."

"Caitlyn's Sebastian?"

Donnie nodded. "Yup. It was the night that Sebastian met Cain. When he first brought him home and then he became obsessed with Cait. Sebastian told me that if I walked away, if I left him to walk into the house, he would never have met Cain and Caitlyn would have gotten to live a happy life with her husband and kids."

"Jaysus ..." That was all Ricky said, his voice trailing off, even though Donnie knew that he had to tell him the rest.

"I saw her and Jessamine in the window. I felt her happiness. It would mean she never came to Ireland. Was never a vampire. And I would die. So I walked away. I left. And then I got my head kicked in again, right in Temple Bar, and Caitlyn never came to save me."

"Fucking hell ... and I thought my vision quest was messed up."

Donnie glanced over at Ricky, who waved a hand dismissively.

"I faced off with me da. That was kind of okay, but then apparently, I'm afraid of myself more than anything. I stood across from me, the me who let the magic in him take control. Then he showed me Zach all grown up, and he drove a knife into my heart. I knew no matter what I did, I could never expect him to do that. I'd rather put a bullet in my head. So I did."

Donnie shook his head, pushing himself off the boulder. "You can never tell her, Rick. Caitlyn can never know."

Ricky shook his head, holding up his hands. "Dude, nuh-uh, nope. Don't ask me to keep that secret for you. I can't. Secrets have bad consequences for me. Besides, those kinda secrets come back to bite you in the ass. You gotta tell her."

A growl of frustration rumbled in his chest. "And what if she thinks that she wishes that fucking test was real? That she had never become a vampire and we had never had a chance? I can live with the not knowing. I can't live with knowing that she hates me because I was afraid of a ghost and not being good enough for her. Would you want Melanie to know?"

"My Lanie already knows I don't think I'm good enough for her. I tell her often enough."

Donnie whirled around with a snarl, ending the conversation as he stalked forward. He heard the shuffle of Ricky's footsteps behind him, following after him, but Donnie had no clue where he was going. There was a large mountain obscured by frost and mist, so Donnie headed toward it, finding a dirt path.

Ricky came to walk beside him as they made their way up the narrow path, and then as if by magic, the mist cleared. A doorway into the base of the mountain opened up. Donnie went closer, ducked his head inside, and all he could see was darkness.

Straightening, Donnie faced Ricky and let out a sigh. "I take it we need to go in there. I think my eyes will adjust but not sure if your eyes are like a normal vampire or more human still?"

Ricky grinned, clicking his fingers and flames danced along the tips, Ricky beamed. "Looks like I got my mojo back. It's okay, darling, I'll keep you safe."

Laughing as Ricky went to the mouth of the cave, then continued on inside, Donnie followed after him, letting the lick of blue flames be his guide. They went down and down along the path, with Donnie listening for any sounds, any scents, but he could only catch his own.

The path seemed to wind downward, as if the way in which they traveled would bring them both down into the depths of Hell itself. Donnie could hear Ricky's heart kick up, though his buddy never said a thing to him about any fears he might have, even though Donnie knew that he himself was feeling the effects of this descent into more and more darkness.

"What I wouldn't give to be sitting on the deck at home, few beers, Ireland vs. the All Blacks on the TV."

Ricky glanced over his shoulder. "The girls staying just for the Haka and then leaving us to our own devices."

"Then coming out to yell at us for breaking a window."

Ricky laughed, the sound reverberating off the walls, making Donnie grin until Ricky stopped suddenly, so unexpected that Donnie nearly plowed into the back of him. Ricky trembled and licked his lips.

"There is something down there." Ricky pointed his finger toward what seemed like a never-ending blackness. Donnie couldn't see or feel anything, but he trusted Ricky and his unique hunger for energy.

Nudging Ricky's shoulder, Donnie took off at a jog, toward the way Ricky had pointed. Ricky was hot on his heels, keeping in step with him as suddenly an archway came into view, a white marble against the opaqueness of the darkness that seemed to ignite the cave into illumination in an instant.

There were runes carved into the marble, but Donnie didn't read runes, and Ricky narrowed his gaze and said it looked like some sort of warning. They exchanged a look, then side by side, they stepped through the archway.

Torches were littered all around the cave, a small waterfall streaming silently down the wall, the lack of sound unnerving as Donnie glanced around the abandoned cave. If he didn't know any better, Donnie would have thought he was standing in a prison of some sorts.

"There's nothing here," Donnie mumbled, his voice a mere whisper, though he wasn't sure why he was whispering.

"Oh, there's something here all right, but it hasn't come to say hello yet. Come out. I can feel you back there."

Donnie felt the sudden shift in the air, like one predator realizing a bigger threat loomed on the horizon. Bracing himself, Donnie edged closer to Ricky, who rolled his shoulders, letting a little bit more power into the flames in his hand.

Time seemed to slow, the sound of a chain being dragged

against the floor of the cave the only indication that anything was happening, and then Donnie saw red eyes before a figure materialized out of the darkness and Donnie flinched.

A teen with inky-black hair, naked from the waist up and a simple cloth wrapped around his waist, stepped forward, his eyes flashing red before they changed to a fathomless black. To be fair, Donnie wasn't sure what was better, the red or the black.

"Is that who I think it is?" Ricky asked.

Donnie didn't say anything, just glanced down at the chains around the kid's ankles and sighed, letting loose a bark of laughter that jerked Ricky's head round.

"Loki doesn't let him loose." Ricky sighed, shaking his head. "We do. She was wrong to blame him."

"You speak of my father like you are friends."

Donnie turned his head back to look at the chained teen, hearing the maturity in his voice as well as the power locked inside him.

"He is. Kind of."

"Have they sent you to kill me? Am I finally to be free of this place?"

Donnie really wasn't sure what they were supposed to do, but Tyr had sent them here for a reason. Odin's fear of wolves was widely known. The very reason Fenrir had been bound was due to the prophecy that Odin would be swallowed whole by Fenrir during Ragnarök.

"I guess we got to get the chains off him."

Ricky inched closer as the teen's lips widened, his teeth more wolf than human. Ricky reached to touch the chains and swore as a shock sent him flying backwards into the wall with a grunt.

"The chains were bound by the blood of Tyr. Only one who carries the blood of the God of War may open the chains."

Donnie glanced over at Ricky, who had gotten to his feet and was brushing dirt off his jeans. Donnie crouched down to inspect the chains. These were chains forged of steel, and as

Fenrir had stated, Donnie could smell the blood on them as if it were as fresh as when it was newly spilled.

"The legends state that the dwarves who forged Mjölnir, who created Loki's scepter and Odin's spear, forged the chains from many a thing. Forged a chain whose strength couldn't be equaled; it was wrought from the sound of a cat's footsteps, the beard of a woman, the roots of mountains, the breath of a fish, and the spittle of a bird, against which it's therefore futile to struggle. Gleipnir is its name."

The hairs on Donnie's neck stood to attention as Fenrir continued to tell his story. "Then Tyr used his own blood so that no other but his blood could release me. Did you bring him to release me?"

Donnie got to his feet and looked at the kid, who was probably centuries older than Donnie was, right in the eyes. "I'm sorry, kid. Tyr was killed by Odin. A lot has changed while you've been locked up here."

Fenrir folded his arms across his chest, tilting his head like a wolf would. "Then the end is here. Ragnarök is upon us. All those who could have released me are dead. My part to play is over."

Ricky glanced at Donnie. "What about Erika?"

"We'd never get her here in time. Tyr should have been more specific about needing someone with his blood before he told Sif to give me the compass."

"And if we managed to get her here, Loki might not let us free him."

Fenrir was glancing from Donnie to Ricky with a blank expression. "Who is this Erika you speak of? And who is she that my father would hold dominion over her?"

Ricky chuckled, shaking his head. "I dare you to say that to her face. Erika is the general of the Valkyrie army and your dad's girlfriend. She is also the only child of Tyr."

"Then the rest are dead?"

The question surprised Donnie because as far as he knew, Erika had no brothers and sisters. Odin had many children, though, like Loki, so maybe there was someone else out there that could help to put hands on the chains at Fenrir's ankles.

"The magic eater does not carry the blood of gods in him. I can scent it."

"Gee, thanks … I'm not sure how to react to magic eater," Ricky said with a flush on his cheeks, but Fenrir wasn't looking at Ricky. He was looking at Donnie.

Then the wolf smiled, and Donnie took an involuntary step back. He had stared down many an unsub. Hell, he had faced down the first vampire ever made, but when Fenrir looked at him, Donnie felt like he was a meal, prey being sized up before he was mauled to death.

"You say Tyr sent you here?"

"Ya, he did."

"Come closer, nightwalker."

Donnie was walking forward without knowing he was moving, as if Fenrir's voice had lured him like a siren to his death. When Donnie was within reaching distance, Fenrir lunged, grabbing Donnie's arm and sinking his teeth into the flesh at his wrist.

Donnie jerked at the pain, trying to yank his arm away from the wolf, Ricky grabbing him by the other hand to try and pull him free. Donnie felt Fenrir lick at the blood that was dripping from the wound, then the little shit let go so suddenly that Donnie fell backwards, landing on top of Ricky on the ground.

Fenrir lifted his head and howled, Donnie's blood smeared on his lips, teeth and chin as he smugly said. "It seems we have a solution after all."

Donnie got to his feet, the wound on his arm already healing to a faint pucker that Donnie was certain would scar, not healed by his vampire healing ability. Then again, it wasn't every day a wolf god tried to bite off your hand.

"It is diluted by human blood and that of the vampire who made you, yet I would know the taste of his blood anywhere."

It took Donnie a couple of seconds to replay what Fenrir was saying before things started to slot into place and he sucked in a breath. Ricky was open mouthed beside him; his buddy having pieced it together before he did.

"Are you telling me that I have the blood of Tyr in my veins?"

Fenrir licked his lips. "I am saying that you are a direct descendant of the God Tyr, by only a generation."

What the hell did that mean?

He must have looked as confused as he felt, because Ricky clasped him on the shoulder, grinning as he said, "Looks like Erika is your aunt. Our family trees are completely fucked up."

Donnie stumbled back, his ass hitting the ground before he could stop it as he tried to understand what was happening. He had lived his entire human life knowing he was unwanted, his poor mother dying in a filthy alley instead of telling her parents that she had gotten pregnant. Caitlyn had gifted him with knowing his mother's family, though their guilt over his mother, Bridget's, death kept them at a distance.

Now, he told himself that he hadn't wanted to know who his father was, that he hadn't mattered, but finding out that not only was Tyr his grandfather but he had a living, breathing relative who was part of their supernatural world, one where they understood him as he was now—that floored him.

"If it is of an ease to you, human females hardly ever survive a birth of one with god blood. It is possible that your father didn't even know who his father was."

It didn't ease him in the slightest, but Donnie got to his feet and looked at Fenrir, his face expressionless, but Fenrir snarled at him again with bloodstained teeth.

"How no one saw that you were of Tyr's blood, I will never know. You look like him now, as you face me."

"I should say thank you for telling me another part of me.

But now that gives me leverage. If I free you from the chains, will you help us defeat Odin? You would have to swear to stay until the battle is done, until we win or we lose. And play a part."

Fenrir's sinister smile felt like ice in his veins as the wolf replied. "Odin was the one who ordered Tyr to bind me here. I have remained here for an eternity, waiting for the day I could exact revenge on the Allfather for his actions. I will play my part, grandson of Tyr. Now unchain me."

Donnie shook his head. "I know the way of gods, Fenrir, so here's the deal. You will swear an oath to me, sealed in blood. Then I will release you and you will help us defeat Odin."

Without waiting for a response, Donnie turned over his palm and sank his fangs into his flesh, then held it out for Fenrir. The wolf did as Donnie had done, biting down into his flesh, and then he clasped his bloody hand in Donnie's.

Donnie's body shook like there was an earthquake inside him, bones rattling, teeth chattering until Fenrir removed his hand and the oath was bound.

"Free me." The growl in the wolf's throat was far from human. Donnie wondered how in hell he was going to get the chains open.

There was no slot for a key, no clasp for him to flick. Narrowing his gaze, he put his hand on the wide metal that ensnarled Fenrir's ankle. When the magic didn't send him flying back like it had Ricky, Donnie knew that the wolf spoke true: He was certainly Tyr's grandson. All of this, getting the compass, making it work, the quest and now this, freeing Fenrir, it all came down to blood, and then Donnie remembered what Fenrir said.

"Gleipnir is its name."

Donnie placed his bloody palm on the wide cuff, then simply said, "Gleipnir."

Magic swirled in the air, and then the chains fell from around Fenrir's ankles, leaving not a mark on his skin as the chains fell away to the ground. Fenrir lifted one leg, then the other. He clicked his fingers, and his body was clad in an all-black ensemble, like he was a member of SWAT. His eyes flared red as he smirked, his eyes looking down at the chains.

"Pick them up, Donnie O'Carroll. We might make use of them yet."

~

"SHIT, SHIT, SHIT ... COME ON, A.K.!"

The shard of Bifrost glass in his hand didn't so much as tremble as Zach glared at it, hoping that he could will it to work, but his best friend still remained in the past. Zach had warded his room to keep the immortal beings from getting in and using him to get to Ash, but he was running out of time, and the wards were being slowly chipped away.

Ash must have done something to mess with the future so badly the fates could not ignore it, and as her accomplice, he was as guilty as she. They had made an agreement, before she vanished into the past without him, that she would come back when he called.

"Fuck this."

Zach pushed away from his desk, opening the secret drawer and pulling out another shard of Bifrost that he had "borrowed." Then he grabbed his shoulder holster, slipping it on over his khaki long-sleeved tee that had a picture of Danger Mouse on the front of it, a present from Ash, who teased him for following after his vamp mom and a love of slogan tees.

Slipping his two guns into the holster, Zach pushed his glasses up his nose and then placed one of the shards into the mechanism at his desk. A whirling sounded as the doors to his apartment blew open, but Zach ignored it as his wall split in two.

He was not Ash to dive into danger with a laugh, nor was he invincible. But Zachary Spencer Moore never shied away from what scared him.

He rolled his shoulders and dove into the split, falling headfirst into the past.

CHAPTER
FIFTEEN

Ash

G rey had disappeared, though Ash knew he was probably lurking around somewhere. After the dead had risen from Hel, the team had taken a few hours to clean and rest, but Ash found herself restless. The shard in her pocket kept heating, as if Zach was trying to reach her, but she couldn't respond without going home.

Ash knew she had to return, especially after her talk with her dad, knowing that her dad, the one in the future, was probably going out of his mind. Ash swept her hair off her face as she looked out of the warehouse to where her grandfather stood, watching, waiting.

She could feel it in her bones that her time in the past was coming to an end. It was as if it sang in her veins, the need to go back to where she had come from, as if home was calling to her.

Picking up her hammer, Ash stepped off the window ledge to the ground, letting the sharp cold of the wind whip against her face. Closing her eyes, she breathed in the scent of rain on the horizon, the promise of thunder rippling against her skin. As a child, she had spent hours sitting out in the rain, staring up at the thunder and lightning and wondering why she loved it so. Then, one day when she had lost her temper and the house had almost caught fire as a flare of lightning seared the roof, her mother had sat her down and told her who she was, who Thor was and why she needed to learn to control her emotions and not let them control her.

The very next morning, the first of her tattoos had appeared. She'd been seven at the time, and it had freaked her dad out. Zach was twelve then, claiming he wanted one of his own. Their parents still didn't know that as soon as Ash had turned sixteen, they'd gone to get tattoos, considering Zach was twenty-one and technically an adult.

Ash felt a presence behind her, ducked before a berserker could claw her back to shreds. She swung Mjölnir wide, sending her grandfather's foot soldier backwards into the path of the dozen others that had converged, as if they had been lying in wait for someone to step out of the warehouse.

Lifting her hammer, the rumble of thunder like the most beautiful of melodies in her ears, she charged at the dozen berserkers with a war cry that was sure enough to alert the rest of those who lingered in the warehouse.

The berserkers were hideous misshapen beasts who seemed trapped in half-wolf, half-human form. Fur matted their flesh, with drool dripping from horrendously formed mouths. They circled her, snapping their teeth at her as she tried to twist and turn to keep them all in view.

Ash spun faster, lashing out with Mjölnir, hitting them square in the stomach, knocking them backward. With glee on her face, she heard her dad call her name, but she dared not glance upward or toward the voice in case she lost her focus.

Others joined in the fray, with Ash catching glimpses of her parents, of Erika and Melanie and Caitlyn all making their way towards where she fought. Ash was transfixed for a moment as Caitlyn lifted a short, curved blade and moved with the deadly efficiency that Ash had been trained with, like a wraith in the night. Her weapon slicing through bone, Caitlyn divested one of the berserkers of its head.

Distraction could get you killed. A blow to Ash's head made

her drop her hammer, claws biting into her flesh as she was dragged down the street, her legs kicking to get free as three berserkers roared into her face, their claws in her head so that she could not even raise her hand for Mjölnir.

She screamed. They seemed to be unsure of what direction they wanted to take her, her body being pulled in three different directions. She felt her shoulder pop from its socket, then she howled as if the moon could trigger her change to wolf, yet she knew changing now wouldn't help her much.

The berserkers snapped at one another, growling and hissing as they seemed to come to some sort of nonverbal agreement, and then just one grabbed her and she was moving in the direction of where Odin stood.

Looked like her grandfather wanted a word after all.

Ash kicked out her foot, smashing in the face of the berserker at her feet. He growled, dropping her legs so that she now dangled along the ground, staggering away as he lunged forward making to grab her again or sink his teeth into her leg.

Stupid fucker didn't get the chance.

His body hit the ground a second after the shot went off, the bullet lodging right between his eyes. The surprise gunshot caused the other berserkers to drop her and spin round, snarls on their faces. She was standing, staring down the barrel of a gun, but she couldn't help but grin like hell.

"Ricky!!!!!" Melanie's voice carried across the street as Ash saw Caitlyn shake her head, a smile on her lips. She saw her tell Melanie who it was, that it was not Ricky, but his son, all grown up, Melanie's eyes going wide as she ran her own gaze over the new addition.

"A.K., duck," Zach barked at her, his green eyes flashing with determination as he lifted his gun-wielding hands up a notch.

She did as she was told, the order coming from the partner she trusted with her life without question. The next two shots hit true as the creatures fell down to the ground, dead. Ash rose up, her arm hanging limp as Zach sheathed his guns away, then practically shoved Ash to lie down on the ground.

Zach braced his foot on her shoulder, angled her arm, his hazel eyes on her as he said, "Ready? On three ... one ... two ..."

Zach pulled and then pushed her arm back into place, and she swore a blue streak at her best friend before she said, "You never wait till three." Ash gasped, rubbing her shoulder.

"And every time you're surprised."

Zach chuckled before he cocked his eyebrow at her. "You don't call. You don't write. You don't answer when I call you. I was starting to think you forgot about me."

Ash threw her arms around his neck, then felt the familiar hands around her shoulders as she hugged Zach to her, his scent as familiar as her own, like fire and fur.

"I missed you."

"I missed you too. We have problems."

Ash detangled herself from Zach as she stepped back. "I know. Grey mentioned something, but I think you need to say hello to some people. Your mom looks like she's about to have a heart attack."

Zach chuckled again, pushing those glasses of his up his nose as he turned, his cat-green eyes brightening as Melanie strode over to him, everyone else not far behind. Melanie was shorter than Zach by a good few inches. She reached up and cupped his cheek.

Zach's smile deepened. "Hey, Mom."

Melanie blinked, her eyes widening as she just stared at him with an open mouth.

Zach glanced at Ash, who shrugged her shoulders. "I don't think you call her that yet, so it's a trip, hearing it for the first time. You should have seen my dad's face the first time I called him Dad. It was worth it to see his face."

"You're—you—" Melanie began, her voice full of wonder. "But you are him as well."

"I think what Melanie is trying to say is that you are definitely your father's son."

"I'll take that as a compliment." Zach replied, then jerked back from his mother to pull out his guns again, popping off two shots before anyone else could react. A lone survivor of the berserkers hit the ground without much fanfare.

"Why didn't you just blow the ears off us?" Her dad asked Zach. Firing a gun right next to a bunch of supernaturals was dangerous. A gunshot could blow out an eardrum, yet they were all unaffected by the two shots Zach had fired off.

Zach seemed to straighten at the sound of her dad's voice, and Ash hid her smile, because as much as her dad was Uncle Derek outside of work, he was still their boss. Zach held out the guns for Derek to take.

"I tinker with things, sir. Cars, weapons, computers. The gun is a prototype of a Glock. I've managed to put a spell into a coil that makes the shot almost silent."

Derek offered Zach a look that was all filled with pride, and she swore that her bestie nearly purred with pride. "Ain't that something. I believe I have you to thank for keeping her safe."

"We keep each other safe, sir. That's what family does. What partners do. I watch her six, and she watches mine."

Derek nodded his approval but said no more as Zach looked pointedly toward the warehouse. He was looking for his dad.

"He's not here, son. He's gonna be pissed he missed this."

"Oh, he hasn't gotten back from the—"

Ash clamped a hand over his mouth and shook her head as Zach's green eyes widened. When Ash shook her head, he seemed to realize what he'd nearly said, and Zach winced.

"See, not as easy to keep your mouth shut now, is it?" Ash said haughtily, a smirk on her lips, considering the lecture Zach had given her about revealing too much. And here he was, not a hot minute in the past and already nearly dropping secrets.

Zach growled at her, ducking under her arm and shoving

her away.. "Well, considering how the fates blew up my apartment door to try and get to you, I think you've done more than keep your mouth shut, A.K."

"A.K.?" Melanie asked softly as she stared at Zach.

Ash held up her finger. "Don't."

Zach rolled his eyes and threw an arm around her shoulder. "A.K. as in Ashlyn, Kyria … but my lips are sealed as to why else I call her A.K."

The ground began to tremble, and they all readied for attack, turning toward the intersection of the street where the roads met. The road did not split like it had when Hel arrived to take the dead back, nor did the dead appear again, but magic was thick in the air.

"I can't deal with dead again. That girl needs to keep hold of her realm a little more," Melanie said as she pulled out a gun and pointed it in the general direction of where everyone was looking. Ash caught the amused look on Zach's face as Melanie stepped in front of him, shielding him, despite the fact that Zach could handle himself.

"It's just like when the kid in class pushed you off the monkey bars and broke your glasses."

"I know, right? When Mom pulled a gun on the banshee, I thought she would piss herself."

Melanie peered over her shoulder at them with a stern look on her face. "I know you two are telling the truth but don't have the brain matter to process it."

"It's okay, Mom."

Melanie didn't get the chance to retort as the air seemed to shimmer and crackle as the appearance of three sisters stole the air from her lungs.

Ash heard her dad call her name. Mjölnir sailed through the air, and she caught it. Her eyes widened at her dad, who had tossed Mjölnir like he had been wielding it for centuries. Even her mom looked shocked as hell.

"Does your dad know he's not supposed to be able to do that?"

Ash shook her head at Zach, considering the last time Zach had tried to lift the hammer, he nearly popped a disc.

Urðr, Verðandi and Skuld stood at the intersection of the roads, past, present and future all equal in their rage as Zach swore next to her, dragging their gaze from Ash to him.

"Zachary Spencer Derek Moore, we have been looking for you," Skuld said, her voice filled with power and age as Zach glanced at her dad, wondering how he would handle the knowledge that Zach had taken his name when he got a little older, such was the influence Derek had played in his life.. Then he turned his eyes back to the fates and his charm.

"Ladies, long time no see. Had I known you were looking for me, I'd have dropped everything ... just for you."

Ash stifled back a laugh as she heard Caitlyn mutter, "His father's son, all right."

"You should not be here, cat. You will return now or we will make you."

That threat came from Verðandi, her appearance nearly the same as the supernaturals who stood around them. But it was Urðr who spoke next and directly to her.

"Ashlyn Kyria Caitlyn Doyle." Ash kept her gaze front and center as Caitlyn whirled in her direction, and the fates kept on speaking, this time in perfect unison.

"You have meddled with the hands of fate when you should not have. You have divulged destinies that you should not have. You have changed the course of the future when you were ordered not to. For that, you cannot go unpunished."

"No. Leave her alone."

Zach was on his knees a heartbeat later, gasping for air and clutching at his throat. Everyone tried to move around her, yet they were somehow frozen. Zach's face turned red, and Ash pushed past everyone to stand in front of Zach.

"He has done nothing wrong. I have. I accept that I must be punished, but please—I will bear whatever punishment if you leave him unharmed."

The three sisters shared a look, then they nodded, and Zach was suddenly gone, vanished as if he had not been gasping for air a mere moment ago.

"He has been returned from whence he came. Unharmed. We will allow you a moment to say farewell, then we will administer punishment."

Ash spun as her parents engulfed her in a tight embrace. "I love you both so, so much."

Her dad gripped her face in his hands, eyes wolf amber. "I am so very proud of you, my beautiful girl. I will love you until my last breath."

Ash was crying now as Derek stepped aside to let Ever embrace her. "Thank you for coming back. For making me see. For letting me love you. I love you."

"Kick his ass for me, Mom. Kick his ass."

Ash nodded to Caitlyn, Melanie and Erika, then lifted her hammer and strode over to where the fates stood. She jerked her chin up and felt the steel of her family at her back as she inclined her head to the fates.

"I'm ready to go home."

Skuld pursed her lips as if pondering Ash's punishment. "Since your birth, we have wondered if the considerable amount of power in you would influence the path of destiny, and it has. You are cocky, unapologetic, reckless and under the false belief that you are invincible."

Urðr looked at the hammer tattoo on her forearm. "Thor was an adult when he inherited the power of Mjölnir, and he took his responsibilities seriously. You consider it a birthright. We will ensure you learn from that misconception."

Verðandi grabbed her arm, and Ash thought she was being burnt alive as she screamed, the tattoo on her flesh searing and bubbling as the fate singed it from her skin. She dropped Mjölnir, her beloved hammer vanishing before her eyes, and Ash cried, for it was like losing a limb.

Her body jerked, the movement taking with it the strength and magic that made her worthy of wielding Thor's hammer. She sagged to the ground, her wolf in her eyes as she searched for the part of her that made her a goddess.

She did not find it.

"You have been stripped of the magic that allowed you to be chosen by Thor. You are still wolf, and you are still Valkyrie. Should you earn the right to be made worthy once again, then Mjölnir will be returned to you. Let us see if destiny is all."

Oh gods, she was dying. This pain, this loss was immense as she staggered to her feet, unable to turn to face the people she loved the most as Skuld clicked her fingers, and suddenly she was standing in the apartment she shared with Zach.

Her legs gave out, too much loss to deal with, as strong arms went around her and kept her from falling to the ground.

"It's okay. I've got you. I've always got you."

She let Zach hold her, tears staining her face, soaking his tee as he reassured her that she was okay, that everything would be okay.

"I am so very proud of you, my beautiful girl. I will love you until my last breath."

Her dad's words played out in her head again, and Ash knew that losing her hammer now didn't mean she had lost it forever. She might know what was going to happen in the past, but the future was still unwritten. Her story was not over yet, and she would be the one to wield the pen and write her own chapters.

When she was done wallowing in her sadness, Ash swept the tears from her eyes, remembering that she was not helpless. She was the daughter of Derek Doyle and Ever Chace, and she would work twice as hard to prove she was worthy.

The door to the apartment swung open, and eyes of dark brown swept over her. "Still alive, then?"

"Fuck off, brat. I can't deal with you right now."

Her baby brother stepped aside as Derek Doyle loomed in the doorway, his eyes a shock of amber, his hair speckled with a little gray around the ears as he glared at Ash with that alpha stare of his.

Ash waved at him, ignoring Gideon as he stuck out his tongue at her while her dad stepped closer. She took a step back as the full force of his wolf bore down on hers, and she knew he was seething with anger right about now.

"Hey, Daddy. Miss me?"

CHAPTER
SIXTEEN

Ever

A nd just like that, Ash was gone, leaving Ever with this overwhelming sense of loss that made her legs quiver. Tears cascaded down her cheeks as Derek wrapped his arms around her, his own skin wet. They stood there, embracing for what felt like an age, before Derek stepped back and cupped her cheek.

"She's not dead, Ever. She went home. She will never be far from our thoughts. But she had to go, and we still get to see her grow up, knowing she is this amazing kid."

Her mate didn't sound convinced by his own words, yet Ever knew he spoke the truth. Ash was punished for her actions. and Ever wasn't even there to help her fix them.

"You are there. The you sixteen years in the future. So am I. We won't let her go through this alone."

Ever barely had time to come to terms with everything when a horn blared in the distance and Ever jerked her head upward.

Odin's horse Sleipnir reared up on its eight legs as her father blew into a horn that Ever recognized. This was the horn that was hung on the wall behind Odin's throne, waiting for Heimdall to usher in the dawn of Ragnarök. Heimdall was dead, so now Odin was sounding the horn himself, Gjallarhorn held to her father's lips as he gave Ever a warning.

War was upon them, and he would meet her on the battlefield.

The Valkyries landed by her side. Few as they were, their loyalty was never in doubt.

"The berserkers have lined Patrick Street, my queen. Marcel and his vampires wait at the other end, ready for your command."

Ever inclined her head to Danae, then glanced at Erika. "You ready to lead your army?"

"I'm ready to lead your army. Side by side. But I think we need to dress for battle."

Ever wasn't sure what Erika meant until Kenzie stepped forward. "We made a stop to Valhalla. Picked up a few bits. Erika said no Valkyrie should ride into battle without the right armor."

Ever took the armor from Kenzie, then turned toward Derek. "If I asked you to stay out of the fight, in case something goes wrong, would you?"

His lips curved into a smug smile. "No Valkyrie queen rides into battle without her champion. You go, I go."

"As do I."

"Same here."

Caitlyn's response came, with Melanie chiming in after her.

"As do I."

Ever turned to see Loki dressed in all his Asgardian finery. His long, black hair was pulled back off his face but left loose. He was dressed straight out of a superhero movie, from the green and black and gold floor-length coat to the black leather pants and top that clung to his lean frame. On his head, he wore his helmet forged from Asgardian gold, the horns stretched out and up.

His scepter was in his hand as he came toward her..

"You vowed to stay out of the fight."

Loki glanced over Ever's shoulder before his eyes of stars and galaxies danced. "I was foolish to think I could remain impartial. Back then, I had not much to lose. Now, there is so much at stake. You have me, sister. I will stand beside you on this night as Thor should have stood beside you against Father."

Ever went up on her toes to kiss her brother's cheek, then left him to have a few words with Erika before they went to war. Inside the warehouse, there was a flurry of activity, as the Valkyries dressed in their own armor, and Ever felt like she was back in one of her past lives, watching her sisters don their shields and weapons before departure.

Kenzie, a warrior herself even if she hadn't been a newly made Valkyrie, wore a skintight bodysuit made entirely of black, yet chose to adorn her shoulders and wrists with Asgardian metal. The others all chose traditional Valkyrie armor, from knee-length skirts and corset-style tops to buck leather pants and full-sleeved woven tops that were made from material that was impervious to a blade.

"Let's get you dressed."

Erika's voice was soft beside her as she led Ever away from the hive of activity. Ever paused to glance at Derek, watched as Erika and Derek shared a look, then he smiled at Ever and turned back to Caitlyn as she strapped a tactical vest to his chest.

When they were upstairs and alone, Erika waited until Ever had her armor set down on one of the camp beds, then they stood facing each other, neither of them knowing what to say to each other. There were millennia of history between them that could not be summed up in the brief time they had to get ready.

"Erika ..." Ever started to say, but Erika clucked her tongue.

"Nope, you don't get to offer me a soppy goodbye. We don't do that. You and me. It's been that way since we first met, and waging war against your father won't change that. You don't get to "Erika "me like this is the end. It's not. Because a Valkyrie does not fear death. Death fears us."

Ever laughed softly. "I only wanted to say thank you. For being there, all this time. Derek might be my soul mate, but you are my soul sister. Two parts of my heart. I am honored to have you stand beside me, Erika."

Erika's jaw was held firm as she stepped forward and untied Ever's hair. "Shut up. You make it sound like this is it. We know it's not. Now let me fix your hair, one last thing. We can't have you riding into battle looking like you've been dragged through a hedge."

Ever was still laughing as Erika braided her hair in the traditional way, then separated it so that she had four separate thick braids hanging down her front. Erika glanced at Ever's armor.

"I think we can do better than that," Erika mused as she went over to a bag and pulled out a sleek back outfit that consisted of trousers and a top. Black boots followed as Erika ordered her to dress. When Ever had pulled on the outfit, she turned back to face Erika.

The top had soft spikes on the shoulders, a crisscross of material across the neckline that nearly covered anywhere she could be stabbed. It was molded to her skin, but Ever knew that it would not impede her fighting.

"One last thing."

Ever continued to look at Erika and let out a gasp. Resting in Erika's hands was a helmet—no, a crown, fashioned from the same Asgardian gold as Loki's helmet with blue jewels speckled in the front and the pieces that curled on the top that resembled a Valkyrie's wings. Blue streaks of lighting made the crown look like it was fractured, yet it was anything but. The helmet was curved to cover her forehead down to the bridge of her nose, curving around the eyes, and then the shape over the ear was fashioned to resemble a Valkyrie's wings.

"Erika … this is …"

Erika dropped to one knee, holding the crown out. "It is a crown worthy for a Valkyrie queen. It is yours, the first and only one for the rightful heir to the throne. This will never be tainted by Odin, for it was forged by master dwarves who listened to the words of those who love you the most and created this for you. Wear it into battle today and know that we stand beside you, with you. Until our last breath."

Erika rose as Ever ducked her head, letting her best friend set the crown on her head, then Ever took the sword that Erika held out for her. A gasp sounded in the door as Ever turned to see Derek leaning in the doorway, his eyes filled with his wolf and other things. She wanted to say so much, but her mate walked past Ever to where Erika stood.

"You might be a Valkyrie general, but you are also one of ours. Family. A member of this team. You never back down, Erika. And put on the goddamn tac vest before I superglue it to you."

Erika rolled her eyes but took the vest from Derek as a horn sounded again in the distance. He kissed Ever's cheek, then left them alone as Erika slipped the tactical vest over her shoulders. She flashed away for a second, and when she returned, she was dressed in all black, with an array of knives and blades on her hip and two guns. Under the vest, she wore the same outfit as Derek, right down to the standard-issue boots.

"Let us join our sisters, my queen."

Ever made to tell Erika she didn't need to call her queen, however, Erika steered her to the stairs, where the entire room fell silent as she descended. The Valkyries dropped to their knees, fists over their hearts. She crossed the floor to them and asked them to rise.

"It has been an honor, my sisters, to fight beside you again," Ever said in the old language, then switched back to English for Kenzie. "We go to war with hearts full and not a trace of fear in our bones. We take with us the strength of those who are awaiting us in the great halls of Valhalla, where we will feast and drink with them again one day. But today is not that day."

"Hail to the victor!" Erika shouted, and the Valkyries cheered in response. The horn sounded again, the battle counting down to the final minute.

"One last thing before we go." Erika pulled out a knife as Danae held a bowl in her hands. Erika sliced her palm, the droplets of blood dripping into the bowl. Each Valkyrie did so, the ancient ritual pebbling goosebumps on her skin. When all of the Valkyries had shed blood into the bowl, and Ever had added her own, Erika dipped two fingers into the blood. Speaking in the old language, Erika streaked two lines down Ever's cheek. "Our blood."

Erika repeated the ritual for every single Valkyrie in the room, then held out the bowl for Ever to dip her fingers in. On their other cheek, Ever repeated what Erika had done, except this time, she said, "My blood."

Erika set the bowl aside and placed her fist into the center of her chest, and they all followed her lead, as they were always meant to do.

"Hail to us, warriors of blood and bone. We are daughters of night and victory. Gaze upon us, masters of fate, and guide us in our victory this night. By the blood of my systirs, I shall not fear death, for the end is only the beginning."

"For Valhalla, for glory," Ever said softly.

"For Valhalla, for glory," they answered, both Erika's prayer and her declaration, for those who were not Valkyrie would not know that the promise was not a path to life but a vow to fight until death and then wait for their arrival in Valhalla.

Turning to Erika, Ever reached out and clasped her forearm. "Lead as you were destined to do and await my arrival on the battlefield."

"Don't be fucking late."

Erika winked as she turned to Derek with a smirk. "Need a lift, Boyband?"

This was part of the plan. One she had discussed with Erika days ago. Erika would be Derek's shadow; Kenzie would be

Caitlyn's, and Danae would shield Melanie. They would fly them to the battlefield and out of it if the situation became dire. The team did not know it, of course, just that they would fly Valkyrie express to the city center.

Derek glanced in her direction as if he knew what she was thinking, and of course, he probably did, her emotions a storm inside her that no doubt leaked down the mate bond.

As Erika rolled her shoulders, her black and blue wings spreading out, Derek held Ever's gaze. "I'll see you soon."

"I love you."

"I know. I love you too."

Then Erika gripped him under the arms and all but dragged him up and out the window. She could hear him swearing like a sailor before the next two pairs followed after them. Then the remaining Valkyrie followed after Erika, and Ever was standing alone in the warehouse.

Or so she thought.

"The shifters have joined in the fray now. So we stand with vampires, shifters, warlocks and witches." Loki said. "I have called upon the frost giants to come stand with us, but it has been so long since I was one of them that I do not know if they will come."

Loki stood in the doorway. Ever turned to face him. The horn blared again as Ever sheathed the sword at her back, readying to spread her wings and fly toward the battlefield.

"Do you remember ancient Greece?" Loki asked her suddenly.

"You mean when we created the Pegasus legend?"

"I think we need to be legendary again this night."

Loki clicked his fingers, and a horse pure as the snow appeared in the warehouse, eyes as clear as the waters of Valhalla. Her wings stretched out, her hooves like thunder against the stone floor. The horse bowed its head to Ever, and she rubbed her palm along its nose.

Ever peered up at Loki. "Then let us go be legendary, brother."

Ever swung up on the horse's back. She grabbed hold of the reins as it reared up, charging from the warehouse as Loki vanished into thin air. Out on the streets, Odin's horn blew again, and her horse took off down the street before stretching out its wings. She flapped them once, twice, and then they were soaring through the air.

The horse moved like it was galloping over sand. Ever steered it toward Patrick Street, where she saw thousands of supernatural creatures standing in formation, ready to jump into the fray as soon as it started. She heard the shocked gasps and felt all eyes on her as she flew on top of her winged horse, like the legends of old, a true Valkyrie riding into battle on a winged horse to claim the worthy for Valhalla.

The berserkers snarled and growled as she flew over them, right toward where Odin sat on his eight-legged horse. Ever stayed in the air, out of striking distance, as she called down to Odin.

"You can still end this, Odin. The way to war has not yet been set in stone. Are you not tired of killing your children?"

Odin didn't even flinch as he lifted his eyes up to look at Ever. "I can always make more children."

And then Ever knew her father could never be reasoned with, that his need for power, for control would always outweigh his love, if any, for his children. There would be no reasoning. There would be no peaceful resolution. Odin would never sing for absolution for his sins.

The descent into hel was truly this easy for him.

"Dressing up as a queen does not make it so, daughter. No more than when you were a toddler playing at being a warrior."

Ever chuckled as her horse snorted. "I am not playing at being a queen, Father. I am one. I have always been so. It is in my blood, in my soul, and no matter what happens this day, I will stand beside those who choose to stand beside me. You, on the other hand, have only hounds of madness to use as your weapons. The gods you claim to be a father to, do not stand by your side. That is what you have been reduced to."

Ever pulled gently on the reins of the horse and flew back to where the supernatural community of Cork and Ireland stood, warriors all ready to fight a war that should never have been theirs. She was proud to call this place home and even prouder to fight alongside them.

"On this night," she shouted, so that every single person with feet on this street would hear her, "we go to war to right the wrongs of a man who has too much power and craves more. I stand with you, brave warriors, and when we are victorious, we shall celebrate like the feasts of old. I am honored to lead you. I fight with you. I will be your sword and your shield."

She was making a vow to them all, right here, right now, and she meant it.

"When you feel weary, I will be beside you, holding you up. If you fall, I will help you to your feet. And if death comes to claim you, I will hold open the door to Valhalla for you, where you will be welcomed as the warriors you are."

Ever landed on the ground, unsheathed her sword and lifted it to the sky. Her heart pounded in her chest as Erika took a step forward to stand beside her on her right and Derek took up a position on her left.

And fate smiled upon them, for destiny was firmly taking hold as the Valkyrie queen lifted her sword higher, her general and her champion by her side.

She had one last trick up her sleeve, one that she had kept secret up until the last second because she wanted to see Odin's face as she finally fulfilled part of her destiny.

Raising her sword higher, she uttered the names of the runes on her sword, in the pattern in which they were always meant to be read. The sword glowed, a light emanating from her right as she opened the doorway from Midgard to Valhalla and called forth the worthy to fight alongside her once more.

Thousands upon thousands of slain warriors filled the streets, sending the berserkers back a couple of meters. The specters flickered to solid. Thor stood with Heimdall and Baldur. Tom came to stand beside Derek. And her fallen Valkyrie sisters charged to the front with a battle cry to join those who they had loved.

Odin's eyes were unreadable as he blared the horn once more, staying where he was as he ordered his berserker army forward.

The sword in her hand glowed, then the gateway closed as Ever roared, "For Valhalla!"

Then Ever lowered her sword and squeezed her legs around the waist of the horse, her Valkyrie answering her cry as she surged forward and into battle.

~

ODIN WATCHED AS HIS DAUGHTER UNLEASHED A BATTLE CRY TO THOSE that stood with her and his slain sons answered her cry also, charging into battle like the true warriors they were. He looked down on them, unrepentant, unapologetic, for he knew that all of this ... all of this death and war was to right the wrong he had done, all those years centuries ago.

His mind cast back to his beloved Frigg as they stood arguing about Baldur, that Odin had not done enough to stop his death, that he, the Allfather, could have stopped it. He had already slipped into the first grip of madness, having sent Tyr to lock up Fenrir, for the prophecy foretold his demise at the teeth of the monstrous wolf. They spoke of Tyr being instrumental in his defeat, and even his son Thor would side against him.

Tyr's death had been an accident, yet it served its purpose, and Odin had not needed to end his life behind closed doors. He had enough death staining his hands that whenever he looked at them, all he saw was the day Frigg died, not slipping into a peaceful death sleep like everyone believed.

She had screamed at him that day when he told her of his plans to take back control of Valhalla from the Valkyries and Freya, to convince her to lay with him again and replenish the ranks of the female warriors. He wanted to wed Ever to Loki, despite the fact they were as close as siblings, yet Frigg had told him that he could not do it.

His mind told him she was working against him, conspiring with their children to overthrow him. His hands were at her throat before he could stop himself, her eyes bulging as he lifted her off his feet, and as he felt the life drain from his beloved, he pulled back.

But it had been too late. Frigg had died, and it was by his hand.

Now, now, he would right his wrong and wipe the murderous stain from his mind and his hands, even if it was his children who bled so Frigg could be reborn.

And they would never know ... they could never know ...

CHAPTER
SEVENTEEN

Ricky

"This is a bad plan."

Ricky shoved his hands into his pockets as Donnie and Fenrir looked at him, having explained their half-assed plan to him for the third time. They both had expressions like they expected this stupidity to work, but Ricky was a little bit more pessimistic about their chances.

"And how do you expect us to get that close to Odin so that this ludicrous plan of yours can work?" Ricky asked Fenrir, the teen grinning in that psychotic way that he tended to do.

"I will bite him and hold him in place while you both do your part."

There was a hint of delight in his tone that Ricky did not like one bit.

Donnie lifted the chains that once bound Fenrir and hoisted them behind his head. "This is why we came here, Ricky. Fenrir was the final piece we needed. The battle has already started. We don't have time to work out every intimate detail."

"You and I both know that this could go horribly wrong." Ricky said.

Ricky knew his fear, knew what his part could mean and what would happen if it all went horribly wrong. If this had been two years ago, he would have thrown every single bit of sense into the abyss, but now, now he had Zach and Lanie to consider. The two idiots would just have to wait while he had a crisis and deal with it.

"I will flash with Donnie to Midgard and then come back for you. We need to catch Odin off guard. We will have seconds before we lose the upper hand."

Fenrir didn't give Ricky any more time to debate as he flashed away with Donnie, leaving him standing at the mouth of the cave for a couple of heartbeats, then the son of Loki was back, grabbing his arm, and then Ricky was standing in the middle of complete and utter chaos.

Cork's Patrick Street was as packed as it was for Paddy's Day, but instead of joyous revelers, the swords of fighting echoed in his ear. He heard the sound of metal banging, cries of pain, grunts, and he could smell the blood and sweat in the air. His eyes darted toward the street, looking for a shock of red hair, but he couldn't see her.

His eyes landed on where Ever was astride a horse with gigantic wings, slicing a path toward her father, who was standing in the middle of the fray, toward the back of his berserkers. He watched with eager eyes, and Ricky sucked in a breath as his eyes focused on a dark-haired form, brutally taking down berserkers left and right, his face streaked with blood and gore.

Odin lifted his spear and aimed at Derek. As Ricky made to call out for his best friend, Fenrir gripped his shoulder. "Wait."

Erika pulled a shield in front of Derek and deflected the Godbolt, nodding at Derek as she kicked another berserker in the shins as it approached. A rumble in the air sounded as the heavens opened, gods of Asgard finally joining in the fray, led by Lady Sif as she dropped down into the middle of the berserkers, sword in hand.

Ricky heard a sharp whistle, jerked his eyes up to see Donnie standing across from him, his brown eyes determined as he motioned toward Odin. Ricky moved when Donnie did, felt

Fenrir at his back as they darted down the city streets. He caught flashes of supes he knew, from Chester to Greg Saunders and Arthur De Valera.

A berserker broke from his fight and lunged at Ricky.

Fenrir unleashed claws and ripped the monster's throat out, blood gushing from the wound as he fell. "That feels even better than I remember."

Ricky wasn't even going to touch that statement with a barge pole.

Donnie had gotten himself into position, ready to do what he needed to do, and then it was all on Ricky, and his heart dropped to his stomach as he wondered why the fate of the world was left to him.

He was not like Derek or Ever or Caitlyn, hell, even like Donnie. He was not a hero. He was flawed and a little broken and battered. He had fallen, and it had taken others to hold him up. He was not the right choice to play the hero ...

He wasn't brave. He was scared shitless.

Then he heard Caitlyn's voice in his head, as she had told Kenzie once, and he listened to her, for she was one of the bravest people he knew.

"To be brave does not mean you are fearless; to be brave means being absolutely terrified but doing something anyway."

Beside him, Fenrir growled, his skin splitting as he changed, matted gray fur covering his body as he grew and grew and grew, then bolted across the street toward where Odin stood. He dove for the god, who let loose a shout and staggered, his horse rearing up and dumping the god onto the street.

Donnie stepped out of the shadows, the chains around his neck as Fenrir circled the person responsible for imprisonment Steam dripped from Fenrir's mouth as Donnie began to speak.

"Last chance, Odin. Call off the battle or it will be your undoing."

Odin laughed right in Donnie's face, the sound bringing a

streak of lightning through the night sky. "What can you do, vampire? You have no power here. You cannot read my mind or walk in my dreams. Those chains you hold cannot hold a god like me. Your defiance is admirable yet completely misplaced."

"I wouldn't say that, and I brought some friends to help me."

Fenrir growled, and Odin went white as a sheet as the wolf leapt forward. Odin fired off a Godbolt that rebounded off the monstrous wolf and almost hit Ricky in the chest, had he not dived out of the way. He stayed where he was, heart in his mouth, as he waited for the signal for him to go.

Fenrir and Odin faced off against one another, Fenrir lashing out with a massive paw to swat Odin back before he lunged. This time, his teeth sank into the god's legs. Odin screamed in pain as steam seared his skin, and despite the fact that Odin tried to fry Fenrir with lightning, the god was unable to dislodge the wolf.

Donnie stepped forward to try and attach the chains, yet Donnie was no match for the god. Donnie crashed backward, slamming into a wall with a grunt, the grunt letting Ricky know that he was okay.

"Let me go, son of Loki. You alone cannot hold me forever."

Fenrir snarled as Donnie got back to his feet. "That's why we brought him."

Donnie pointed in Ricky's direction as fear grasped its fingertips around his spine. His heart was beating so fast and hard, Ricky thought he might be having a heart attack or an anxiety attack or both and it would just stop.

"To be brave does not mean you are fearless; to be brave means being absolutely terrified but doing something anyway."

Ricky pushed down all of his reservations and stepped out from where he was hiding, letting his magic flare in his eyes as he crossed the road and faced Odin, who laughed at him.

"You are nothing but a mere warlock. You cannot stop me."

Ricky quirked a brow. "You say mere warlock like it's a bad

thing. Like I have no power. Everyone has power if they believe it enough. Have you ever wondered what it's like to be powerless? To not rely on what you were born with and be completely and utterly human? Let's see how that feels, shall we?"

"I am the father of all, the beginning and the end. You cannot stop me."

Ricky reached for the hunger inside him, letting loose the noose of control he had since he became a vampire. His magic licked at the magic that was Odin's, liked the taste of it and wanted more of it. It was not willing to wait any longer.

"Pucker up, motherfucker. This is gonna hurt."

With Fenrir still holding Odin in place, Ricky reached out and dragged Odin down to him, kissing the asshole smack on the lips, and then he fed.

Ash and Loki had been fast food compared with the immense magic reservoir inside Odin. As Ricky drank, he saw the dawn of time, the creation of the realms. He saw life and death and gods and monsters. He learned Odin's greatest shame, and he continued to drink and drink until his own skin felt as if it would burst from the magic contained inside him.

Ricky wrenched his lips from Odin's with a groan, his hands going to his head as magic pressed against his skull, trying to find a way out. He dropped to his knees, flames erupting over his skin, the scent of burning flesh making him want to be sick.

Or maybe that was because he was trying to contain a god's power in a body not meant to wield it.

Lifting his head, he watched as Donnie clanked the chains around Odin's ankles, the god laughing as he said, "Those old things cannot hold me. They can only be activated by the blood of Tyr. I do not think the Valkyries will make it before my powers are reborn and I make you wear your innards."

Donnie chuckled, then he sank his fangs into his wrist, letting the blood drip into his palm. Then he clasped his hands together, letting blood smear both hands. Donnie placed them on the chains and growled, "Gleipnir."

Fenrir let go of Odin as the chains flared, then Ricky heard a snick as the locks engaged and Odin was trapped in chains that suppressed his magic and could only be unlocked by the blood of Tyr. The god tried to pry his legs free, staggered and went to his knees on the ground, his eyes wide as he regarded Donnie.

"Looks like we didn't need Erika this time, for I am the grandson of Tyr and one of two people who can unlock the chains."

Ricky sagged, letting his ass hit the ground as the magic waged its own war inside him as it tried to get free. Hands to his head, Ricky tried to stay calm, to control it, but when he placed a hand on the ground to brace himself, the concrete cracked under his touch, fracturing the road and leaving a serious fixing job for the council.

"He was not built to contain the power." Smirked Odin. "The blood of the gods does not run in his veins. Release me, and I will take it back before it kills him."

Donnie crouched down in front of him as the berserkers, realizing that Odin had been defeated, began to retreat, running down alleys and streets to flee from the war. A victory cry sounded as Ricky scooted away from Donnie.

"Mate, I don't think this is gonna end well." Ricky scoffed.

Donnie glanced at Fenrir, who had changed back to his teenage self and was quite content to simply walk circles around Odin.

Ricky blew out a breath, and thunder rumbled above him. "Well, that's new."

"My magic will flay him alive, boil his organs to ash," Odin said. "You must give it back and release me."

Ricky let a burst of magic out, and it hit just shy of Odin's feet. "No can do. Looks like I die and take the magic with me."

Ricky heard footsteps behind him as he let loose a scream,

the magic infusing every part of his being, an undiluted source as thunder roared and lightning ripped apart the skies. He heard Donnie telling people to back away as Ricky felt his toes curl as if the magic was a pleasure in itself, at the feel of unnatural power in him as it sought destruction and death.

Ricky got to his feet slowly. Then reached for the spear that Odin once wielded. The power in him made him a god amongst men, one who should be bowed before and worshipped. Lifting the spear into the air, he called forth the lightning, and it came to him, tickling his skin as bolts hit him like a shock to the system.

And he felt himself smile.

It reminded him of the way his alt self had smiled, that smug smile that said Ricky was not strong enough to withstand the storm, but Ricky had weathered many a storm, and this was a piece of cake compared with everything else he had been through.

And he knew deep down he would put his gun to his temple and pull the trigger before he became anyone's bitch.

He wanted to expel it, to rid himself of this power, but he wanted to keep it all to himself as well. It was his now. He had claimed it. He had taken it, and it was his.

The age of the new gods was upon them, and he would rule them all.

Ricky shook his head, fighting thoughts that were not his as Odin smirked.

"You cannot wield my powers, boy. It will be the death of you."

Ricky staggered forward, his hand at Odin's throat, the touch singing his flesh as he leaned in and whispered, "My da used to call me boy too. He was also an asshole. Tell me, Odin, how did it feel when you wrapped your hands around your wife's throat and strangled her? Did it make you feel powerful, to take another's life that you claimed to love like a mere human would? How does it feel to lose, knowing that everyone will know your secret?"

"A man cannot tell secrets if he is dead, and you will be soon."

Ricky dropped Odin and pressed his fists to his temples, the pressure building again. This was way worse than the time he went self-destructive and blew up a hotel. It was worse than coming down from a high and jonesing for a fix. This was like his insides were being ripped apart and he couldn't stop it.

Turning away from Odin to where Donnie was looking at him, Ricky gritted his teeth as he grunted out, "I told you this was a bad plan."

"You can do this. You know you can."

Ricky wasn't convinced as his bones quaked. The magic seemed to sink into his bones, and he creaked like an old staircase. "You look after her for me. You tell her that she is everything to me."

"Ricky."

"No, Donnie. You tell her. And Zach. You raise him like he was yours and Caitlyn's, you hear me? You tell him I was a hero and I loved him and I love her."

"Don't ... Ricky ... don't you dare!"

"No choice, mate. The magic wants out, and it feels like it's quite happy to wrench it from me. I need to figure out how to get rid of it or else I'm a goner."

Donnie looked around, as if he searched for something or someone to take the magic from Ricky. He hated to be the bearer of even worse news, but Ricky only knew how to siphon the magic, not dole it out.

But that was a good idea, right—even a smart one.

Odin had said it himself. Ricky's body was not built to contain the power. The blood of the gods did not run in his veins, but he knew a few people who fitted that profile. And if not one body, then what about a few?

Everyone needed a power boost every now and then, right?

"Donnie ... gimme your hand."

Donnie didn't even hesitate, the mad bastard, as Ricky pushed a sliver of magic into his buddy, who jerked on the contact until Ricky yanked his hand away. The tension in his head weakened but didn't leave him.

Next, Ricky grabbed Fenrir and gave him a little jolt of Odin's power. The wolf's eyes flared red. He heard Donnie call for Erika, for Loki, for Ever. Then he called for Caitlyn and Kenzie, all of whom had the blood of gods in their veins.

Ricky fed them all a little sliver of power, and the buildup of power ebbed and flowed inside him. Ricky had almost depleted himself, but the vampire side of his nature did not want to let the power go. It clawed at him from the inside, dragging a growl from his lips as he clenched and unclenched his fists.

Donnie stepped forward and gripped his elbow. "Give me more, Ricky. Come on. Get it out."

The others had not seen Ricky give him the first dose of power. Caitlyn snarled that it would kill him. Ricky felt a wave of pride inside him as Donnie, who finally knew all about who he was, where he came from, peered over his shoulder with a massive grin and declared, "I am the grandson of Tyr. I can handle a little more."

He heard Erika's sharp intake of air as Donnie turned back to Ricky.

"You don't have to kiss me again, do you?"

"Fuck off," Ricky bit back with a shaky laugh, then he sucked in a breath, pushing the last remnants of Odin's power into Donnie. The vampire grunted as he yanked his hand back and Ricky dropped to the ground.

He lay on his back with a groan, staring up at the sky, his brain and bones a little mush as he struggled to stop his heart from racing and his lungs from burning. Then Donnie was standing over him, then Derek, Caitlyn, Erika, Ever, Kenzie, and finally, the most beautiful vampire in all of the nine realms peered down at him, her eyes wet with tears.

"I told you the plan would work," he groaned, trying to sit up as Donnie barked out a laugh and Ricky decided to take a little nap.

CHAPTER
EIGHTEEN

Ever

E ver glanced down the street where the last of the
berserkers were being taken out by the supernatural
community. The battle seemed to have lasted for days, yet Ever
knew, thanks to Donnie and Ricky, it had only lasted hours.
Everyone she cared for was safe, and those who rose from
Valhalla to fight alongside her needed to be returned to
celebrate.

She had yet to look at her father. Donnie picked Ricky up in
his arms, the warlock out cold. Erika took him from Donnie,
saying she would flash him to his mom's. Loki offered his hand
to Melanie, who glanced from Ricky to Caitlyn.

The vampire cupped Melanie's cheek. "Go with your
husband. You have both played your part. We will see you soon."

Melanie nodded her head hurriedly, then slipped her hand
into Loki's. He was only gone for a minute when he returned
with Erika by his side. Erika nudged Loki's arm, then came to
stand beside Ever.

"Well, that was a bit anticlimactic."

Ever laughed, shaking her head as she stared at the fallen,
who stood waiting for her next order. Tears filled her eyes as
she saw Thor incline his head, Tyr fist a hand over his heart and
Heimdall lift the Bifrost sword. Tom Delaney smiled at Ever as
she lifted her hand into the air, and as she slowly lowered it, the
fallen began to vanish, one by one, until they disappeared.

Ever glanced up at the sky, the first rays of the sun heating her skin as she heard the army of vampires suck in a breath and rush off to seek cover. Donnie told Caitlyn to go as he grabbed onto Odin and pulled him toward a building that would shield him from the sun. Fenrir had Odin gripped by the other shoulder, a flash of red in his eyes.

Donnie kicked open the door to the shop, then slipped inside as the sun illuminated the streets and the true devastation of the battle unfolded. Ever watched as vampires burned to ash under the sun, the wolves pulling their own dead from the streets, leaving bloodstains on the road.

The warlocks and the witches chanted. The berserkers' bodies dissipated as if they had never been fighting, as if they had not ripped throats apart, broken bones with teeth and killed for a purpose that led to bloodshed.

Ever stepped inside the shop and, for the first time since the battle ended, took stock of her father. His hair was matted with blood, his face looked haggard, and blood soaked the end of his robes from where Fenrir had bitten him to hold him in place.

He had magic inside him, but the chains that Tyr had forged to contain Fenrir for millennia would contain that also. It was better than he deserved, her father, for all of the death, all of the sorrow. For the countless times his actions had meant that she lost someone she cared for. Ever's pain, Thor's, Loki's ... the fact that Erika's mother had hidden her from Odin with Freya. And Freya, who made them into the warriors they were today by making them hate her ... they were all victims of a tyrant who had to be stopped.

Ever lifted her sword, swung before anyone could react. Derek's voice was a bark of authority, and she let the blade graze her father's throat. Odin looked up to hold her gaze with this smirk that made her think, made her see clearly.

He wanted her to kill him.

The tip of the blade kissed the side of his neck, blood welling from the strike as Ever gritted her teeth. The smile fell from his lips as Fenrir put an arm on Ever's shoulder.

"Odin cannot be killed without the entire fabric of seven of the nine realms collapsing onto one another, including this one. His blood, his bone was woven with that of his brothers to create the nine realms. His brothers are dead, so if you kill him, you do exactly what he wants and end the world."

Odin's smirk of satisfaction was enough to convince Ever that Fenrir was right. Odin couldn't die, but he did have to be punished.

Ever pulled back her blade, glancing at Fenrir. "Do you have a suggestion?"

The wolf god's expression went sinister, and Ever could see the part of him that terrified Ash. "I happen to know a place."

Ever turned to Derek, his face covered in blood, his arms littered with scratches and battle scars that would heal in no time for him. She hugged him fiercely, telling him that she would be back. Derek inclined his head to them all as Caitlyn drove up in a tinted car.

Derek paused, looking to Donnie, but the vampire shook his head. "I need to see this through."

Derek ducked out and the car left, leaving Ever with Odin, Erika, Loki, Donnie and Fenrir. Danae appeared in the doorway, the rest of the Valkyries landing behind her.

"Help make sure the berserkers have all left the city and the barriers have been lifted. We will return soon."

"Yes, my queen."

When the Valkyries took to the skies once more, Ever turned to face the immortals standing with her. "How do we get to where we need to go?"

Fenrir inclined his head. "Since Ricky gave us a little power boost, let me lead the way."

Fenrir waved his hand, magic saturating the air as a portal opened, and Fenrir, Odin still held in his grasp, stepped through. They followed after him, standing inside the cave where Fenrir had been kept secret for almost his entire life.

"Tyr, the wily old bastard, kept you hidden here? Does the dragon still guard the forest?" Loki asked his son.

Donnie laughed. "She sure does. Made a pass at Ricky."

Fenrir pushed Odin farther into the darkness of the cavern, the god falling to his knees in the dirt. He lifted his head, face enraged as he spat out, "This will not hold me. I am the creator of all the realms. Tyr's powers are not enough to hold me."

Loki chuckled, the sound like music in the darkness. "Niflheim is one of the only two realms that you did not have a hand in, so it is the perfect place to put you. If my son could not break free of the chains that Tyr had fashioned, then I have no doubt they will keep you here."

"I will be released, and I will have vengeance. I will hunt down your children and your children's children and forge new worlds with their bones. I am the Allfather. I cannot be beaten. I cannot be kept prisoner!"

Ever shook her head at the man who was the greatest legend in all Norse mythology, who had Vikings and shieldmaidens pray to him before battle. The old man who glared at them now had no power, and while there would be many who would never know the story and song of Odin the defeated, Ever would make sure that her descendants would.

Donnie reached for the chains. Taking the farthest length, he looped it through a bracket built into the ground so that Odin would have limited movement. Odin reared at Donnie, only to be stopped short of being able to touch him. He grunted as the chains kept him within a small circle of the cave.

"Someone should stay and watch over him."

Loki's words were quiet, as if he himself was offering to stay here to guard Odin.

"Nah, I'll do it," Donnie said, his face determined. "It's my blood that binds him. It should be me."

Erika rolled her eyes. "If that's the case, I should be offering too, *nephew*. But you have a very scary mate at home who I do not want to have to tell that you are staying in this land of mist and fog for eternity."

Erika's emphasis on the word *nephew* cracked a smile on Donnie's face as Fenrir watched the interaction with curiosity.

"I shall do it."

Everyone turned to look at him as Donnie shook his head. "Nah, you just got free. We can't ask you to stay in a place where you were held prisoner for a minute longer than necessary."

Red flashed in Fenrir's eyes. "Would I be welcomed back in Asgard by the gods? Would I blend in with the humans and live like them? I would not be a prisoner here but a warden, free to leave whenever I please. I do not think the world is ready for me to walk amongst them."

Ever and Erika exchanged a look, then quickly schooled their expressions as Fenrir turned to look at them. Loki stepped forward and held out his hand to Fenrir.

"I would like to come visit you, stay with you for a time. If it suits you. I'm sure Hel would like to see you also."

"Perhaps. Now be gone. I tire of you already."

Fenrir's body rippled, bones cracking and molding as he changed into his wolf form, forcing them out of the cavern as he lay down, blocking the doorway and Odin from view.

Ever flashed away first, back to the warehouse, then Loki with Donnie and Erika. The warehouse was empty apart from one lone figure, who turned, her face smeared and her hair mussed.

"Odin is defeated then."

Lady Sif came forward, sheathing her sword as she held out her arm to Ever, who gripped her elbow.. "He is. And now he is in a place where no one will find him."

"Then we will prepare a feast to toast your ascension to the throne as Queen of Asgard."

Ever glanced behind her, then back to Lady Sif. "I was not the one to bring Odin to his knees. It was the vampire and the warlock. One of them is the rightful heir to the Asgardian throne. I already have two realms to watch over. A third would be pushing it."

Lady Sif stared at Donnie, who gave a nonchalant shrug of his shoulders. "I have no desire to rule. I'm content where I am. I can also vouch for Ricky with a polite no thanks."

Ever felt Lady Sif stiffen as if she did not know how to proceed. "Then who will lead us?"

With a smile on her face, Ever gripped Lady Sif's arm tighter. "My brother once told me the day a young fierce Asgardian warrior put him on his back and held a blade to his throat that he would make her his wife and one day queen. Thor may not be here to take the throne, but you are. And you will lead the gods until his sons are able to take the throne."

A smile tugged on Lady Sif's face as she took in the information. "Yes, indeed. Thor should be the one taking his rightful place as king, but I will do my best to rebuild what Odin broke. Perhaps with a little help from our friends."

Lady Sif let Ever go, and then she vanished, leaving Ever with a sense of peace that she had not felt in a long time. Setting her sword down on the table, she leaned against the arm of a chair as she looked up at Erika before saying, "What now? What do we do now that there is no war to be won?"

"There will always be wars, Ever. Mankind was not built for peace. We will do as we have always done, ferry the souls of the worthy to Valhalla. I don't know about you, but I think it's time the Valkyries lived a little."

Narrowing her gaze, Ever asked, "How'd you mean?"

"I mean," Erika replied with a quick glance at Loki, then Donnie, "you have a mate and a gorgeous little girl. I have Loki and a brand-new nephew to spend time with. The girls don't have that. We spent our entire lives training for a war that's over. I think that we need more Valkyrie, and that means the girls need to live a little."

As if sensing that they were being discussed, the Valkyries strode into the warehouse and stood in line before Ever. With one final glance at Erika, Ever turned to address them.

"Odin is defeated, and the war is won. The time for change has come. While Valhalla will always be my home and I am only a flash away, my life is here, with my mate and my daughter, until she comes of age and becomes Midgard's protector."

The Valkyries looked at one another as like they were unsure what they sound say, when Danae spoke up, "Then the general will remain with us in Valhalla?"

"You do not have to remain in Valhalla. It is time to live. To forge your own destinies." Ever watched their confusion, but then Erika stepped forward.

"I'm staying here. I have long-lost family to get to know, and despite the fact I'll be working for Boyband, I want to stay an Agent. Danae, you have proven yourself worthy of keeping the Valkyries in check. You will be my sergeant at arms."

Danae, who had spent a considerable time fighting with Erika as teens, widened her eyes and then fisted her hand over her heart. "I am honored and I am proud to serve you both."

Ever shook her head. "There is no serving. There is no more bowing. Go out into the many realms and live your life. Search for love and know that Valhalla will always be your home. Replenish the ranks with your daughters, and we will do what we were always meant to do: ferry the worthy to Valhalla, where they will feast with their brothers and sisters once more."

Almira opened her mouth. "I could travel to Rome like I have always wanted and play tourist."

Ever smiled as she inclined her head. "And so you will."

"And I could learn to drive a car really fast, as if I were flying!" exclaimed Rebekah, glee in her face and eyes.

Kenzie looked a bit lost down at the end, so Ever went to

stand with her, conscious that Donnie was also watching the interaction.

"What say you, Kenzie?"

Kenzie frowned, her dark eyes narrowing. "I have yet to master my new strength. I want to train like my new Valkyrie sisters did, on the sands of Valhalla, so I can be just like them. Less of an outsider."

"I will train her. And perhaps the general can come and train when she can." Danae offered, nodding her head at Kenzie.

Ever smiled. "I think that can be arranged. Erika can bring Caitlyn by at night so you can learn to fight using both your natures."

Kenzie grinned, holding out her fist to Danae, who looked puzzled for a moment, then bumped Kenzie's fist. Then the newest Valkyrie turned, jogging outside before she took to the skies. Ever watched as the Valkyries all flashed away, and she let loose a sigh of relief.

Removing her helmet, Ever held it in her arms as she turned to look at Donnie and Erika, who stood looking at one another.

"How did you know? That we were related?" Erika asked him, folding her arms across her chest.

"It wasn't until Fenrir bit me and told me that I believed it. I mean, the hints were there, but as someone who knows very little about his past, finding out the god of war is your granddad never ran through my mind." The vampire flashed his teeth as he looked down at Erika.

"Don't start calling me Auntie Erika or some shit."

"Once you don't start calling me nephew every time you get mildly annoyed at me. But I would like to know that side of me …when you have some time."

Erika rolled her eyes. "You're family. I always got time for you. But not right now. Right now, I want to get naked and have spectacular sex that blows my mind."

Donnie winced and shook his head. "Too much information."

Erika laughed as Loki wrapped an arm around her waist, and they vanished from view, leaving Donnie and Ever alone.

"I can never thank you or Ricky enough," Ever said. "I feel a little defeated myself that it was not I who saved the world but you and him."

Donnie shrugged, folding his arms across his chest. "It was a group effort. When you think about it, every single moment in all of our lives led to this, this victory. You had to die to find Derek this last time. I had to die to find Cait. If Ricky hadn't've died, then he couldn't have siphoned Odin's power. Fate may be a fickle bitch, but she finally got it right."

Donnie saw her flinch at the mention of fate, and she told him about Ash and how the fates had come back to get her. At the end of the tale, Donnie was smiling.

"Those kids, they got this. Because they were never left alone like I was. Those kids will save the world because they have all of us to help them. She's doing just fine, Ever. I promise."

"When they tell this story, Donnie O'Carroll, in centuries to come, when they speak of the time of gods and monsters, they will speak of the two friends, family chosen not of blood, who risked it all to save the world."

Donnie shook his head. "Whatever you say, don't say that to Ricky. I love the bastard, but he's going to be hell to live with, especially if he gets a hero complex."

Ever laughed, knowing that the vampire was right. She held out her hand to him, which he took. "Then let's keep that between you and me. Now shall we go track down our mates?"

Donnie winked, and his smile deepened, creasing his cheeks. "Hell ya. Let's go. I have lots to tell my mate before the sun sets."

CHAPTER
NINETEEN

Melanie

Ricky still hadn't woken by the time the sun set for the night, and Melanie was able to open the heavy curtains to gaze outside. Donnie had stopped by to check on Ricky, hugged Melanie so hard that her bones creaked before leaving to see Caitlyn.

Diane had ordered them all to stay, citing that she loved having the house full as they recovered from the events of the last few days. Melanie had been terrified, watching Ricky struggle with the powers inside him, his skin turning a sickly color that had frozen her to the spot. She began to worry about having to live without him, how his mom would deal with his loss, how the team would feel. And Zach ... she couldn't even think about poor Zach.

When Erika and Loki had flashed into Ricky's mom's kitchen, asking where she could put Ricky, Diane had paled until Melanie stepped forward and said that Ricky was just sleeping, ignoring the tremble in her voice as if saying the words might convince her that Ricky would be okay.

Killian had been the one to take Ricky from Erika, heading up the stairs and into Ricky's room. Melanie stepped inside, after Killian, a slight smile on her face as she caught sight of the music and movie posters on the walls. A guitar leaned against the wall.

Killian had laid Ricky down on the bed with care, then he

had turned to Melanie and asked her if she needed anything. When she said no, he had lingered like he wanted to say something, and then he had.

"He'll be fine. Ricky always bounces back. He was always better at finding a way. Forging his own path. When Da was at his meanest, Ricky always made sure that he focused on him, never me. He thinks I never saw it."

Killian walked over to look out the window before he continued. "I blamed him for leaving me behind. I know he had to leave or one of them would be dead. Da spent so much of his time hating what Ricky had done that he didn't bother with me. Every time Ricky was on the news, every time the team solved a case, Da would be livid because Ricky was out there proving him wrong."

Striding to the door, Killian paused to look at her. "He jumped in with Sadie because he thought he wanted normal. What he never had in this house. Sadie never fit him as much as you do. You pull when he pushes. You don't give him an inch. I saw the way he looked at you the night he turned up here with Zach. I was jealous, and I lashed out. I'm sorry."

"It's okay, Killian. If it helps, I know even if he doesn't say it that leaving you here with Xavier was the hardest thing to do."

Killian glanced at Ricky and smiled. "I understand now. But I'm glad he has you."

Melanie had spent the rest of the day pacing the floor, wearing a hole in the carpet even as others stopped by to check on Ricky. Every time someone opened the door, she expected bad news or another megalomaniac god trying to remake the world. Her nerves were shot. In the end, she growled at them all to go away and she would let them know when he was awake.

Now, after umpteen hours of watching and waiting, Melanie peered out the window again, closing her eyes with tiredness both in her bones and in her soul. She really needed him to wake up soon or she was going to be a wreck.

"I never had such a beautiful girl in this bedroom. I must still be dreaming."

Melanie spun round at that delicious husky tone to see Ricky's eyes open and looking at her with a dash of mischief that she loved, even if he looked tired. He pushed himself up, leaning against the wall as he scrubbed a hand down his face.

"How long was I out, babe?" His question was spoken like he had not just woken up after sucking a god's power and almost dying, like it was the morning after a bender with Donnie and he was nursing a hangover.

"Just a couple of hours," Melanie said quietly as she walked over to the bed, sat on the edge with her leg turned toward him.

Ricky being Ricky, he lay his palm on her thigh with a glint in his eyes "Fancy making my teenage fantasies come to life and make out with me?"

He wiggled his eyebrows, and Melanie started to laugh before she remembered what had put him in the bed, unconscious, and she punched him in the arm.

"Hey, what was that for?"

"You just had to go and play the hero. You could have killed yourself with that idiotic plan of yours!"

Ricky frowned for a second before he tugged on a strand of her hair. "To be fair, I was totally against the plan to begin with, but Fenrir said it would work, so we had nothing to lose."

Melanie felt tears wet her eyes. "I'm getting really tired of almost losing you."

"Gods, I love you, Melanie Newton."

"Moore."

Ricky glanced at her in surprise. "Pardon me?"

"Melanie Newton-Moore. I tried just Melanie Moore, but it sounded like a bad DC comic book character. I didn't like how it sounded, so I went with the double barrel."

From the smile that lit up Ricky's face, her warlock vampire was delighted at the addition to her own name. "I like the sound of that. Sounds sexy as hell."

Melanie laughed as she bent down to press her lips quickly to his, felt his hand in her hair as he deepened the kiss with a growl that sent a shudder through her. Ricky bit down gently on her lower lip, tugging playfully as he swept his tongue into her mouth.

Melanie could see where this was headed, knowing full well her husband had the ability to make her forget where she was until someone managed to creep up on them. She gently placed her palms on his chest and pushed away from him.

"Your mom could walk in at any second."

Ricky groaned and thumped his head back against the wall. "I really want you naked."

"Couple of hours won't change that." She chuckled, taking his hand in hers. "Tell me what happened."

And so Ricky told her, and she listened as he told her about him and Donnie traipsing through the forest to him getting propositioned by a dragon, which had her growling like any mated vampire would.

"I told her I was happily mated and in love. No need to growl at me."

Melanie rolled her eyes, leaning into him as he pulled her into his lap, her head falling to his shoulder. "We had to pass a test, us both. I saw me da, faced him as he told me I was worthless. I guess he still haunted me, in a way, but that paled in comparison to what I had to face next."

Ricky shifted, his hand on her thigh as he sighed. "I didn't realize I was fucking terrified of myself. Of this unknown power in me that means I drink energy. I didn't want to revert to form, to who I was when I was high. I figured I had replaced the addiction of pills to chasing this new high. I can't deny it's a rush, babe, every time I drink."

Melanie didn't say anything, just listened as Ricky continued, knowing he needed to tell her how he was feeling. She would sit and listen to him talk for hours, if it made him feel better, and then she would call him an idiot and tell him that it was not the same and she loved him, like she had always done and always would.

"Lanie, I faced myself, and it was weird, but then he showed me what I could become, this asshole who forced his kid to kill him. That would make me no better than Odin. I couldn't let that happen."

"So what did you do?" she asked against the curve of his neck.

"I put a gun to my head and pulled the trigger."

Melanie jerked upright. "You did what?"

"Turns out self-sacrifice was the test."

"What did Donnie have to do?"

Ricky kissed her jaw quickly. "Not my story to tell. He needs to talk to his mate."

Ricky kissed her jaw again, and Melanie rolled her eyes. "Are you trying to distract me from overthinking about what you just told me?"

"Maybe." His answer was said in a teasing tone. "Is it working?"

Melanie shook her head, her chest feeling like it would burst from happiness as a short tap sounded on the door before it opened to reveal Killian carrying a tray of tea, toast and a bottle of blood.

"Mam was pacing with the baby and she heard talking, so I brought some food. For both of you."

Melanie smiled at Killian, having had a conversation with the warlock during the day, when he had sat with Ricky so she could shower and change. She hoped that the two brothers could form a new relationship now that the weight of Xavier Moore was lifted from their shoulders.

Ricky sat up straighter when Melanie slipped off his lap, as

Killian came in and set the tray down on the side table. Ricky grabbed some toast and bit into it without a word as Melanie thanked Killian for the blood.

"How are things going with Freya? The last time, she was only scowling a little bit."

Killian laughed, a rich sound, as Ricky looked at him, puzzled. "She's warming to me. I know it."

"But … you're gay?" Ricky made it sound like a question as he set the toast down and stared at his brother.

Killian rolled his eyes. "No, big brother. You saw me once with a guy, and you assumed I was gay. I like men, and I certainly like beautiful women."

Ricky continued to stare at him, and Killian rubbed the back of his neck before he turned. Ricky shot from the bed. "Kill, wait."

Killian slowly turned as if he expected a blow of words from Ricky. Instead, Ricky held up his hands in apology. "I'm sorry. I'm an ass. It's cool, yano. Guys, girls, goddesses. I don't care. If you're happy, it's all good. Thanks for looking after the furball. Maybe, when the dust has settled, we could go for a pint, you and me?"

"I'd like that. Plus, now that I stepped away from the Phantoms, I was considering signing up for the guards. Spoke to Derek about it already."

"I'm not sure the team can handle another Moore with devilish good looks. This'll be fun." Ricky teased.

Killian was still laughing as he left. Ricky turned back to Melanie when a flurry of footsteps alerted him to an incoming visitor. Zach raced through the door and was clambering up his body before Ricky had time to brace himself.

"Dad!"

Ricky squeezed his son tightly until Zach squirmed and said, "Dad, you're squishing me."

Balancing Zach on his hip, he tickled him. "Well, we can't have that now, can we?"

Ricky glanced over at her, his eyes filled with love, and she blew him a kiss. Zach's stomach growled as Ricky poked his tummy, and their little cat laughed.

"I think we better go see if Grandma has any food to feed you."

Zach rested his head on Ricky's shoulder, and Melanie strode over, pushing the little guy's glasses up his nose. He frowned at her as Ricky kissed her cheek.

"That's gross," Zach said with a mock growl.

Both Melanie and Ricky laughed as Melanie ducked her head and kissed Zach, the sound of his cute little purr reminding Melanie that she still hadn't told Ricky about grown-up Zach.

Sensing Melanie's unease, Ricky turned to her with a raised brow.

"He came back to get her ... Ash ... and he was so like you. I don't know how Derek and Ever dealt with it. I didn't know what to say, and then they were gone. He looked for you. But he seemed to know where you were. I'm sorry you didn't get to see him."

Ricky hoisted Zach up a little. "Would it have been cool to see him all grown up? Hell ya. But I lost five years with him. Now, now I get to be his da, do it right. I would have liked to see that I didn't screw him up and know I was going to do okay by him, by Sadie, but I can wait to see it."

"You did good. We did good. We will do good ... and now even I'm confused."

Ricky laughed as Zach tapped him on the chin. "Dad, I'm hungry."

"Then let's go get you some food, little man."

Ricky held out his hand, which Melanie took, and they walked downstairs to where Melanie could smell breakfast being cooked. They followed the scents to the kitchen, where it seemed that Diane had roped Derek into some cooking.

Ricky set Zach down on the chair next to Killian, then walked around to where his mother was frying up enough sausages to feed an army. He leaned down and kissed her cheek. "Need any help?"

Diane reached over and patted her son on the cheek. "You always cremate the sausages, so you could set the table. Derek is doing a fine job as my sous chef."

Ricky chuckled but did what he was told.

Melanie ruffled Zach's hair, then glanced up to see Derek watching her. "Where's Ever and Ash?"

Derek smiled, and Melanie considered how young he looked when he smiled, when you looked past the wisdom in his eyes and the scarring at his throat. "Ash is sleeping, and Ever is getting some much-needed rest. Caitlyn and Donnie are also resting, but I'd use that term lightly."

Melanie must have looked horrified at Derek's casual innuendo because Diane smacked Derek behind his head as if he were one of her boys, and the werewolf had the good grace to look sheepish.

Ricky was laughing to himself as he set the table, and Melanie sighed at Derek. "I expected that kind of thing from him but not from you."

Derek shrugged as if it was nothing. "I guess Ricky's had an influence on me."

"That might be the sweetest thing you've ever said to me, D. Is that your way of asking for a kiss too?"

Derek growled, throwing a tea towel at Ricky, who ducked to avoid it. Melanie picked it up off the ground, then slapped it against Ricky's arm at the exact same time as Diane clipped Derek round the ear again.

"He started it," they both said in unison, then burst out laughing like the two of them were teenagers.

Melanie wasn't sure she had ever felt so normal in all her life.

Derek brought his plate of bacon over to the table as Ricky set down a slice pan. "I spoke to the commissioner early on the phone. He thinks we need to expand the current gardai force with more supes. Caitlyn agreed for us to use the warehouse, and he wants me to lead it."

Ricky inclined his head at Derek as he sat down in his chair. "No better man for the job. Sarge would have been proud."

"Every captain needs a lieutenant."

Melanie's eyes widened as Ricky spluttered, "Me? Why me?"

"I need to keep my partner close, to keep me grounded. Every single member of the team will be within my inner circle, if they want it. We will have a lot to do, though. If you're up for it?"

"You got it, D. Anything you need."

Derek turned to her then, another smile on his face. "I guess I'll have to convince you to stick around as well. Just to keep us in line."

"Melanie won't be going anywhere, Uncle Derek," Zach said. "She's gonna be my vamp mom."

Derek let his eyes slide from her to Zach, then back to Melanie, who remembered what Ash had said to him as she ruffled his hair again. "That's right, kid. I'm not going anywhere."

Zach jumped down from his spot, grabbed some bacon and patted Derek on the leg like he was comforting him. "See, Uncle Derek. Mom's not going anywhere."

Diane came over with the sausages. "Right now, you lot, dig in."

Melanie wasn't really in the mood for food, even if she had started to make little attempts at picking at solid foods, but Ricky and Derek had no qualms even if Ricky paused to cut

Zach's sausages into little bits. She leaned against the counter, watching until she felt a tap on her shoulder.

Turning slightly to see Diane holding out a glass of blood, Melanie took the glass from her mother-in-law and offered her thanks. Diane patted Melanie's cheek and said very softly, "Thank you for loving him. For loving them both."

Melanie looked over to where Ricky was buttering some bread for Zach, then he glanced over at her and winked.

"He makes it easy. They both do. And I'm glad he has you again. He never said, but I know he missed you."

Diane didn't say anything, just took a mug from the counter and sat down at the table, watching as the boys tucked into the food. Melanie stayed where she was, drinking her blood and wondering how she got so lucky.

For years, she felt like she had been a ghost in her life, living day by day knowing she wanted more, needed more. It took being turned into a vampire to make her finally start living, and Ricky was a massive part of that. She had found her family, her tribe.

Ricky glanced over at her with that twinkle in his eyes.

"I love you," he projected to her in his mind, and she said it right back to him, that smug satisfaction as infuriating as it was charming.

And she wouldn't have it any other way.

CHAPTER
TWENTY

Caitlyn

C aitlyn had just left Derek as she checked on the children when both Donnie and Ever appeared on the landing. She watched Donnie's expression as he ran his eyes over her, relief flashing in his eyes as he stepped away from Ever and came towards her. She had kept her feet planted on the carpet as her mate cupped her cheek, shuddered and just muttered, "You're here. You're still here."

Donnie had kissed her then, stealing any response she might have offered or any questions that she may have asked to know what had put that haunted look on his face. Instead, she had placed her hands on his hips, pulling their bodies flush against one another.

With a growl of lust, Donnie had kept on kissing her, backing her toward the bedroom door, with Caitlyn opening it. Once they were inside, the door was quickly shut, and then there were a lot less clothes and a lot more skin. They had spent the rest of the night and half the next morning as such.

Now Caitlyn was sitting up in the bed, watching as Donnie slept with one hand on her side of the pillow, the other under his head. His eyes were shut, yet she could feel his emotions through the bond as he twitched. She had yet to speak to Ricky and ask what had happened, but it must have been something to send little pinpricks of sadness and pain down the bond.

A rap of knuckles sounded at the bedroom door. Caitlyn got

up from the bed, dressed quickly in a pair of leggings and one of Donnie's tees then padded barefoot to the door and cracked it open a peep to see Melanie standing there, looking sheepish.

Caitlyn stepped out into the hallway so as not to disturb Donnie, closing the door softly behind her.

"I'm sorry to disturb you, but you have a visitor in the front room."

Caitlyn offered Melanie a warm smile. "It is all right. I was awake. If Donnie comes looking for me, would you tell him where I am?"

Melanie nodded, then walked beside Caitlyn as she made her way down the stairs, pausing at the door of the living room when Caitlyn asked her, "Has Ricky spoken of what happened to them whilst they were gone?"

With a small nod of her head, Melanie chewed on her bottom lip before she glanced toward the kitchen. "Just his stuff. He didn't break Donnie's confidence, but if what happened to Ricky is anything to go by, I think Donnie has a story to tell when he wakes up."

Caitlyn watched as her sired child strode away, heard her peal of laughter from the kitchen before she opened the living-room door and stepped inside.

Marcel turned as she entered, once more dressed impeccably, his handsome face brightening when she entered. Caitlyn lowered herself into one of the armchairs that faced a roaring fire, tucking her legs underneath her as Marcel then took a seat opposite her. Caitlyn rested her cheek on her hand and smiled at Marcel, who studied her with open curiosity.

"You almost seem relaxed."

Caitlyn chuckled softly. "I'm afraid that all my high lady manners have mostly gone out the window, living with all the young ones."

"If it means that your face is alight with happiness, then it is not something I can disapprove of."

Caitlyn rolled her eyes before she asked, "Why are you here, Marcel? I would have thought you would have returned to Paris."

Marcel leaned forward in his seat, resting his elbows on his knees. "When I came to your mating ceremony, I was awash with anger. I cast aside all that you helped me achieve because you would not offer up the girl to me. Had it not been for that girl, what skills she had, both myself and Mateo would be ash on the wind."

Closing his eyes for a moment, Marcel then opened them, those dark brown eyes filled with sorrow. "We have both lost too much to let old vengeance ruin the friendship, the bond we shared since you took me from the streets. I wish I had not been so easy to dismiss it, but I have spent the time since our last encounter replaying that night in my head, and I am sorry for my part in all of it."

Caitlyn lifted her head. "Marcel, you came when I called. That was enough. Actions, they do always hold more weight than words ever do. Just like I would come anytime you asked me to, if you needed help."

"Then I can go back to Paris with my heart full, knowing that one day, maybe soon, you might come and visit us back home."

"Ireland is my home now, Marcel. My family is here. The man I love is here. Paris might be where I came from, where I survived the darkness, yet I am home here. But I may still visit one day."

"And bring your niece with you, if you can. I fear Mateo is quite smitten with her."

Caitlyn chuckled softly, a smile tugging at her lips as Marcel rose, and she followed his lead, waiting until he opened his arms to step into the embrace. She patted his back as she whispered, "You will always be part of my family, Marcel. If you should fancy ever swapping Parisian wine for Irish stout, you will always be welcome here."

Marcel was laughing as she showed him to the door, closing it with a firm snick, then turned to see Derek standing in the hallway. Caitlyn strode to him, then leaned against the staircase.

"You two made peace?"

"Yes, it appears Kenzie proved herself, saving Marcel during the fight."

Derek let his lips curl into a wolfish smile. "Diane was worried you and Donnie would starve, so they nominated me to check on you. You guys need anything?"

"Not right now. I think I need to speak to my mate and not be … distracted."

Derek huffed out a laugh, running his hand through his hair. "Okay, but I want to run something by you both, when you have time."

Derek left her then to head back upstairs, where she found Donnie sitting at the edge of the bed in just his boxer shorts, his eyes staring out the window as she entered. When Caitlyn closed the door, Donnie's shoulders sagged.

"I don't know how to tell you what happened. I don't know what to say that won't get you retreating into yourself."

Caitlyn carefully walked toward Donnie. "I had this feeling in my chest while you were away that I was about to lose you. That I hadn't said all that I wanted to say. That I love you. That I would be shattered beyond repair if I lost you. That I had not told you any of that recently. Did I feel that through the mating bond?"

Donnie was silent for a long time before Caitlyn kneeled down in front of him and rested her head against his leg. Her mate reached out and played with the strands of her hair.

"Did Ricky tell you guys what happened during our test?"

Caitlyn shook her head, afraid to say anything, especially when Donnie let out a relieved sigh. "I don't want to tell you."

"It cannot be that bad, Donnie. We have no secrets, you and I."

As he continued to play with her hair, Donnie started to speak. "The compass led us to Nidhug, the dragon that guarded the forest of your greatest fears. I half expected it to be like I have to fight my way out of a pit of snakes or something, but this forest, it gets inside your head, your heart and soul and presented me with the thing I feared the most."

Caitlyn turned so that she was facing him, scooting back as Donnie joined her on the floor, shivering, though she knew he was not cold.

"And what were you most afraid of, mi amour?"

Donnie lifted his eyes, as if he needed to see her reaction as he said, ever so quietly, the name no more than a whisper between them, "Sebastian."

Caitlyn startled, her eyes widening. "I do not understand why you would be afraid of a dead man."

Donnie shrugged, and Caitlyn saw him bite the inside of his mouth, like he was trying to think before he spoke. "I know it's not rational, Cait. But we mated quickly, and then I fucked up. I guess I felt insecure, like I was gonna be that kid again that never got adopted. Who was left alone in the home. That you would see sense and leave me, in the end."

With a shake of his head, Donnie continued, his fists clenching and unclenching as he spoke. "Sebastian—well, the test version—he showed me how you first met. He told me that you had too good a heart, collecting strays, and it made me feel like I was a stray."

"I have never made you feel that way." Caitlyn heard the ice in her tone, tried to soften it. "You were different."

Donnie thumped a hand down on his thigh. "He took me to the house, your house you shared with him. I heard the easy laughter, felt the love inside that house, and it broke my heart. I felt jealous that Sebastian had that piece of you, but I knew you had to go through what you did to end up with me."

Caitlyn blinked the tears in her eyes away before Donnie glanced at her again.

"Sebastian offered me a choice. Let him walk into the house that night, the night he first met Cain, and none of it would have happened. You would not have suffered, and you would never know. You would never have found me in that alley and made me into a vampire. You would not have known I love you."

Caitlyn sucked in a breath, for a split second wondering if Donnie had failed his test. Because she was still here, with him …

Donnie shook his head, having heard the thought in her mind. "I didn't fail. I walked away, Cait. I left Sebastian to go into the house, even if it meant I was going to die. Even if you never knew me, I wanted you to be happy. I left Paris to walk into that street in Temple Bar and got my head kicked in. But there was no avenging angel to save me that night because you died happy as an old woman and were never reborn as a vampire."

Donnie held her gaze as tears began to stream down her face, and hurt flashed across his face. Silly man, darling man. Who would have given up everything for her … so she could have been happy?

She reached for him, her mate, who darted upright and strode to the window, his back to her.

"I'm sorry it wasn't real. I'm sorry I couldn't fix it for you."

Caitlyn got to her feet, walked over and wrapped her arms around Donnie's waist, pressing her lips to his spine. "There was nothing to fix. I am exactly where I am meant to be. Would you have thought I would make a different choice if it was offered to me? Do you think I would have replaced the grief for my babies with my grief for you and Melanie? Non, you gave up a chance of happiness for me."

"But I considered not walking away, Cait. For this split second, I was selfish and didn't want to walk away, because like I told him, as much as I felt like the other man, I didn't want to be without you. Then I felt like a bastard because I didn't matter, in the grand scale of things ... I didn't matter."

Caitlyn felt her heart break, and she wondered if it was her fault that he felt this way, that she had made it so that he thought himself insignificant in their relationship. She made to answer him when Donnie tensed.

"And now that I have his powers to dream walk, I'm terrified that you will look at me and only see Cain."

Caitlyn growled and spun Donnie round so he would see her eyes and know she spoke the truth. "Cain used his powers to invade my dreams and force my will. You, my love, have seen inside my head for decades and have not once forced me to do anything when I said no. You saw inside my mind that I ached for you and still, you held me when my nightmares were too much to bear alone. Not once did you take or use that power against me."

Caitlyn ran her palm up his chest, her mate's body trembling slightly at her touch. "You would never invade my dreams for what I give freely to you. My body, my heart, my soul is yours, Donnie. And if I have to spend the next century proving it to you, then so be it."

"But ..."

She pressed a finger to his lips. "No. The past, it happened. I died under the city I called home, but I was like a wraith, waiting to be swallowed up. I began to live the moment I happened upon a sexy-as-sin rugby player and had to make him mine, like I had done with no other before him."

Donnie shuddered, then lowered his head to the crook of

her neck, hugging her to him. They stayed like that for an age, until Donnie stepped back, his eyes full of tears.

"I can't believe Erika is my aunt."

Caitlyn smiled, patting his chest. "I think it is a good thing to have found that part of you. I also think Erika might be happy to know that despite losing Tyr, she has a little part of him alive to call her kin."

"Like you and Kenzie."

Caitlyn smiled at her mate as she took a step back. "Exactly." She walked over to the duffel on the floor and removed some clothing for Donnie. "Derek would like to speak to us. I'm sure it will be about the expansion, but before we agree to anything, I have something to ask you."

Donnie's eyes narrowed. "Anything. My answer will always be yes."

Caitlyn ran a hand through her hair before leaning her hip on the dresser. "I think it is time I buried the past. I would like to sell the house in Paris. Perhaps to the family who has worked in it for generations."

"Don't sell the house because of me, Cait."

"Non," Caitlyn said with a shake of her head. "I have been considering it for a time. I was wondering if you would like to see the world with me? I remember you saying that you had traveled quite a lot when you were human yet had not seen many places. The war is won. I think we could do with a few months of downtime."

Donnie crossed the room in three strides, cupped her face in his hands and kissed her hard once before he stated fiercely. "I would walk into the fires of hell if it meant I could be with you. I would very much like to see the world with you."

Donnie released her only to dress, then they walked down into the kitchen, where Derek sat with a tablet in his hand, Ash resting in his other arm. Ricky was brewing coffee, slid them a mug as Melanie beamed over at them.

Caitlyn smiled as she took her mug and sat down at the table. It had not been two years since things had started to change, when Melanie had died and become a vampire. They had been through the wars between them, yet when Caitlyn considered it, the five of them had been there at the very start, with Sarge, and it was a miracle that they had mostly come out unscathed.

A hand fell on her shoulder, and Caitlyn glanced up at Donnie with a sad smile.

"I've already got Ricky and Melanie on board, but how about you two?" Derek interrupted her thoughts and glanced up, patting a hand on Ash's tummy as she whimpered before drifting back to sleep. "I need people I can depend on to help me get this off the ground. Sarge had a lot of plans for expansion, and now that we have the warehouse, we have the chance to bring more supes onto the force."

Donnie glanced at Caitlyn, letting her decide what she wanted to do. Caitlyn reached up and squeezed his hand. "Mon loupe, we would be delighted to continue the good work that P.I.T. do when we return from our travels. I have some things I need to do in Paris."

"You're leaving?" Melanie asked, her tone sad, her eyes even more so.

"For a time. But Cork is where our family is. We would not be able to stay away too long."

Derek nodded his head. "I'll hold you to that. Sarge was pretty clear in his instructions that we do this as a family. I texted Erika, and she's in, once we allow her time to check in with things in Valhalla. Kenzie will also have a place once she spends some time training with the Valkyries."

Ricky nudged Donnie's shoulder as he passed. "You owe me a pint before you leave."

Donnie lifted Caitlyn's hand to his lips. "Sure, Ricky. I'm

sure Josephine's is having an open mic night this weekend. We could get the band back together."

Ricky held out his fist for Donnie to tap, and Caitlyn lifted her gaze to meet Melanie's, who rolled her eyes as if to say, *These two.*

Caitlyn sat back and sipped her coffee as Ricky told Donnie of places he needed to visit on their travels, from Berlin to New York, offering names of bars and restaurants. Derek caught her gaze, lifted a brow.

She lifted her mug to let him know that she was happy, her eyes falling to the sleeping child cradled in Derek's grasp. She sipped her coffee again, her entire body feeling relaxed for the first time in what felt like forever.

Donnie peered down at her, his eyes filled with love and devotion, and Caitlyn smiled back, hoping that her eyes told him how she felt, how much she loved him.

His expression told her he saw it.

His kiss told her he believed it.

And for the first time in Caitlyn's life, she was excited for the future, for what was to come. Her demons may have been vanquished, even if the hurt remained. Yet, with Donnie by her side, she felt like the darkness in her soul would be quietened.

She loved him … truly loved him as much as he loved her. Love conquered the darkness. Love had been victorious.

And in the end, that was all that mattered.

CHAPTER
TWENTY-ONE

Ever

Her sword swung toward the berserker, lodging in its chest. The creature roared, spitting drool into her face that made her want to swipe it from her skin, but Ever yanked out the blade, and her next swing severed its arm. They kept coming, the berserkers. She feared the battle would not be won.

Ever patted the rump of her horse, and it galloped away, vanishing as quickly as it had appeared. Taking off at a run, she slid under the body of another berserker and twisted her wrist to slice through flesh and bone before Erika lifted off the ground and decapitated it.

Back-to-back, they turned, then took out two more berserkers. Ever's head darted to the right, her eyes falling on Marcel, the vampire who had traveled from Paris to fight beside them. A berserker had him pinned to the ground, its twisted and gnarled teeth snapping as it lowered its mouth to tear chunks out of the vampire, while the other vampire with the cheeky smile tried to get to him.

Ever was about to head over to assist when she spotted a lush mass of feathers in an obsidian color come down, the glint of metal as Kenzie swung her scythe and separated the head from its neck. The head bounced as Kenzie dropped to her feet, held out a hand to Marcel. The vampire looked like he was going to refuse, then gripped Kenzie's hand tight.

They shared a look, then Marcel nodded as Kenzie shot up off the ground again, grabbing Mateo's berserker by the shoulders before she dropped it from a height and Mateo sliced into its carotid.

Ever looked around her as Thor fought alongside Baldur, Tyr fought alongside Loki. They were beating the forces back. They had a shot at winning this.

Then Ever heard Erika shout, her sister pointing to where Donnie squared up to Odin before the monstrous wolf appeared, seizing Odin between his jaws, and then Ever felt powerless as she watched Ricky step up to Odin with that cocky grin of his. She was even more shocked when Ricky pressed his lips to her father's, Odin's magic being siphoned into the energy vampire.

Ever blinked at the sound of the door opening, angling her body to smile at her mate as he entered, ready to place their sleeping daughter into the cot that had once been Ricky's and Killian's. Once he had made sure Ash was settled, Derek kissed her lips.

"Did you get them all on board?"

"Caitlyn and Donnie are going to take some time out, but they will be ready to start. They deserve some time to just be."

Considering Caitlyn had waged her own war long before Ever had appeared on the scene, she was happy for the vampire and her mate. And now that Erika and Donnie were related, it only forged the bond that Donnie was family, like the rest, as if he too were her nephew.

"I know that Erika plans on staying, dividing her time, but we haven't discussed where we go next."

Derek's eyes held a hint of amber as he looked into her eyes, yet Ever kissed his jaw before she spoke. "Valhalla is only a thought away. Danae can run things on a day-to-day basis. I'm not sure what Freya intends to do, but my place is here with you. It's nice that we can flash to Valhalla any time we need a weekend away."

Derek, ran his palms up and down her arms. "I think you could convince her to stay, if you asked her. The way her and Killian have been throwing glances at one another, I think she would stay. She was even civil with Samhain. Diane said that she was very attentive with Ash, even Zach, though I do not think a woman alive could say no to that kid."

Ever laughed, shaking her head. "It seems that even you aren't averse to his affections either, Uncle Derek."

"I would have been less floored if you hit me with a two by four."

Derek rested his nose in her hair, inhaled her scent and then sighed. Ever stepped back, ready to ask Derek what was wrong, when there was a knock on the door. Derek kissed her forehead, then walked over to the door and opened it.

Freya stood on the other side, her hands in her pockets, her face that unreadable mask as Derek inclined his head and stepped out. Freya stayed standing in the doorway as Ever placed a blanket over Ash, who immediately fussed until Ever removed it.

"You used to do that. Even as a toddler, you would kick off the blankets during the night, and no matter how many times I tucked you in, you would wriggle free within minutes."

It was the most Freya had ever said about when Ever was a baby. Ever had not heard the softness in her tone before, and when Ever glanced up at her birth mother, there was a flash of regret before the mask was back.

Freya stepped into the room. "I have spent some time with Diane, speaking with her. I have made some mistakes, Ever. More than a few. I hope you will realize that what I did, how I was, it was to protect you and the girls. I could not let myself feel love for you when Odin would have used it as a weakness."

Ever peered down at Ash, her heart constricting at the reminder of the teen who had returned to where she had come from, and though Ever could not imagine not showing Ash all of the love she had for her, she had also almost made a terrible choice.

Freya had made a terrible choice, but what if the alternative was worse?

"The cloaking spell will evaporate once I leave the house. She won't even feel it."

Ever leaned against the other wall. "What will you do now?"

Freya craned her neck, her expression serious. "In truth, I am unsure what I can do now. When Odin handed Valhalla to me to look after under the promise that he would bed me, in order to birth a Valkyrie who would one day be queen, I buried parts of me that I do not think I can reclaim. When Odin saw the affection I had for you, when he began to use it against me, I shut down."

Shifting her weight, Freya sighed. "Valhalla has its queen. It has its general and Danae to train the new Valkyrie, when you find them. My time as Valhalla's gatekeeper is over. Though I do not belong on Asgard, I do not belong anywhere."

"You could stay?"

Her mother blinked, as if surprised by Ever's words. "I beg your pardon?"

Ever smiled, glancing from Ash to Freya. "I understand you better now. You have the chance to be the doting grandmother Ash needs. You have time to find who you are without Odin. We have time, you and me, to work through things. You could be part of our family, if you want. And I'm sure Killian would be delighted to know that you were hanging around."

"Killian is far too young for me." Freya grunted, causing Ever to laugh.

"I am centuries older than Derek, even if I have been reborn six times. Loki is older than Erika. Caitlyn is older than Donnie, and Ricky is older than Melanie, though in vampire terms, she's technically older than him. You have spent too much time alone, mother. Maybe a little sexing by the young warlock would do you some good."

Freya rolled her eyes. "I have not lain with a man since your father. It was not an enjoyable experience. Though I did quite like sex before him."

Freya, goddess of love in the eyes of mothers, narrowed her gaze as she pondered Ever's words. "I would like to visit my granddaughter and you. If that would be all right."

"I would like that very much."

Freya inclined her head, then retreated out of the room before she flashed from view. Ever was happy that Freya would be back, had already had a conversation with Samhain and had promised to sit down with her next week to talk things through.

"It looks like you are repairing hearts and minds all round, sister."

Ever rolled her eyes as Loki appeared, draped on the bed, wearing a Marvel Studios tee over well-worn jeans. His black hair was pulled back off his face as he looked at her, obviously amused.

"Freya did what she did. We have all done things we regret. Tell me, if you had known all that would happen, would you have set the curse in motion?"

Loki pondered her question, tapping his fingers to his chin. "I try not to think of what-ifs and maybes, Ever. We lost our dear brother, yet I finally got Erika to see me, and you have your little family. Those around you are happy, content. Had I not cursed us all those years ago, we might not have had the power to defeat him."

"That was all Ricky and Donnie."

"Perhaps. It was as the fates designed it to be. It was not the gods who saved the world but those called monsters by the humans. I think, considering all that could have happened, we should be happy with the win."

Ever heard Ash whimper, touched her fingers to the toes of her little feet, and she settled again. "I'm not sure why Ash thinks you let Fenrir out, but I think she would be upset to know that it was Donnie."

"Then we will have to wait and see what happens in the future. Perhaps we have changed Ash's fate by winning. If we can stop her from traveling to Niflheim, then we can keep them from crossing paths. But you know as well as I do, Ever, that if it is meant to be, it will be."

Loki shifted to stand, smoothing down his tee.. "Now I have left a sleeping Valkyrie and Goddess of War in my bed, and I can feel her beginning to stir. I will take my leave."

"Wait, Loki, before you go."

The god of mischief halted, tilting his head as Ever began to speak. "Neither of us is religious. Me and Derek. But we wanted to have people Ash could rely on. Most Catholics have two godparents, but we might end up with a few. Derek and I would like you and Erika to be one set. Should anything happen to Derek or me, we need people who understand her powers."

Loki arched his brows. "I have not exactly been a great father."

"But you are an exceptional brother. And now an uncle. Perhaps, just like Freya, you have time now to dedicate it to your children. Or any that may come along the way."

"I am honored. As will Erika be. I am very proud of you."

Then Loki flashed away, leaving Ever alone with a smile on her face. "I love you too, brother."

Ever made sure the monitor was on in the room, checked the windows and doors and acknowledged she might be a little paranoid before she closed the door and headed down to the kitchen, where everyone seemed to be gathered.

Melanie and Ricky were on the floor, surrounded by an army of Legos as they built something with Zach. Caitlyn sat perched on Donnie's lap as they looked over some paperwork Derek passed them. He caught her eye, smiled, then nodded at something Caitlyn said to him.

The moon was at her highest tonight, not full, but she felt it coming. There was no thunder, no lightning, no storm on the horizon. All was calm as she looked outside to see Killian sitting in the grass, Freya beside him, even if there was a space between them.

Derek looked over his shoulder at the pair before he turned to Ever, a smile playing on his lips. "Killian just asked her if she had a mobile he could text her on. Freya looked puzzled until he asked her if she had ever sexted."

Ever burst out laughing, setting down the monitor as Ricky said. "He's definitely my brother."

Derek leaned back in his chair, rolling his eyes as Ever pushed her thoughts down the mating bond and into her mate's head. *Did you ask yet?*

I was waiting for you.

Her mate smiled as he closed down the laptop, reached out his hand to Ever, and she slipped her hand in his, fingers grasping one another.

"We know that life is never certain. Sarge's death proved that. But now with Ash, we wanted to make sure that she had family around her if anything was to happen to either of us," Derek said as Ricky frowned.

"Nothing's gonna to happen to you, D. Your mate was already a badass, and now she has a little extra oomph. Don't be getting all morbid and shit."

Derek rolled his eyes, resting his hand on Ever's thigh. "My mate was always a badass, as is yours, buddy. Now shut up and let me get a word in."

Ricky made as if to speak, but Melanie clamped a hand over Ricky's mouth to let Derek go on. Ever leaned her head on Derek's shoulder as he said, "Family, this one we have all chosen, is the most important part of our lives, and we want Ash to have that. We've already asked Loki, and Ever will ask Erika, but Caitlyn and Ricky, we wanted to ask you to be Ash's other set of unofficial godparents."

Caitlyn looked delighted; her eyes filled with a quiet determination that Ever knew would be such an inspiration to her daughter. Ricky just looked stunned, as if he didn't believe that they had even considered him. His mouth opened, then closed. The motion repeated, yet not a sound came out.

"I think you broke him," Melanie teased as she nudged her husband. "Ugh, this is where you say thank you."

"Derek ... I ... I mean ..."

Derek held up his hand. "Before you say anything, before you argue our choice, let me tell you that we were both in full agreement. You are not the young man with a chip on his shoulder who joined the guards anymore. You fought tooth and nail to be the man you are today, the husband and father they deserve. And you just about helped Donnie save the world. I could ask no better man."

Ever saw the wetness in Ricky's eyes, heard him sniffle before that cocky smile returned. "Donnie was the best sidekick I could have asked for."

"Fuck off, mate. I'm nobody's sidekick."

Zach turned round and wagged his finger at Donnie. "That's a bad word, Uncle Donnie. You shouldn't say things like that or Auntie Caitlyn will have to put you in time-out on the naughty step."

They all laughed as Donnie pressed a kiss to Caitlyn's neck before he looked at the kid with a serious expression "Okay, kid. I'll watch my language."

That seemed to appease Zach, who went back to his Legos, not paying any attention as Donnie winked. "I think I'd quite enjoy being put on time-out by you, Cait."

Caitlyn rolled her eyes as Ricky muttered, "Save it for the vacay, you two."

Ever glanced out the window behind her as Killian lifted the back of Freya's hand to his lips, grinning when Freya snatched her hand back and disappeared into the night, removing the spell and Ash's aura spilled over her and Derek, whose eyes flashed amber, as Freya's spell broke,

"When do you leave?" Ever asked Caitlyn, who smiled back at Ever.

"Tomorrow night," came Caitlyn's response. "I must pay a visit to Chester before we depart or else he may have a canary if I simply up and disappear."

"Any destination in mind yet?" Derek chimed in, opening up his laptop again, another email flashing on the screen.

Donnie answered this time. "I'm thinking of a beach somewhere. A few nights by the ocean with Caitlyn in nothing but a bikini sounds like fu—" Donnie broke off as if he caught himself before he swore, then rephrased his words. "Cait in a bikini sounds like a little slice of heaven to me."

"There are a few very secluded cabins in Valhalla if either of you wanted to stop by and visit Kenzie. Just give me or Erika a call and we can flash you there. If you give us enough time, we can make sure the cabin is sunproof."

Caitlyn offered her thanks, then rose, bending to kiss Zach before she and Donnie left for the night, heading back to the house to pack and have a little privacy.

Zach yawned not long after. Melanie took the child in her arms on his request for a story before Ricky tidied up the mess on the floor, offering them a cheerful good night as he left them alone in the kitchen.

"I thought they'd never leave." Ever's mate's growl was the only warning she got before she was astride his lap, his lips on hers, hands in her hair as Derek kissed her like a dying man needed air. It was a kiss of all tongue and teeth and possessiveness until Ever was dizzy and pushed him away with a playful swat.

Derek's wolf was in his eyes as he kissed her hard once more, then shifted slightly so Ever could tell exactly what he had in mind.

"I am so glad you walked into me that day on campus, Derek Doyle. Even if you were a grumpy ass most of the time."

Derek nipped at her chin. "We may need to have a discussion on this, mate of mine, considering it was you who bumped into me. Can't have you telling our grandkids untruths about how we first met."

"Grandkids?"

Derek chuckled softly, his hands cupping the side of her neck. "Hell ya. I have generations of agents to bring into the force. We've got Zach and then Ash, but we could do with some more family members on the team."

"Lots of grandkids means more kids."

"Six sounds like an okay number." Derek laughed at her shocked expression.

"Six?"

"I'm a wolf, babe. We like packs. I need my own little squad."

Ever leaned in to the curve of his neck, licked the spot where Derek's pulse thrummed, then bit down gently before she whispered in his ear. "Then I think you need to convince me, Mr. Broody Agent."

Derek barked out a laugh, then kissed her again as if they had forever to play with each other, to kiss and touch and love.

Because that's exactly what they did have now … forever.

EPILOGUE

Derek
11 months later

D erek growled as he cut the video link on the conference call, closing his eyes to rein in his temper at the hoops he was being dragged through. He knew he was asking for a lot, more funding for a growing department, but the numbers justified his ask of government for an extra grant to expand the Paranormal Investigations Team countrywide.

Since Derek had taken control, supernatural crime was down fifty percent.

In the ten months since Derek took over the running of the new standalone branch of the Gardaí, applications had come through fast and in great quantities to join. He had requests from many large cities and counties to come and train or give a briefing on the need for more supernatural boots on the ground.

Dublin had been the first to get on board, with their captain coming down to shadow Derek and the team for a whole month before he agreed that as the country's capital, Dublin needed more qualified guards to deal with supernatural offenders.

Derek was already stretching himself thin, and now, with the fact that the bearcats in government and the supernatural council could not agree who should fund the training in Derek and Ricky's plan, it meant that it would take longer to get things off the ground.

He was lucky that he had Ricky, who had taken to training the newbies like a duck to water. His easygoing yet stern attitude, or Dad mode, as Melanie liked to call it, made him extremely well-respected and liked among the new class of recruits.

Derek was respected by them as well, but they were also a little afraid of him, considering he was the boss and ultimately, he had the final say as to whether they joined the team or not.

And then there was Erika.

Derek snorted as he remembered the recruit who had pissed himself because Erika got in his face when he made a smart-ass remark that there was nothing a girl could teach him at the shooting range. The Valkyrie had smiled, then proceeded to pull a gun from her hip and empty the clip into the bullseye.

They used Erika to help Ricky train the newbies and scare the wrong ones out of the program. She enjoyed it a lot more than she should.

Derek glanced at the clock on the wall as the phone on his desk rang, his PA on the other end.

"Sir, the meeting with Arthur De Valera has been pushed to Friday. Mr. De Valera sends his apologies, but his mate had a difficult early birth last night, and he cannot leave the county. He wanted to offer his apologies, but you were on the phone with the Taoiseach."

Derek thanked Melissa, then asked her to send a hamper to Arthur and his mate. He hung up the phone, glancing at the clock again with a sigh. Getting to his feet, Derek strode over to the window and glanced out at the city of Cork.

Since Odin had been defeated, since the war was done, things had been blissfully normal, with the team dealing with the usual nasties and garden-variety monsters. Ricky, Melanie and Zach had stayed in Caitlyn's home while she and Donnie traveled, and their home was ready to move into, right next door. Himself and Ricky were just adding the finishing touches to the paint and they would be good to go.

Caitlyn and Donnie had kept them updated on their travels, and he had never seen the two look so happy. Melanie had asked, well, demanded that the new P.I.T. have a dedicated computer science department, and when she was not training the recruits, that was her contribution.

Once a hacker, always a hacker.

And Derek ... gods, he was deliriously happy. They had bought a cottage not far from the rest of the team, with a massive patch of land where Derek and Ash could run during the moon or whenever the fancy took. Ever had taken time out to be a full-time mom, as Derek had his hands full with getting the new headquarters up and running and assembling new recruits.

Ever spent her time between Cork and frequent trips to Valhalla, with Derek often joining them, especially since there was no phone signal there and he could relax. He enjoyed his sparring sessions with Erika, though he'd never tell her that.

The first class had trained for ten months and had recently graduated, with Ricky's brother Killian at the top of the class. Derek had wondered if it would be awkward with Ricky training his brother, but Ricky and Killian had grown close, with the two of them spending most Saturday mornings doing extra training at Ricky's mom's house.

Every Friday night, when the kids stayed at Grandma Diane's, they all gathered together in one place, unless the team was in the middle of a case. Caitlyn and Donnie even joined them via video. Just last Friday, Ricky had hosted a barbecue where everyone turned up, even Loki, who was rather amused as Ricky thought he could beat the god at poker.

Now Ricky owed Loki a favor of his choosing, anything he wished.

"I see that you still are as broody as when I left, mon loupe."

The words were said in a teasing tone as Derek turned to see his oldest friend standing in the doorway. Derek ran his gaze over Caitlyn, her features relaxed, a shimmer of light in her eyes that was no doubt in part down to the vampire being greeted in the halls. Dressed in tight black jeans, a tee that smelled like it was Donnie's and a leather jacket, Caitlyn watched him with an amused look.

"Please tell me this is not a flying visit and I can put you two on the payroll Monday morning."

Caitlyn chuckled as she came forward, pressed a kiss to each of his cheeks, and then, when he opened his arms for a hug, she stepped into them without a flinch or any reservation.

"We would not miss Ash's first birthday. Plus, Donnie has been asked to help coach Zach's rugby team. He forced me to come back."

Donnie's chuckle rumbled as Caitlyn stepped out of Derek's embrace. "Oh ya, like I had to force you. I'm not the one who had the flights booked before I'd even said yes."

Derek and Donnie exchanged a hug, clapping each other on the back as Derek asked how their trip to Paris was. Donnie and he shared a look as Caitlyn said, "Paris was lovely. We visited Marcel, and I signed the house over to the family who have taken such good care of it since I left."

Donnie cupped the back of her neck. "We also purchased a small plot and reburied Caitlyn's Sebastian and Jessamine. Got a nice little headstone so Cait can go visit whenever she wants."

"Where the fuck is my nephew!"

Donnie chuckled as he rolled his eyes, turning just as Erika walked into Derek's office. "Of course you'd come see him first. Does blood mean nothing to you people anymore?"

"Dude, we went to Asgard last week. I haven't seen Derek in months."

Erika laughed as she inclined her head to Caitlyn, then

shifted her eyes to Derek. "Ricky wanted to know if you would come down and cast your eyes on the recruits."

"Have you made someone cry?" Derek taunted with the hint of a smile on his lips.

The Valkyrie rolled her eyes. "Relax, Boyband. No tears or urine have been spilled tonight ... but it's still early."

They all laughed as Erika grabbed Donnie by the arm and pulled him down the corridor. They vanished down the stairs, leaving Caitlyn alone with him.

"You doing okay after Paris? You know you don't have to keep up pretenses with me."

Caitlyn offered him a warm smile as she began to walk out of the office, Derek falling into step with her. They reached the stairs before Caitlyn responded to his question.

"I have laid my ghosts to rest. Being in Paris, it stirred some things in me that caused me some nightmares, but Donnie has been my rock. I may never traverse the catacombs again, yet I think I could go back to Paris, if I wished to."

They descended the stairs. Derek inclined his head to the double doors to their right. Caitlyn smiled at the name over the door, Sergeant Thomas Delaney Training Centre. "Fancy coming to check out the recruits with us? I'd appreciate your input."

Caitlyn tilted her head. "Ricky has done a good job with the last batch. I'm certain he has done so once more."

Derek shrugged his shoulders. "We have a few vampires this time round. I'd like to see how they react to the vampire queen. See if they are unnerved."

Caitlyn chuckled as Derek held open the door. Ricky stopped to give Donnie a punch. Melanie jogged over to Caitlyn and threw her arms around Caitlyn's neck.

"Oh my god, I've missed you guys!" Melanie exclaimed as she stepped back, her bright smile lighting up her eyes.

"We have missed you, too. We will catch up this evening, oui?"

"Absolutely." Melanie replied, pulling out her phone. "Let me tell Kenz that you are back and maybe she can slip out for a couple of hours. You should see how much progress she has made, Caitlyn. It's remarkable. I mean, she was kick-ass before, but now ... Even Derek offered her lots of money to come back."

Melanie slipped the phone back into her pocket, striding across the hall to the bleachers and plonking down. Ricky, who had been standing by Donnie, jogged up the steps to kiss her full on the mouth, earning a whoop of whistles from the recruits. Ricky winked over his shoulder at them.

"Don't hate the player; hate the game."

"Okay, Kanye, back to work," Melanie rolled her eyes as Ricky strode back down, his face turning serious as he came to stand by Caitlyn and Derek. After Ricky and Caitlyn hugged, Ricky telling Caitlyn that Zach was all excited about seeing her and Donnie this weekend.

Caitlyn glanced over to Donnie, then back to Ricky. "Thank you for asking him to help with the little one's team. He has been elated since you called."

"I'm not exactly an expert, so having Donnie around will be awesome. The school is thrilled to have him on the training team."

Ricky folded his arms across his chest, the muscles bunching. Caitlyn walked over to sit on the benches with Donnie and Melanie.

"We've got a handful of good potentials, D. I think the harpy has a few temper issues so not sure if she will pass. There's one kid, one girl who I really like. She has instincts and smarts you just can't teach."

Derek flashed Ricky a grin that was all teeth, rubbing his neck, feeling the marred skin under his fingertips as he replied. "Then let's see if I can pick her out."

Ricky stepped forward, clapped his hands together and whistled. The ten recruits lined up in formation, legs apart and arms clasped behind their backs. Derek scanned his eyes over the group, who all looked to be in their early twenties, but Derek knew one or two of the vampires were years if not decades older.

"All right, ladies and gentlemen, this is the last exercise of the night, and we are gonna play a little game called tag."

The recruits looked at each other, puzzled, but this was a tradition that each and every class had to take part in, like it was a rite of passage.

Ricky glanced to his left, and Erika flashed into view. Some of the recruits instantly paled as Erika appeared. Ricky chuckled as he held out his fist and Erika bumped it.

"The aim of the game is simple, folks. You just have to catch Erika before she tags you out. This is a test of your senses, of your ability to think on your feet. You need to be able to make decisions on the fly or you might end up dead. It can literally be the difference between taking your next breath and a place on the memorial wall."

Derek knew that Ricky was being blunt, but it was one thing to deal with a human assailant. Wrangling a rapid shifter was different than a coked-out human. The recruits would learn both sides, like Killian's class, which was working with the human patrols right now.

Erika rolled her shoulders back, then vanished before appearing on the other side of Ricky. "If I take your ribbon, that means sit your ass down and watch and learn."

"You will have ten minutes to try and catch Agent Sands." Ricky continued. "This is like tag rugby, people, no claws or weapons. Anyone who doesn't follow the rules or doesn't want to, don't let the door hit you on the ass on the way out."

Ricky handed the recruits a colored ribbon, which they fastened to their loop belts, and Erika did the same. As the recruits started muttering, Ricky lifted his hand and gestured to Derek, then to the vampires on the benches.

"Do not embarrass me. Watching you are the best of the best. I am the cop I am today because of them. I did exactly what you guys are going to do today, and I never looked back. But I promise, if you lot show me up in front of the boss, I'm gonna make you do the bleep test until you vomit."

The recruits groaned but readied themselves, separating out. The vampires formed a little trio, huddled together, thinking that mass strength could win. The four shifters also joined forces, the two harpies sticking together so that left one lone girl standing on her own in the center of the hall, her face relaxed, but she had that quiet determination in her eyes.

She was the smallest of the recruits. Her blue eyes blinked twice before Ricky shouted go, and she stayed where she was. The rest of the recruits started running about the place, expending energy, and Derek knew they would tire long before the general of the Valkyrie army. Erika had the vampires' ribbons in the first five minutes. One kicked a bin over in temper, and Derek nodded to Ricky that he was to be cut.

Derek folded his arms across his chest as the young woman watched every place that Erika appeared, ignoring the chaos around her as Erika grabbed one of the harpies' ribbons, then ducked, rolling to catch the other before she vanished from view.

Holding back his enthusiasm, Derek now watched the young woman and remembered a certain warlock who had done exactly what this girl was doing to win his own game of catch. Ricky had only told them no claws or weapons, but he never mentioned magic.

The girl's eyes opened, ice forming before she lifted her hand, and then as Derek saw her mentally count to four, she crouched down and iced the floor around her just as Erika appeared to grab her ribbon.

Erika slipped on the ice, and the girl snatched Erika's ribbon. Then, right before Erika fell on her face, the girl reached out a hand to steady Erika so she would not hurt her. When Erika was steady again, she glanced down at the ribbon in the young woman's hand, her smile brilliant.

"Well, I'll be damned. Good job."

Erika high-fived her. A blush darkened the girl's cheeks. Derek clapped, and Ricky looked proud as punch. It was then Derek noted her appearance, from the slant of her nose to the thin, firm line of her lips. He moved forward to congratulate her, offering his hand and a warm smile.

"Congrats, recruit. That was quick thinking."

"Thank you, sir."

Derek tilted his head to look at her. "Do I know you?"

"No, sir. We've never met before. But I know all about you. My uncle used to tell me stories about you and your team. We moved back to Cork just before the longest night, and I joined up as soon as I was allowed."

The girl clasped her hands behind her back. "My name is Cara Delaney, sir. Thomas Delaney was my uncle."

Derek glanced at Ricky, who looked like an idiot being all smug back at him. Derek turned back to Cara with the warmest of smiles on his face.

"You didn't use Delaney on your application."

The girl shook her head. "No, sir. I wanted to be chosen on merit, not on my name."

"Well, I'm glad that there may be another Delaney on the team soon. Keep up the good work, Cara."

The girl was looking behind Derek, her eyes wide. "Um, sir ... there's a toddler in the training center."

Derek glanced over his shoulder to see a small, chubby, blond-haired toddler waddling her way to him, her amber eyes bright and her laugh infectious.

"So there is ... excuse me a second."

Derek closed the distance in two strides, then dropped to one knee so that Ash could wrap her tiny little arms around his neck before he stood.

"Dada, look!"

Ash held up a pony with wings that had him laughing. His daughter wasn't even one yet, but she was shifting, talking and walking mostly now. She pranced the pony up onto Derek's shoulder and neighed, before resting her head on his shoulder, like she had done since the day she was born.

"Who gave you the pony, Ash?"

"Uncle Lolo! It's pink!"

Derek rolled his eyes at the mention of Ever's brother Loki. He tended to spoil the girl, but hell, Zach and Ash were both spoiled by them all. He wasn't one to argue when just two weeks ago, Derek built a treehouse in Ricky's garden with specialized cat-climbing stairs for when Zach was in cat form.

Shifting Ash so that she was balanced on his hips, her head still resting on her shoulder, he watched as Ricky dismissed the team, stopping to have a few words with Cara that had the girl flushing red.

Coming to a halt by the rest of the team, he dropped a kiss to Ever's lips before Ash was squirming in his arms, her own little ones held out ... but not toward her mother or Caitlyn but toward Donnie.

Donnie scooped her up, then hoisted her up on his shoulders, then galloped around the floor, all while Ash laughed so hard, she hiccupped.

"She's not even one yet, and she's already enamored with my mate."

Erika snorted at Caitlyn's statement. "He probably doesn't even realize it. When he was in Asgard, he spent hours letting the kids tell him stories from our history. He played with them, and all I get now is 'When is Donnie coming back to visit?'"

They all laughed as Donnie threw Ash up in the air, and

while Derek's heart plummeted to his stomach, he knew Donnie would never drop her. Ever snaked her arm around his waist, leaned her body against his. "I have to go collect the cake before the store closes. You guys free for dinner tonight?

"We've gotta collect Zach from Diane's, but dinner sounds good."

They glanced over at Donnie and Ash as Ever sighed. "I can't believe it's almost been a year since she was born."

Ever didn't have to say it, but he knew that his mate was thinking about the teenager who had been with them a short time yet had left such an imprint on them. It was almost a year since Odin had been locked away, and he seemed to be where he was meant to stay. Those with the blood of the gods in their veins seemed to have no ill effects from taking in some of Odin's power.

"I think the fact that it has been a year since we saved the world deserves a pint or two," Ricky mused, his lips curling up on the edges.

"Did someone mention pints? Those Europeans don't know how to pull a proper pint," Donnie groaned as he handed Ash back off to Derek.

They all laughed as Derek glanced down at Ever, his mate up at him, and he wondered just how in the hell he got so lucky. Derek would always be grateful to Sarge for bringing him onto the team, then sending his grumpy ass to the college that day.

When he had started on this road, he was content to be a lone wolf, but these people were his pack, his family. Derek looked at all those around him, at his mate, his daughter, and felt happiness like he never had before. He was never alone, always surrounded by those he claimed as his own. The war might be over and victory theirs, but the future was looking good now. The end really was only the beginning.

ACKNOWLEDGEMENTS

Thank you so much to CTP Publishing for allowing me to share my stories and characters with the world.

Marya,
I am in awe of how you take my jumble of ideas and make every cover into a cover that gives Of Gods and Monsters that epic movie poster look!

Melanie,
Therapist, sounding board, person who notices weird stuff no one else will and more importantly, my friend. Thank you for all that you do and for being who you are. Xx

Massive thanks have to go to Chris Kridler, for her masterful editing and preparing Of Gods and Monsters for everyone to read.

Special note of thanks to Ashley Brilinski for proofing Of Gods and Monster for me.
You might know the books better than I do at this stage!

I cannot let this book go by without a special shout out to Greg Newton
for his epic voiceover skills for the cover reveal video!
It means a lot that you took the time to work on this for me!

I feel extremely lucky to have such supportive parents.
Thanks for the cups of tea and the snacks when I am off visiting
fictional worlds!

LJ and Taylor,
I love you both to infinity and beyond x

I am blessed to have a fantastic circle of friends.
Thank you all for supporting me.

Muser Fam!
Thanks for being such a big part of my online family!

And last but definitely not least,
To the readers,
This ones for you guys!

Character Playlist

Ever

- American Horror Story Cast - Gods and Monsters - From "American Horror Story"
- Anavae – Afraid
- Evanescence - The Game Is Over
- Lorde - Everybody Wants To Rule The World - From "The Hunger Games: Catching Fire" Soundtrack
- PVRIS - No Mercy Ever
- SVRCINA – Battlefield Ever
- Madalen Duke - How Villains Are Made
- Tommee Profitt - Tomorrow We Fight
- Alibi Music - Ride of the Valkyries
- Saint Agnes - And They All Fall Down
- Nothing More - Go to War
- The Rigs - All the King's Men
- Hidden Citizens – Immortalized
- Within Temptation - Endless War
- Dead Posey - Head Of The Snake
- Ruelle - Game of Survival
- Ruelle - The World We Made
- Grace McKagan – Surrender
- M.I.A. - Bad Girls - Ever
- M.I.A. – Warriors – Ever
- Nightcore Reality – Astronomical
- Amon Amarth - Guardians Of Asgaard

Derek

- Lana Del Rey - Gods & Monsters
- Battleme - Hey Hey, My My
- Phlotilla - Going Down Fighting
- Thirty Seconds To Mars - This Is War
- SAKIMA - Death Is in the Air
- Thirty Seconds To Mars - Hail To The Victor
- Refused - REV001
- Chase Holfelder - Nothing's Gonna Stop Us Now
- R.E.M. - It's The End Of The World As We Know It (And I Feel Fine)
- Frank Carter & The Rattlesnakes – Battlefield
- System Of A Down - Protect The Land
- Black Sabbath - War Pigs
- Radkey – Underground
- Bugzy Malone - Don't Cry
- Anderson. Paak - CUT EM IN (feat. Rick Ross)
- IDLES – War
- FEVER 333 – SUPREMACY
- Tom Morello - Can't Stop The Bleeding (feat. Gary Clark Jr. & Gramatik)
- Foo Fighters - Waiting On A War
- You Me At Six – SUCKAPUNCH
- Róisín Murphy - Kingdom Of Ends

Donnie

- A Day To Remember – Mindreader
- Jake Bugg - Rabbit Hole
- Young Guns – Daylight
- Ozzy Osbourne – Goodbye
- Fall Out Boy – Centuries
- Fall Out Boy – Immortals

- Nothing But Thieves - Holding Out for a Hero - From the Trailer for "Vikings" - Series 2
- Enter Shikari - Sorry You're Not a Winner
- Aviators – Godhunter
- Chase Holfelder - I'll Be There for You (Theme from "Friends") - Minor Key Version
- Bring Me The Horizon - Kingslayer (feat. BABYMETAL)
- AC/DC - Code Red
- Michael Kiwanuka – Hero
- Volbeat - The Devil's Bleeding Crown
- 8 Graves - Bury Me Low
- Gerard Way – Brother
- Royal Blood – Typhoons
- Imagine Dragons - Whatever It Takes
- Architects - Death Is Not Defeat
- Fall Out Boy - Thnks fr th Mmrs

Ricky

- Imagine Dragons - Nothing Left To Say / Rocks – Medley
- Nothing But Thieves – Painkiller
- alt-J – Tessellate
- Sia - The Greatest (feat. Kendrick Lamar)
- Muse - Apocalypse Please
- Barbie Sailers - No Time to Die
- Imagine Dragons – Radioactive
- Chase Holfelder - My Way
- Hidden Citizens - Paint It Black - Epic Trailer Version
- The Offspring - You're Gonna Go Far, Kid
- Imagine Dragons – Monster
- Ruelle - Live Like Legends

- AC/DC - Kick You When You're Down
- grandson - We Did It!!!
- Tom Grennan - Something Better
- Papa Roach - The Ending
- cleopatrick – hometown
- Palaye Royale - Tonight Is The Night I Die
- Gerard Way - Here Comes the End (feat. Judith Hill
- Architects - Black Lungs
- FINNEAS - American Cliché

Ash

- AWOLNATION - Lightning Riders
- Macklemore & Ryan Lewis - Can't Hold Us - feat. Ray Dalton
- Labrinth - Earthquake (feat. Tinie Tempah) - Radio Edit
- Black Peaks – King
- Random Recipe - Out of the Sky
- Eminem - Kings Never Die
- DE'WAYNE - National Anthem
- MISSIO - I Don't Even Care About You
- AC/DC – Thunderstruck
- Against The Current - that won't save us
- Holy Wars - LITTLE GODZ
- All Time Low - Monsters - Prblm Chld Remix
- MISSIO – Wolves
- JJ Wilde - The Rush
- Black Honey - I Like The Way You Die
- Quinton Brock - To the Moon
- Kierra Luv - Do It Again
- UPSAHL - STOP!
- Holy Wars - Tainted Love
- Rezz - Sacrificial (feat. PVRIS)

Melanie

- Agnes Obel - Fuel to Fire
- Fall Out Boy - Dance, Dance
- DeathbyRomy - Don't Fall For Monsters
- Låpsley - Speaking of the End
- Tommee Profitt - Shoot To Kill
- Tommee Profitt - In The End
- Arrested Youth - Riot!
- IAMX – Bernadette
- Eurielle - City of the Dead
- Faith Marie – NVM
- Nothing But Thieves - This Feels Like the End
- Saint Raymond - Solid Gold
- Royal & the Serpent – Choke
- Lady Bri - This Will Be the Day
- Swet Shop Boys – Zombie
- Poppy - All The Things She Said
- BONES UK - I'm Afraid of Americans
- Twenty One Pilots - The Run and Go
- nothing,nowhere. - upside down
- Vanic, Skyklar Grey - Fucking Crazy (Remix)

Caitlyn

- Bea Miller - to the grave
- The National - You Were A Kindness
- MILCK - This Is Not the End
- Becky Shaheen - Stand up and Fight
- Alibi Music - Beautiful People
- Hidden Citizens - The One to Survive
- MISSIO - Bottom Of The Deep Blue Sea
- Pim Stones - We Have It All
- Ashley Serena - Lullaby of Woe

- Foreign Air – Monsters
- Ozzy Osbourne - Today Is The End
- Neoni - Carry on Wayward Son
- The Coronas - Heroes or Ghosts - Acoustic Edit
- Meg Myers - The Underground
- Ruelle – Empires
- Damned Anthem - The Final Countdown
- Harry Hudson - Meet Again
- Vanbur - Through the Dark
- Bush - Flowers On A Grave
- Eminem - Black Magic (feat. Skylar Grey)
- Hayley Williams – KYRH
- Hayden Thorpe – Diviner
- Vinyl Sky - Human Heart

ALSO BY SUSAN HARRIS

THE EVER CHACE CHRONICLES

Skin & Bones, book 1

Collateral Damage, book 2

Smoke & Mirrors, book 3

Night of the Hunter, book 4

Never Back Down, book 5

Shortcut to the Grave, book 6

Arsonist's Lullaby, book 7

Of Gods And Monsters, book 8

DEFY THE STARS

A Tale of Two Houses, book 1

Until Death Do Us Part, book 2

In Defiance of the Stars, book 3

Shattered Memories

THE SANGUINE CROWN SERIES

Chaos Theory, book 1

REBEL COUNTY SERIES

Rebel Racers is part of the Rebel County Universe which will span at least four different businesses, with intersecting timelines, and characters popping up when you least expect them.

THE REBEL RACERS TRILOGY

Available Now:

Adrenaline Junkie (Rebel Racers Book 1)

All or Nothing (Rebel Racers Book 2)

Crash and Burn (Rebel Racers Book 3)

THE REBEL ROCK TRILOGY

Available Now:

Centre Stage (Rebel Rock Book 1)

Strings Attached (Rebel Rock Book 2)

Make or Break (Rebel Rock Book 3)

Coming Soon:

REBEL INK TRILOGY

REBEL BOOKS TRILOGY

About the Author

Susan Harris is a writer from Cork, Ireland and when she's not torturing her readers with heart-wrenching plot twists or killer cliffhangers, she's probably getting some new book related ink, binging her latest TV or music obsession, or with her nose in a book.

Susan LOVES connecting with her fans!
www.susanharrisauthor.com

Thank you for reading *Of Gods And Monsters*; I hope you enjoyed my book!

Want to be the first to know when I release new books? Here are some ways to stay updated:

- Sign up for my email list so you can find out about new releases.
- Like my Facebook page.
- Visit my website: www.SusanHarrisAuthor.com/
- Connect with me on Spotify

If you loved *Of Gods And Monsters*, please tell your friends about my book and consider leaving a review. Reviews are like potato chips; you can't ever have enough of them; thanks for reading my book!" ~Susan Harris